Dear Reader,

We're ba-ack! After the success of last year's inaugural Shadows collection—not to mention the stellar performance of our full-length Shadows books—we could hardly let another haunting season go by without three more darkly romantic tales, written by some of the best writers in the business. And look at the treats (no tricks, I promise!) we have in store for you.

Kathleen Korbel's "Timeless" will intrigue and entrance you with its tale of love that knows no bounds—not even time!

"Devil and the Deep Blue Sea," by Carla Cassidy, forces a woman to match wits with the devil himself—and with a devilishly handsome man.

Finally, let Lori Herter introduce you to "The Phantom of Chicago," a hero whose subterranean lair becomes an unlikely—and irresistible!—setting for romance.

Three top talents, three terrific—and terrifying— stories. So lock your doors, turn on all the lights and prepare for a passionate good time as you take a walk on the dark side of love, with Shadows as your only guide.

Happy hauntings!

Leslie Wainger
Senior Editor and Editorial Coordinator

SHADOWS

'93

A Romantic Collection
from the dark side of love ...

KATHLEEN KORBEL
CARLA CASSIDY
LORI HERTER

Silhouette® Books

Published by Silhouette Books New York
America's Publisher of Contemporary Romance

SILHOUETTE BOOKS
300 East 42nd St., New York, N.Y. 10017

SHADOWS SHORT STORY COLLECTION

Copyright © 1993 Harlequin Enterprises B. V.

ISBN: 0-373-48263-9

TIMELESS
Copyright © 1993 by Eileen Dreyer
DEVIL AND THE DEEP BLUE SEA
Copyright © 1993 by Carla Bracale
THE PHANTOM OF CHICAGO
Copyright © 1993 by Lori Herter

CONTENTS

Timeless

KATHLEEN KORBEL

CHAPTER ONE

Genevieve O'Shea Mallory was afraid to go to sleep. It wasn't that she was afraid she wouldn't wake up. It wasn't that she couldn't sleep at all. It was that she dreamed.

It was *what* she dreamed.

Gen had been back at the old house for exactly five days, and for each of those five days—deep in the night, when Gen couldn't protect herself against the turmoil that had driven her here—she'd had the nightmare.

Each night, hard into the darkness, she'd awakened tear-streaked and sobbing, desperate to blot out the sights and sounds that followed her from sleep. Stunned into shaken silence by emotions she couldn't remember ever having felt in her waking life. Increasingly obsessed by the irrational conviction that there was something more to the dreams than just the bubbling up of grief and guilt and old terrors.

Each night she woke plagued by the suspicion that something in the old house itself was creating these dreams, something so embedded in the wood and metal and memories that it had finally escaped to torment her. Something that waited for her here, where her grandmother and great-grandmother had watched the sea before her.

Straightening from the old rocker she'd curled herself into, Gen walked out onto the porch. It was going to rain. She could feel it in the gusting sea breeze, could taste it in the humid air. The world around her shuddered and whispered, and the clouds raced in from the sea.

She loved storms. She loved to watch them whip the water into a frenzy and torment the trees. The sky split open and the earth answered, and Gen stood outside on her porch, at her home, on the island that had belonged to her family since before the Civil War, and sang back.

But not tonight. Tonight the storm seemed to have invaded *her*, as well, stirring her up as much as the ocean beyond her door. Her heart was beating faster, as if she was waiting for something. Her palms were sweating. She couldn't go out, and she couldn't stay still.

And she couldn't go to sleep.

Gen took one more look up into a sky mottled by tumbling clouds and faint moonlight and headed back in to call Annie. It was only eight p.m. on the other coast, and she'd promised. And if there was one thing Gen could pride herself on, it was that she never broke a promise to her daughter. That had been Michael's specialty.

"Hello, Mom. Is my girl there?"

Three thousand miles away, Gen's mother could be heard rustling to attention. "You're calling late tonight."

"I was out walking on the beach."

Gen could hear the worry in her mother's voice even before she admitted it. "Are you okay, honey?"

Gen knew better than to even hesitate. "I'm fine, Mom. Really."

But then, her mother didn't know the truth. She didn't realize that after only five months, Gen was finished mourning Michael's death. Or maybe she'd never mourned at all. She'd lost Michael a long time before the plane crash that had taken his life. Watched helplessly as the man she'd once loved succumbed to the pressure of power and opportunity, inexorably changing into someone she didn't know anymore. Someone she liked even less.

Just as she had every day since the Georgia State Police appeared at her door, Gen tried to call up Michael's handsome blond features, the same sharp brown eyes and mesmerizing smile that had been reproduced on Annie to enchanting effect. But Gen couldn't quite see him anymore. His face was fading, had been fading, and she wished with all her heart she could say she was sorry.

She wasn't so much. What she was, was afraid. But that wasn't something she could admit to her mother or her daughter. Her mother had never understood, and her daughter would understand all too well.

"Mommy? Hey, guess what? I got to see some seals today. It was so cool!"

Even with the acid of unease building in her chest, Gen couldn't help but smile. Annie was her baby, her friend. Her gift from a dying marriage. Nothing was more important in her life than the trust of that little girl, who had lost so much already.

"That's neat, baby. Are you behaving?"

Gen could imagine the scowl. "Aw, Mom. Gram says we can go horseback riding tomorrow." A pause now, just like always. "Are you okay?"

Aching now, sharp enough to take her breath. That her little girl should worry about her. Gen wished she could tell someone how she felt. She wished she could explain the conviction that she was being watched in her empty house, that the dreams that plagued her meant something more.

She wished she could explain the fact that when she should be healing, she was becoming obsessed with the sight of a blue-eyed stranger she met only in her sleep.

"I'm really fine, honey. I just needed to get away from all the hassle from Dad's business. You know."

"Yeah, Mom. And I'm really glad I got to come here. It's just..."

Gen closed her eyes, wishing she could dispel the sick sensation. Wishing she understood it better, that she hadn't handed it on to her little girl, that irrational terror of abandonment.

"Do you want me to come out?"

The answer was quick and sure. "No, Mom. Really. I'm..." Suddenly that little voice was even smaller. "Is it okay if I'm happy I'm here at Gram's?"

Gen pressed her fingers against aching eyes. "Of course it is, honey. You've been planning this trip for a year. I'm glad Gram got to fly back on the same plane as you."

"You're not sad?"

"I miss you. But I'm really happy that you're having fun. Besides, you're only gonna be gone another week. And you know the deal. I'll call every day before ten. If you need me, call right away and I'll be on the next plane. Okay?"

"Oh, Mom, you don't have to..."

More definite now, brooking no argument. "Okay?"

And Gen heard the relief. "Yeah."

It made her want to cry. "We're gonna get through this, little girl. You and I. Together."

"Always?"

"Always and forever. And that's a promise."

Gen heard the pause, wished Annie wouldn't continue. Knew she needed to. "But Dad said the same thing."

And Dad was gone. Gen felt her stomach cartwheel, felt the sudden urge to look over her shoulder.

There in her comfortable, spare house, where generations of O'Shea women had watched the ocean, Gen battled the sudden devastation of abandonment. She talked to her daughter, knew own her mother was no more than a pause away, and yet she couldn't get past the sudden, certain conviction that she was all alone. She felt like a six-year-old again, desperately searching the crowd in a busy shopping mall, knowing with sick certainty that she'd been left behind.

Outside, the wind began to whine. One of the big old live oaks that backed the house scratched on the wall in protest. The ocean grumbled. Gen squeezed her eyes shut, terrified. Shaken. Dreading the end of the call, when she would have to face her own failings again. When a strange dream would begin to whisper at the edge of the shadows.

"How many days, Annie?" she asked, because she couldn't really answer her daughter any more than her mother had been able to answer her when her own father died.

It took Annie a second, but she answered. "Seven, Mom. And if you want me home, I'll come right away."

"Thanks, sweetheart. Now let me talk to Gram."

Her mother returned, sounding just as brisk and pragmatic as always. "Have you had any luck straightening out Michael's affairs?"

Gen sighed. "No. That's one reason I escaped. He left things in a real mess. I've been talking to everybody from his lawyer to the bank examiners, and they can't straighten out his records."

"Well, they'll probably get everything tied up while you're gone. You just rest and take care of yourself."

"I will, Mom. Thanks."

"I never wanted this to happen to you, honey. Never."

Gen couldn't think of anything to say. Her mother's voice was suddenly so intense, so abrupt, as if there was so much more to say that she couldn't manage. For a moment Gen wondered if her mother remembered all her old fears after all.

"I know that, Mom. And I love you."

"Me, too, Genny. Take care."

"I will. And Mom—?"

"Yes."

"Did we have anybody in the family in the Civil War?"

Gen heard the surf and imagined it on the other end of the line. "Why ever would you ask a question like that?"

Gen lied. "Oh, I don't know. I read something. About the Battle of the Wilderness, I think. Does it ring a bell?"

Another silence. "Don't think so."

Her mother had never been much for family history. Gen knew less about her own grandmother than about the Renaissance artists she'd studied in college. But she had to ask. She had to know before she slipped back into the dream, that same damn dream that had plagued her every night she slept under the roof of O'Shea's Seven Oaks.

She had to have an answer to the question of why she didn't grieve more for her own husband than she did for a man she'd never met, who lived only in her imagination.

"Okay, Mom. Thanks."

They talked for a while longer, but Gen could keep her mother on the line for only so long. So she signed off and hung up, and looked around at the house she'd fought to save.

Silence. Such a comfort, usually, an isolation that countered the intensity of her job as a securities broker. Old, worn walls that had withstood everything from hurricanes to negligence. A potpourri of furniture left by succeeding generations. History.

Maybe too much history. Maybe that was what was plaguing her. She'd had the dream when she'd come here before, but only occasionally. Not every night. Not following her into the day, nudging at her during phone calls and walks on the beach, as if the fantasy was more warning than escape. As if it was a portent.

Gen shook her head. That was ridiculous. She was a businesswoman, not a fortune-teller. She'd rescued the house from family indifference for the escape, for the wonderful soothing comfort of the sea. Not because it had any special meaning or message for her.

Certainly not because it had any kind of ghost to commune with.

Even so, it took her two glasses of wine to get up the nerve to go to sleep. Outside the wind notched up another key, and the grass sang like a violin section. Far in the distance, thunder muttered and the ocean answered. The house groaned, as if it resented the newest onslaught. Gen pulled up the covers and tried her best to relax.

As always, the dream began in hell.

She heard it first, smelled it, saw it. A long, large building with worn wooden floors. An old warehouse, maybe, with high, grimy windows and bare white walls. Nothing to dull the echoes, no shield to hide the sights.

But Gen didn't really notice them. Not the rows and rows of cots swathed in mosquito netting, not the sighs and whimpers and cries of the men stretched out there, lined up on the floor, staining the old wood with their blood. Not the stench of death that permeated the very walls until it couldn't be scrubbed clean. She didn't take the time to stop for them, this once, even though her apron was stained and torn from her efforts. She lifted a hand to brush damp hair out of her eyes and hurried on.

Looking. Desperately searching before it was too late.

"Rafe," she muttered to herself again and again as she looked into each soldier's gaunt face and then ran on. A plea, a prayer. "Rafe, please be here."

Genevieve O'Shea Carson Mallory knew nothing about the Civil War. But the Genevieve in this dream knew that she was in Richmond. She knew it was 1864 and Lee and Grant had been fighting over a stretch of woods that began at the Wilderness and marched inexorably her way. She'd seen the bodies, the horrific wounds suffered there, heard the unbelievable stories of dead carpeting the beautiful woods along the way. She knew that the South, her South, would soon die. But right now, she didn't care.

"Rafe, my God, please . . ."

Her eyes filled with tears. Her hands clutched the full skirts of her dress, and she ran on, her heels clattering, her heart stumbling with dread certainty. She knew he was here. She was terrified she wouldn't find him in time.

"Gen . . ."

Genevieve shuddered to a stop. He was there, propped against a wall in the corner. Not even afforded a bed. Not needing one for long. Gen cried out, an incoherent rasp of grief that seemed to rend her in two. She bent to him, gently, and held his ashen face in her hands.

"Oh, my love . . ."

"Thank God, Gen," he managed with a weary smile. "It is you."

She smelled the gunpowder and grime on him, the sweet stench of the whiskey they'd given him to ease the pain. She heard the terrible rattle of his breathing. But she saw only his eyes, those sweet sky blue eyes that had so enchanted her. The grim set of that proud jaw, the tumble of raven black hair that she loved to sweep her hands through. She sobbed and bent to pull his emaciated body into her arms, knowing there was nothing else she could do. Knowing that her world had ended.

"Don't die," she begged, nestling his head against her breast, stroking that hair that was now so dank and limp. "Please, my love. Don't die."

"Oh, Gen," he whispered, really smiling, even with his hands at his belly to hold his life in for just a little while longer. "It won't...be so...bad...."

Her tears mixed with his and stained the floor. "I can't live without you."

"You...won't, girl. I'll never...really leave...."

"You will. Oh, you will, and I can't bear it." She pulled him tighter, protecting him against death, rocking him to ease the terrible pain.

"I won't...ever. It's a...promise...a solemn..."

And he was gone. Her husband. Her life. Deserting her when she needed him the most.

"No, Rafe, no! Come back!"

Gen came awake with a start, shaking. Sweating. Sobbing as she never had for Michael. The storm had broken, the thunder ferocious in the deep night, the lightning looking so much like the shudder of field artillery on a ridge. The house shook and the trees shrieked. A shutter banged somewhere, and the lights had gone off.

Gen scrambled to her feet. She couldn't stay there. She couldn't stay still, not when she was certain that she still felt the weight of that man's head on her chest, felt the life drain from him.

She knew it was guilt, she knew it, over not having grieved more for Michael. It was the terror of abandonment that had followed her from childhood, showing up again in a horrible way. The song of her losses, from her father to her husband to her best friend, Eddie, who'd died trying to pull her from the pond when she was seven.

It didn't matter. Whatever fomented these dreams left her sick with loss and wandering in a house that seemed to groan with almost human agony. Shadows writhed and climbed the walls. Beyond the dunes, the ocean roared, and the storm battered the windows. Gen was terrified of it, because it sounded just like a battle, and Gen had never heard a battle before. She was alone, yet she could have sworn that footsteps followed her from that terrible hallway where the dead still beckoned to her.

"That's quite enough," she said aloud with faint determination. "It's time to do something."

Maybe it was this house that was infecting her. Maybe it was all the detritus of the past that had been collecting untouched in the attic all these years. Well, maybe it was time to face the problem head-on.

She was going to go up to the attic and look for ghosts.

Another bolt of lightning split the night. Gen jumped, her heart slamming against her ribs.

"In a minute," she amended sheepishly. "After I have another glass of wine and go watch the storm."

Cowardice won out. Gen ended up downstairs on the porch, letting the rain pummel the rest of the fear out of her.

Lightning snaked along the oceanfront a hundred yards away with a terrifying crack and sizzle. The huge live oaks that had given the house its name clattered against each other, straining to be free of the wind. The Spanish moss that festooned them danced like mad spirits in the dark.

Shadows fled with the blue-white flash of lightning, and Gen lost her breath.

There, on the beach.

Something.

Something moving.

She waited, hand to mouth, thick red hair plastered to her forehead until she had to wipe at it, just as she had in her nightmare. Her heart outpaced the thunder of the ocean, and her chest burned with fear.

Another flash of lightning, and she saw it again. A body. A man's body, halfway between her house and the furious waves.

"Oh, God," she moaned, looking around, as if she'd find some help. But she knew she was alone. No one inhabited Little Cyril Island but her and, during the day, the state wildlife commission. She'd inherited it and kept it that way to preserve the rich ecosystem on the little coastal island. She'd preferred it that way, too, until now.

He was moving, just a little. Gen didn't take any longer to consider the matter. Whipping her afghan off the rocker, she ran.

The sand was wet, and the wind tore at her nightshirt and hair. The lightning sent out searching fingers, but it didn't find her. She stumbled and ran through the sea oats until she reached the prone man.

The naked prone man.

It cost her a second, wondering. She looked up and down the beach, but there was no boat. No wreckage of any kind. No other way he could have arrived on her island. It didn't matter. He was hurt. Gen bent down and flipped him over.

And leapt back to her feet with a cry.

The man lying unconscious on her beach was the same man she'd held in her dream.

CHAPTER TWO

She didn't need to open his eyes to know. For the past five nights, she'd held him in her arms, stroked his brow, wrapped her arms around his chest and tried to hold on to his life by the sheer force of her will.

But there was more. There was the certainty that she knew that body. Had gloried in it, first shyly, catching glances over the top of a fan, then, more boldly, in a dance or two. And then . . .

Dear God, what was she thinking?

"Get up," she commanded nonsensically from where she stood frozen by his side.

He never heard her. Then another bolt of lightning showed her why. There, along his left temple, was a ragged gash, a wound of some kind. Gen immediately bent back down and gave in to some awful instinct.

"Don't die," she pleaded, her hand to his bare chest.

She felt how cold his skin was where the rain pattered against it. She reached out shaking fingers to find a thready pulse at his throat. She battled the overwhelming conviction that she had once possessed that hard, athletic body as only a lover could, had buried it on a stifling summer day when even the birds were silenced by the weight of what was happening.

"Please," she whined uselessly. "You have to help."

He didn't.

Gen looked around again, this time for some kind of transportation. A board, a raft she might have left here before. Anything on which to drag a body up the dunes. For a second she thought she saw something flicker by the back of the house, but it must have been a reflection off a bottle or something. There was no one on the island but her, no kind of help, and she needed some way of getting Rafe off the beach.

Rafe.

She looked down, stunned by her own assumptions. She'd already named him. God, this was getting too hallucinatory. Next she'd look down and find herself in hoops and gray serge.

In the end, Gen called on old first-aid classes. The fireman's hold, guaranteed to get just about anybody out of a building. Or off the sand, she hoped as she pulled his limp body up to a sitting position and wrapped it in the thick afghan before attempting to haul the deadweight over her shoulder.

The storm was passing through, leaving behind sleeting rain and dropping temperatures. But that wasn't why Gen was shivering. She was suffering from reality shock.

She kept expecting to wake up yet again, and she didn't.

It took every ounce of her strength, but with a lot of hauling and straining and not a little cursing, Gen got the injured man up to the house. She even got him up the stairs before completely giving out. That left him dripping water on the polished floors and her gasping for breath.

And then she looked, to find that she'd left him crumpled in the corner of the living room. Just like...

She couldn't consider why she had to do it, but she did. By the time Gen finally finished, her unexpected guest had been settled on the middle of the floor, wrapped in dry blankets and cushioned on a sacrificed pillow for warmth.

It didn't help. The sense of déjà vu was so strong, it actually took her balance. Gen knew what to do to help this man as much as she could, but she couldn't for a good five minutes, until she could open her eyes without feeling the nausea of dislocation.

She could still smell that place, could hear the lost moans of the dying. She could feel that terrible grief exploding in her chest, and she knew better.

Maybe if she called Annie everything would right itself. Gen would turn away from the phone and find that her visitor had vanished like a well-behaved hallucination.

She didn't think she'd be so lucky.

"Don't..."

Gen was all set to get some supplies from the bathroom. The raspy mutter pulled her to a dead stop.

"Don't what?" she demanded, crouching down next to him.

His features pursed, as if in concentration. He groaned and moved just a little.

"Die..." He sighed, as if it were the heaviest word in the world.

Gen just stared at him.

"Please, my love," he said quite clearly. "Don't die."

Gen ran.

She stood in the bathroom for a very long time staring in the mirror.

"He's not there," she insisted to the wild-eyed redhead in the mirror. "You'll walk back out into the living room and he'll be gone. Something you ate...or drank.... Anything."

The redhead obviously didn't believe it. Her moss green eyes were wide with terror, her skin almost as pale as her patient's.

"You've been having a rough time of it lately," Gen assured herself out loud, as if her voice would add credence to her thoughts. "The plane crash and the memorial service and Annie. All that mess with the bank. The insurance on Tom and the plane. You have a right to be a little...upset."

Upset. What a nice, calm word for *psychotic.* Just how *did* she explain what was lying out on her floor?

How did she make anybody understand that she'd evidently conjured this man right out of her nightmares, just to prove to herself that she wasn't stable enough to be alone?

Gen squeezed her eyes shut and took a long breath. She thought of trying another glass of wine and decided against it, if for no other reason than the fact that if her patient out there was real, she was going to have to keep a cool head around him.

She'd get him stable and call for help. After the squall passed, the Coast Guard could land somebody out here to take him to a hospital.

That was it. Action. A plan. Gen took another breath, but she still couldn't quell the disorientation, the terrible fear that her sanity had just slipped a very big cog.

"Don't die," the man in her living room had pleaded. The same words she'd uttered in her dream. It simply couldn't be.

In the end, she made it back out there with bandages and blankets and hot broth. Gen looked down at the chiseled features of the man on her floor, at the curl of hair that was visible above the line of the blanket across his chest, at the wide shoulders and callused hands that had seen real work.

Farming, if she remembered.

She didn't. She swore she didn't.

But when she bent down to take care of that slash along his temple, her hands were shaking.

"It's time to wake up," she informed him briskly as she knelt alongside him, pouring hydrogen peroxide onto a rag. "You have a hell of a lot of explaining to do. After all, this is private property—kind of. Not someplace I'd expect a stranger during a storm."

Her hands couldn't seem to stay away from his skin, from the delicious silk of that blue-black hair that tumbled over his forehead and curled at the back of his neck. Gen wanted to trace the hollows of his cheeks and reassure herself with the bulk of his arms. Instead, she dabbed at the wound and murmured when he flinched from the pain.

"Please wake up," she pleaded, lifting his head to towel his hair dry before trying to bandage the wound. "I think there's a lot you and I have to talk about."

He muttered something, frowning. He shifted uneasily, but there was nothing that helped Gen. Gen was tall, about five-ten. She figured he must be well over six feet, well muscled and trim. She wanted him to open his eyes so he could prove to her that he didn't have the most sinful smile God ever put on a man. She wanted to believe that she wouldn't know the sweet, melting joy of recognition when he finally opened his eyes to her.

She didn't want the dream to mean anything.

When she sat to lift his head into her lap, Gen had to take a minute to squeeze back sudden tears. It had seemed so real, after all. And now she was holding him again, just like before. And it felt the same.

No, it felt better, because she'd felt him die, and he was back.

She wrapped quickly, talking to him the whole time, and then picked up the soup to warm him. He was still so cold, shivering from exposure. Muttering again. Restless. Even so, he swallowed when the broth slid down his throat. He seemed instinctively to nestle closer, which Gen tried desperately to put down to a search for warmth. He moaned again, but the sound was much more of relief than distress.

Gen yanked the phone over to where she sat. She lifted the receiver, anxious to deliver her problem into other hands. She heard the throb of silence where a dial tone should have been and moaned herself.

It was going to have to be the old backup radio, and that was in the den. When her patient woke up. After he explained just how he'd ended up on her beach without any clothes.

Probably shot by a jealous husband. On a boat. In the sound. At midnight on a Tuesday. Gen bit back more tears of frustration and bent back to her task.

"Come on," she urged as he swallowed. "You don't know how important it is to talk to me. Please. Come on, Rafe, wake up."

She didn't even notice her slip this time, or the fact that it produced the biggest response yet. She saw his eyelids flutter and then open, and found herself falling right back into that sweet sky blue she'd thought she'd only imagined.

Then he smiled, and her world tilted into impossibility.

"Oh, thank God, Gen." He sighed in relief. "It is you."

And he closed his eyes again.

CHAPTER THREE

"What am I gonna do?" Gen demanded yet again. Still in her bare feet, her T-shirt molded to her and her damp hair itching the back of her neck, she stood in her den with the radio mike in her hand.

It was dead. Not that she should have been surprised. The radio was a relic, and she'd just never seen fit to get a new one.

But this wasn't the time for it to break down. She had to get that man out of her house. Off her island. She had to get in touch with the real world before she got back and found out it wasn't there anymore. Had never been there. Suddenly, as the wind began to whine again and the rain clattered against the tin roof, Gen wondered if she wasn't trapped somehow, lost in time, where the Civil War still raged outside her door and her daughter hadn't been born yet. Might never be born.

That was ridiculous. All she had to do was get back to the mainland, and she'd find that everything would be all right. Back in place, with this man just an incredible coincidence. A scientist who had suffered from the storm while studying the coastal islands. A neighbor from across the channel, blown off course and shipwrecked. Something.

The problem was that until the storm eased and her patient woke up reasonably coherent, she wasn't going anywhere. She only had a moped to get around the island on, and a little power boat over by the research station at the other end of the island to get back to the mainland.

Modern amenities had come to the island with the research facility—phone lines and electricity and one partially paved road up by the salt marshes. But it was still an island, no matter that it was separated from the mainland by no more than marshes and estuaries. Gen was stuck right where she was until the weather eased a little.

She hoped her patient survived.

She hoped she survived her patient.

Gen took another quick look into the living room, where usually she only saw wicker furniture and a motley accumulation of seascapes on the walls. Now those were joined by a man lying on her floor, a man who set off bells in Gen she hadn't even known she had. A man who had single-handedly upended her universe more than all the deaths and desertions she'd suffered in her life.

He'd called her by name. By name, for God's sake, when she would have gladly sworn in court that she'd never set eyes on him before in her life. In this life, anyway.

But that was absurd.

What was she going to do?

"Gen . . ."

She moved without thinking.

His voice was so deep, like the growl of the surf against rocks. His face was so weary, as if he'd struggled for a long time against something. Gen wanted to ease the lines of strain that marred his forehead. She wanted to pull him back into her arms.

She crouched down next to him, preparing to demand answers.

"I can't . . . I . . ."

She squeezed her eyes shut a moment, held her breath. Knew she didn't have a whole lot to lose, and sought her answers.

"Rafe?"

His eyelids fluttered again. His hands clutched at something she couldn't see.

"I'm sorry, girl. I'm sorry."

Gen didn't think she could be more afraid. "Rafe, it's me. Wake up."

She even nudged him, which probably wasn't therapeutic in anybody's book. But she wasn't a nurse, no matter what she seemed to suddenly remember. She was a businesswoman, and TLC wasn't one of the degrees she'd earned.

"Rafe, please," she begged, easing down to a sitting position for what looked like a long wait. "Talk to me."

He surprised her yet again. With no more than a sigh, he opened his eyes and looked at her.

And Gen felt her own breath catch. Snagged deep in her chest by a storm of emotions she'd thought she only imagined being so powerful. Joy, desire, relief. Love.

It couldn't be. She didn't even know him.

And yet she felt as if she'd loved him for the longest time.

"Rafe?" Her voice this time was small, uncertain. Tears burned the back of her throat.

His answering smile was the sweetest thing she'd ever seen. The most sinful.

"It *is* you," he murmured, lifting a hand to his head. "I thought I'd dreamed it."

Yeah, Gen almost answered out loud. *Me, too.*

"What happened?" she asked, instinctively brushing a lock of damp hair back from the sharp white of the gauze that circled his head.

He opened his mouth to answer. He looked at her, looked away. Looked back.

"I . . ."

Gen found herself leaning closer. "What?"

His face puckered, and he closed his eyes. Gen was afraid she'd lost him again. She found herself actually reaching out to him, when he gave a shuddering sigh and opened his eyes again.

"I don't know."

Gen wasn't sure whether she felt better for that answer, or worse. But didn't people with head wounds often forget how they happened? Didn't it always come back to them eventually?

"You don't remember?"

He didn't look any happier about it than she was. "No. Don't you know?"

She did her own pausing. "Uh, no. No, I don't. I just found you on the beach. Can I ask a silly question?"

His only answer was a small shrug.

Gen screwed up her courage and asked, "How do you know me?"

And suffered her fourth or fifth surprise of the evening.

Suddenly he looked like a child who had wandered into a strange place. "I don't know."

Gen definitely was not in the mood for this. "What do you mean, you don't know?"

He didn't answer her right away. Instead, he evidently decided it was time to try his hand at sitting. Gen tried to restrain him and was brushed off. Then she wondered whether she was going to need a basin or something. What little color he had in his face drained right out, and he swayed alarmingly, even still sitting on the floor.

"Lie back down," she commanded, ready to push.

He shook his head, eyes closed, hands bracing himself on either side. "No. I have to get up."

"But you've been hurt. And I can't get you to a doctor."

"Probably a good thing." He took another few deep, steadying breaths, as if he was preparing to launch himself straight to his feet.

"You can't get up yet," Gen insisted.

He gave a little shake of his head. "I hate being on my back."

And that was when Gen noticed the scar, the one she'd missed before. Long and lethal looking, wrapping the side of his torso and disappearing beneath the wool of the blanket. Old. She wanted so badly to ask. She didn't.

"Well, hold on to the blanket, then," she advised. "I can't keep you and your modesty up at the same time."

That got his eyes open again. And then focused in the direction of the meager covering. His expression folded into one of confusion.

"What—?"

Gen couldn't help but grin. "It was going to be my next question. How you ended up in the middle of my beach in a storm, naked as the day you were born."

His eyes, when he turned them to her, were frankly astonished. "I have no idea." Then he gave in to that lopsided smile that was so endearing. "Do you think it was worth it?"

Gen couldn't withstand his charm. "I think you'd have to ask whoever else was involved."

He wound up shaking his head again, although Gen wasn't sure whether in consternation or wonder.

"I'd like to get to a chair."

"How 'bout the couch?"

He looked over at her. "The what?"

Gen pointed. He nodded.

They made it. Barely. Gen wasn't in the kind of shape it took to keep a very large man upright. Nor had she ever really needed the skills before. Michael had no more than matched her height. Michael had also never seen fit to lose control enough to need assistance of any kind.

In the end, they made it without too much trauma. He sat, and Gen sat alongside him, trying to be unobtrusive about getting her breath back.

"Now then," she decided with much more confidence than she felt, "I think it's time for some answers."

Gen couldn't believe she'd actually said that. The last thing she really wanted was answers. She couldn't even handle the question.

He simply looked over her way and gave another of those weak, self-effacing smiles. "I wish I could help."

"You have to help," she insisted shrilly, before finally getting her distress under control. "If you can just tell me who you are. Uh, where you're from, that kind of thing, you know. Maybe I can get in touch with the authorities and let your family know that you're okay."

Rafe just rubbed at his head, right over the mysterious injury. The one that looked suspiciously like a gunshot wound.

But that wasn't where he'd been injured. He'd been injured right where that other scar—

Gen stiffened. "Your name," she suggested.

He looked out the darkened window, as if the answer were waiting on the deck. "My name."

Gen's chest was beginning to hurt. "Come on, I'm not in the mood to play games here."

"I am not," he said, turning helpless eyes to her, "playing games."

"Then tell me."

He shrugged. "I can't."

"Because?"

Another small movement, this one of frustration. "Because I don't know that, either."

Gen didn't remember getting to her feet. Suddenly she was there, though, vacillating between fright and flight. "What do you mean?"

"I don't know it. Not who I am, or where I came from, or how I got here."

Gen might have considered this funny if there had been any witnesses. If she hadn't just lost her husband. If she hadn't had those damn dreams.

If she weren't so compelled by a man she'd never met.

"What *do* you know?"

He smiled, and she thought her heart would break. "You." Then he motioned around him. "This place... although it's different somehow."

Gen looked around. "Different how?"

But he couldn't tell her. "It just is. I'm sorry."

She sighed and sat back down. "Not half as sorry as I am."

He reached out a hand. "You don't have to be afraid of me," he assured her gently.

Gen looked down at his hand. It was well used, bruised and callused and strong. A beautiful hand. The kind of hand she'd want comforting her, caressing her, caring for her. The kind of hand a woman would sell her soul to know.

She looked up into his eyes and felt that unnerving stumble of her heart. There was such beauty in those blue eyes, such joy and life, and there, deep, the shadow of sadness to make them so much richer. Not just a lake, but a lake with bewitching reflections.

She wanted to cry. She wanted to believe that this all made some kind of sense. The kind of sense she understood in her humdrum day-to-day world, where the most exciting thing to happen was her daughter's dance recital. Not ghosts and premonitions and haunted houses. And yet her house *was* haunted. Haunted by a man with the warmest smile and gentlest hands she'd ever known.

Well, if you're going to have a hallucination, you might as well have one that's fun, she thought.

"We have to call you something," she said simply.

He gave another shrug. "Any suggestions? Nothing sounds right."

It was Gen's turn to smile, although there was very little amusement in her expression. "You answered to Rafe."

His eyebrows went up. "Really? Okay."

Gen nodded, businesslike, as if the right attitude alone could push some semblance of order back into her life. "Good. Well, then, I don't know about you, but I've had a really long day. Would you mind if we got a little sleep? It probably couldn't hurt you, and it would certainly help me a little."

He thought about it for a minute. "It's going to storm again."

Gen listened to the pitch of the wind. "I don't think we ever stopped having the last one. It'll probably clear out by morning, and then we can figure a way to get you off the island."

He nodded. "That's fine. I think."

Gen was about to get up when he laid a hand on her arm. "Gen?"

She turned, bracing herself with the sweet light in those eyes. "Yes?"

"I know you, and you seem to know my name. Why don't you know who I am?"

It took Gen a very long time to furnish him with an answer, simply because she didn't have one. Not one that would make any sense, unless this man had, in fact, materialized from her dream. Or he was a delusion. If he was a coincidence, as she suspected—as she desperately hoped—tales of Civil War battles and abandonment neuroses would just aggravate his head injury.

"It's kind of a long story," she finally hedged. "Maybe I'll give it a try after I've had some sleep."

If I've had some sleep, she thought miserably. If a person's dream is sitting on her couch, will he still end up in her subconscious? Definitely the research topic for the night.

"Gen?"

She closed her eyes, knowing that she simply couldn't pursue this right now. "Yes?"

"I need some clothes."

That got her eyes open. It actually got a laugh out of her, as well. "My God, you're right. I don't have anything."

Anything except what might be in those trunks she'd been intending to search.

Gen finally shrugged. "I'll work something out in the morning, if that's okay with you. You can sleep in the extra bedroom."

Sleep. Should she wake him periodically during the night? She'd learned that in the first-aid course, too. But then, if she woke him and something was wrong, what was she going to do about it? Gen gave in to another sigh, this one sounding even wearier than the others. If she was going to be subject to inexplicable hallucinations, couldn't they at least be easy ones? A walk in the park, a night at an exclusive restaurant, that kind of thing. She had to live hers as Cherry Ames, Civil War nurse.

Rafe seemed to think about Gen's offer for a moment, his brow pursed, his eyes dark. Then, looking suddenly vulnerable, he offered another of those small shrugs. "I guess that would be okay. I can't seem to remember anything important I need to do."

Gen tried to encourage him with her best smile. She'd been married eight years, and had never once been struck by the overwhelming urge to comfort a man. Not like this. But there was something about the helpless frustration in this strong man that compelled her. She didn't care, suddenly, who he was or why he'd ended up here. She decided, without even realizing it, to give in to the madness. No matter what else was going on in her life, or anybody else's, this man was here and he needed her help.

This man who gave her memories she shouldn't have.

This man who made her body remember, too, in ways it never had.

She knelt back down before him and put her hands in his. And when he looked up at her, she smiled. "We'll figure it all out, Rafe. I promise."

Seemingly almost against his will, he nodded back. Looked at her. Looked hard, as if he could plumb the depths of his own consciousness in her eyes. It took everything she had in her, but Gen held still. Withstood the onslaught of now-familiar emotions, instinctive responses that seemed older than her soul. Willed herself to silence even as her heart thundered in her chest and her palms began to sweat.

But when Rafe lifted his hand to her cheek, Gen couldn't resist. She closed her eyes and nestled against his touch.

"Oh, my God..."

That brought her eyes open again to find that his were startled, turbulent.

Gen held on more tightly to the one hand she had, uncertain what she wanted from that look. "Rafe? Have you remembered something?"

For a second, he didn't answer. He simply kept staring at her, his gaze somehow shrouded and distant. Gen could feel a faint trembling in his hand, and was unsettled anew.

"Rafe?"

He came back with nothing more than a faint shudder. Met her gaze with urgency, the crystal blue of his eyes suddenly seething.

"Gen, I remember..."

Her heart stumbled, righted. She almost held her breath. "What?"

He grabbed hold of her other hand, as if to keep her where she was. "Why I'm here."

She couldn't stand this. Lightning shattered the night outside, and thunder cracked. The storm was back, and with it the howling, angry wind.

"Why?" she demanded, holding him as tightly as he held her.

His expression didn't ease. "To save you."

CHAPTER FOUR

Gen blinked in confusion. "Save me? From what?"

Again that distracted expression, as if he was searching somewhere inside himself. He spoke with a thrumming of urgency that was transmitted right through his hands. "I...I don't know. Damn it, I don't know. I just have this...feeling."

Well, Gen knew all about feelings. She also knew that Rafe was beginning to look really pale again, and that worried her more than his assertion.

"Rafe, it's okay. You're here now. You'll probably remember after a little sleep."

"But, Gen..."

She pulled a smile out of somewhere. "Let me put it to you this way. If I do need help, you're not going to be in any shape to provide it until you've had a little rest. Now, how about some sleep, and we'll worry about it in the morning? Believe me, Rafe, nothing much can happen until the weather clears."

He didn't look happy. "Do you have any ideas?" he asked. "Any reason you could be in danger?"

Gently she shook her head. "None," she said simply. "I'm not a spy or a member of the Mafia. I'm just a mother with a little time off before I have to get back to work."

That seemed to provoke a new concern. "A mother?"

Gen found herself frowning at his reaction. "Yes. I have a five-year-old daughter named Annie. She's in Oregon, visiting her grandmother."

"Annie...Annie..." He ended up shaking his head. "God, I wish I knew why that meant something."

This time it was Gen who reacted. "She's not in trouble, is she?"

Rafe shook his head. "No. No, it's not that." Pulling a hand away, he rubbed at his eyes, and Gen saw that his hand was still shaking. "God, I wish I knew. I wish I could remember something!"

Gen tried yet again. "You remember me. The rest will come."

He pulled his hand away and challenged her. "You're sure?"

And Gen, not knowing what else to do, smiled. "Of course. It works that way in the movies all the time."

She'd thought she'd get acquiescence out of him. Instead, she got another frown.

"The what?"

Which brought her back to a dead stop. He wasn't being funny. "The movies," she said deliberately.

He just shrugged.

Gen shrugged back, deciding that she really didn't want to deal with that right now, either. Maybe it would all make more sense in the daylight.

"We'll talk about it later," she offered. "Now, let's get to bed."

And for the first time since he'd opened his eyes, Rafe shot her a real smile. A four-point dazzler that took the stuffing right out of her knees and set up a weird harmonic of reactions in her. Tinglings and warnings and yearnings racing along nerve pathways that had never spoken before.

At least, not that she could remember.

"Alone?" he asked, his voice laced with every innuendo a man had used since crawling up from the slime.

Gen wanted to giggle. She wanted to preen and flutter and melt. Gen, who drove a Volvo station wagon and bought her business suits from Anne Klein. Which just proved how far removed from reality this little episode had taken her.

So she smiled back in the best quelling fashion she could manage right then, even with her heart doing triple time and her hormones coming to sudden, breathtaking life. "Trust me, Rafe. Neither of us is in any condition to do otherwise."

She got him to bed. She got herself to bed, after closing down the house and making sure everything that could be blown away in the new, more intense storm wouldn't be. And then she lay there in the dark, listening to the dissonant chaos around her, and shook.

Her windows faced the water. The wind battered them with rain and salt spray driven all the way across the dunes. The water thundered, and the thunder cracked and snarled like a live thing. The lightning never seemed to stop, so that even if Gen could have closed her eyes, she couldn't have slept.

It was never a consideration.

The minute Gen crawled into bed, the fear struck. That old terror, let loose in the dark, that nameless, floating phantom that had accompanied her through childhood and still sat on her shoulders as an adult. The ridiculous, infantile conviction that she'd be abandoned. That everyone would die, one after another, leaving her at a string of grave sites, the only one left to place flowers and grieve. All alone, finally, with her island and her silence.

It had been with her as long as she could remember, even before her father, before Eddie. Gen remembered it, long, terrible nights when she'd begged for her father to come sit with her so she would know that he wouldn't disappear. Days spent listening to her mother trying to convince her that she was just being a foolish child, that of course the people who loved her wouldn't just die.

But they had, one after another, just as she'd known all along. And Gen lived in daily, hourly fear that the worst was yet to happen.

And now she knew what the worst would be. She lay in the bed that had held her grandmother and her great-grandmother and her great-great-grandmother, and she knew that what she'd been waiting for was this man to appear. She'd known from her first memory that there would be someone in her life whose leaving would shatter her. She'd thought her dreams of Rafe had simply been reflections of that. They hadn't. They had been warnings.

It was so stupid. She was a grown woman. A woman of the nineties, who had never, not even in the years when she really loved Michael, lived or died by a man. She even admitted to herself that Michael's death had left her with no greater emotion than relief at her refound independence.

She swore that the only person she couldn't lose was Annie.

And yet, the minute Rafe had opened his eyes, she'd recognized him. Not as the man in her dream, but as the person she'd feared all those years. The single human being who seemed to tap into that deep place in her that held instincts she'd never been able to name. Primal memories so powerful that Gen couldn't believe she hadn't heard them before.

But she had, in different ways, faint and troubling, as if she'd only heard them from far off, like fading explosions from a very old sun. Echoes so deeply ingrained that they had altered the tenor of her life without her even realizing it, until the sun returned from its distant orbit to surprise her with its terrible power.

And so she lay in bed, watching the spectacular assault of the storm, listening to the old house protest and fight back, and the terror grew in her like a cancer. Because all she could think of was that, as surely as Rafe had appeared, he was going to leave.

And that his was the leaving she wouldn't survive.

The storm must have eased during the night, because Gen finally drifted into an uneasy sleep. She didn't have the nightmare, just a jumble of disjointed dreams about Annie and her father. She even heard Michael whispering to her, deep in the night, and he hadn't disturbed her dreams for a long time now.

The day never seemed to really dawn; the night just eased into an indistinct gray. By then Gen was wide-awake again, staring out her window at the angry, churning sea and the scudding clouds that seemed to skim the heaving waves. The storm had eased. It hadn't finished. Gen relented and tuned her portable radio to the weather station—and lost a little more of her equanimity.

They weren't riding out a storm. They were seeing the advance squall line of a hurricane that was threatening the coast. Gen rubbed at her weary eyes. Just what she needed. A hurricane, and no way off the island. When she'd arrived there hadn't been a breath about it, or she wouldn't have ever come. If she hadn't been plagued by those stupid dreams, she would have paid more attention to the world around her.

She had to figure a way to jimmy the temperamental two-way radio back to life, if only to get hold of Annie and let her know that everything was okay. If worse came to worst, she'd go over and break into the wildlife station. They probably had a radio that was the model of modern efficiency. Gen simply could not let Annie worry about her. Especially after all the times she'd sat at the edge of her little girl's bed stroking her head and promising that she would never be alone.

First things first. The storm shutters needed closing, and the generator needed checking. And then, before she went traipsing around in her sou'wester, Gen would have to figure out exactly what to do with her guest.

She found him standing in the living room, where he was enjoying the view out the floor-to-ceiling windows along the oceanfront wall. Gen had had them installed when she renovated the sagging, empty house. She'd also bowed to common sense and given them good, stout shutters, in preparation for the kind of news she'd just had. But they had yet to be really tested.

Rafe didn't move as she neared. She wondered if he knew she was there. He was so still, standing with his arms down, his head up a little, as if he was searching the ravaged sky for answers. He'd fashioned a wrap with one of the big bathroom towels, leaving his back and shoulders bare. Gen couldn't take her eyes off them, off the solid, uncompromising lines of him, work hardened and sleek. Warm as life against her hands. Protective, rather than intimidating, even when he was angry.

She lifted a hand to her mouth, as if to hold back the memories just the sight of him seemed to provoke. A small house with a hardwood floor and stone fireplace. The sun beating down on his glossy hair and tanned face. His smile at her approach over the hard, dusty ground.

But it couldn't be. It couldn't.

Could it?

"Have you remembered anything?" she asked, her voice husky with denial.

He didn't even flinch. Just shook his head, as if the weight of that admission was too much for words.

"Does anything look familiar?"

His shoulders lifted just a little as his head came down. "That," he said, still watching the ocean.

"What kind of impressions do you get from it?"

Another small silence, as he assimilated the question. "I was happy here."

Gen didn't know how to answer him. She didn't know what other questions to ask that might pry something loose, so she retreated to the pragmatic.

"How's your head this morning?"

He shrugged.

Gen was well acquainted with shrugs like that. "Well, don't worry. Aspirin is something I have plenty of."

This answer was a nod.

She tried again. "Are you hungry?"

That turned him around, produced a halfhearted smile. "Starving. But I'm not at all sure I'm dressed for the occasion."

Gen stopped a moment, considered the view. Agreed. She wanted to smile in return and couldn't. It was just too much. The sight of those arms, and knowing somehow that they had held her. That terrible scar she knew had killed him . . .

She looked up to his face and wondered how to tell him that the last thing she wanted to do was go searching around in the attic. She'd never known the women who had given her their names and customs. In the same vein of ignorance that seemed to run through her family, she'd never thought she needed to. Now that she knew better, she suddenly didn't want to. She was afraid. Somehow, whatever waited for her in the attic had everything to do with who faced her in the living room. She was sure of it.

In the end, she managed a smile of sorts. "You're right. Unfortunately, I doubt you'd fit into anything of mine, and the only other clothes available are stored in trunks that date back at least fifty years."

"Your husband?"

"Died about five months ago."

Rafe ducked his head a little in embarrassment. "I'm sorry. I didn't mean..."

Gen offered him a smile. "It's all right. Really. We'd been...estranged for a while. How 'bout that aspirin, and I'll go hunting upstairs for you?"

He had no choice but to follow her toward the kitchen. "He didn't leave any clothing here?"

Already reaching into the cabinet, Gen smiled. She just couldn't see Rafe in the surgically tailored three-piece suits and Izod shirts and Dockers and Topsiders Michael had worn in Atlanta. They would have suffocated the man, sucking the very vitality from him. She saw him in hard-worn jeans and T-shirts, a sport coat thrown on if it really became necessary. Whatever Rafe really was, he wasn't a banker.

"No," she said as she offered him pills and water. "Michael never stayed here. He only visited twice, once when I got the place and once about a week before he died. He didn't like idle hands or sea air."

"You stay here alone?"

"Annie and I. It's my family's home. Passed down through the women, kind of, only my mother never really wanted it. So I took it."

Aspirin still in hand, Rafe looked up toward the front of the house, where they could just see the view. "I'm glad."

Gen looked the same way, saw the same wild ocean and sand, the gnarled live oaks and hoary Spanish moss, envisioned it at its best, with seabirds in flight, gulls and terns and herons, the dolphins that sometimes came to call, the sunrises that were straight out of an impressionist painting. She thought of what she would have lost without it all, and she found a smile.

"Me, too." And with that she turned back to the task at hand. "Now, you see if you can scrounge up something to eat in here, and I'll go up and try and find something in a size...tall. Okay?"

He nodded. And Gen did the last thing she wanted to do. She went in search of her ancestors.

The attic was reached by a little ladder that pulled down from the ceiling of her bedroom. Gen had known all along that it was there. The workmen who had redone the house for her had reported on the pile of unused furniture and storage chests that resided in the dim, low-ceilinged space, but Gen had never had even the slightest inclination to go up and wade through it all. History had never been a topic of interest to either side of her family. Her father, when asked, had laughed and said that he came from a long line of horse thieves. Her mother had simply said that she came from a long line of plain, hard-working people. No kings or visionaries or warriors. And Gen, never so much a curious child as an obedient one, had never thought to search further.

Like her parents, she had spent most of her time concentrating on the present and future. Schooling, career, marriage, family. Her history was tucked away in the attic, where it belonged. She kept it out of some kind of respect, but that didn't mean she wanted to try on old hats with ostrich feathers and pretend she was visiting the queen.

Which meant that she was climbing into unclaimed territory. It was hot up here, close, with frail, uncertain lighting from a single bare bulb and the constant complaints of the house overhead. The rain spattered against tin like ricocheting bullets, and the wind probed weakened corners for entry. Shadows ruled in the musty room, giving Gen the creeps.

The workmen hadn't lied. There were probably some valuable pieces up here, the detritus of over a hundred and fifty years of collecting by the various O'Shea's Seven Oaks that had occupied this site over the decades since that distant O'Shea ancestor decided he could make a go of this isolated place.

But Gen was only looking for trunks, boxes, anything that might hide apparel that would fit a man of Rafe's size. Suddenly she wished she knew a little more about her family. It would at least be helpful to know whether any of them had been his size. Or almost his size. For all she knew, the men married to the various O'Shea descendants had all been jockeys.

Gen stood where she was for long minutes, trying desperately to get up the courage to open even one of the old steamer trunks that cluttered the floor. There was an old bicycle up here, a hat tree and three very old hunting guns. Hatboxes and baskets, all tidy and untouched, as if deliberately put away for good along with their owners, so that the next occupants wouldn't be touched by them.

Gen was genuinely spooked by the place, especially knowing that she'd lived within ten feet of it off and on for the past six years. No wonder she had strange dreams in this house.

She should have come up here. She should have laid more claim to her heritage than saving it for a summer home. Well, she'd do better for Annie, she swore. That is, if she ever got the nerve to look at it now.

"Gen?"

She jumped at least a foot.

"Don't do that!" she demanded, even as the bandaged head appeared through the trap.

He was looking around. "I was getting a little chilly. Thought I'd lend a hand."

"You eat already?"

His answering smile was sheepish. "I . . . uh, can't seem to figure out anything down there."

Gen didn't want to hear that, either. "Well, be careful. I have no idea what's up here."

He climbed up the rest of the way, and Gen was reminded just how little he wore. If it hadn't been close in here already, it was now.

Damn it, hormones had no place here. She had business to attend to. It ended up that they did serve some purpose, though. To escape their effects—not to mention their surprising temptation—Gen finally turned with a vengeance toward the first trunk.

"Hopefully it wasn't just the women who kept their clothes up here," she offered briskly.

Rafe ducked to keep from hitting his head on the rafters. "I can't see myself in hoop skirts," he admitted.

"Not if you're going to help me batten down the house," she retorted, hands on the trunk, arms tingling with something she didn't really want to identify.

"Batten down the house?"

She nodded. "Sorry, I should have told you. It seems we're going to be stuck here a little longer than I thought. We might be visited by the edge of a hurricane."

Rafe took a moment to consider that. "I see." Then he took to looking around.

That left Gen with nothing but the task at hand.

The trunk she'd chosen was old, battered. It had been a beauty once, though, with brass fittings and a lovely arch to the lid. Gen just hoped nobody had locked it.

Nobody had. With unusual timidity, Gen wrapped
her hands around the sides and lifted. It opened easily. Gen was glad. At least she was spared the creepy
sound of creaking hinges. That would have been all
she needed, especially up here.

There might not have been noise, but there was
something. Some... feeling, as if whatever had been
courting her in her dreams had lived here all along,
and that she was truly letting it loose. Pandora's box,
with its humors, whether good or ill, set free to wreak
their havoc. Gen felt it along her spine, at the base of
her neck. Frissons of apprehension. Whispers of
emotions, like the frail attar of long-pressed flowers,
sorrow and joy and pain, escaping into the air as if
they had waited a long time to be shared. Gen fought
an unholy urge to run. Instead, she looked inside.

"Dear God..."

Right there, on top of the trunk, on top of the first
trunk. Moth-eaten and old, ripped and stained and
darkened from the smoke of a thousand guns. A long
gray wool uniform coat, its twin row of buttons still
shining dully, its sleeves decorated with elaborate
frogging, as carefully folded as a christening gown, the
old sabre reverently placed alongside. Gen couldn't
breathe. She saw that jacket and knew exactly where
the scars had come from, each and every one. She
knew the feel of that heavy wool, the weight of the
sabre as a woman stretched around a handsome man
to clip it on. She saw where the blood had poured

through the gash in the side, and fought sudden, hot tears.

"Fourth Georgia," she heard over her shoulder in an awed whisper.

For a moment, it didn't register. Then Gen was whipping around on her heels to find Rafe's attention on that coat, his expression pensive, his eyes almost dreamy.

"What?"

He started, almost as if coming out of a trance. He looked down at her. "Fourth Georgia."

"Fourth Georgia what?"

"Regiment. Until Spotsylvania, anyway."

If Gen had been a woman to swoon, that was the moment she would have done it. Spotsylvania was a town in Virginia, southeast of the Wilderness, where some of the fiercest, most horrific fighting of the Civil War had taken place. Where, on May 12, 1864, Rafe had been mortally wounded.

CHAPTER FIVE

"How do you know?" Gen demanded softly as she climbed to her feet.

Rafe still seemed caught in that other world. "Know? I recognize it."

Gen took a careful step closer. "What about Spotsylvania?"

He snapped to attention. "Where?"

"You just mentioned Spotsylvania. What about it?"

For a second, Rafe looked trapped—caught between sleep and waking, perhaps. "I did?" he finally asked.

Gen motioned down to the old coat in her trunk. "You looked at that coat and said that it belonged to someone of the Fourth Georgia Regiment. Why?"

He frowned at her. "Why are you so upset about it?"

"Because..." Because it didn't make sense, any of it. Because Gen was caught in a house in a storm with a man who shouldn't exist, fingering evidence of a dream that seemed to have materialized. Because she wasn't enough of a believer in things that go bump in the night to understand all this, much less believe it.

"Because," she said very carefully, "I think that coat fits you perfectly."

It was Rafe's turn to look confounded. "Does that make sense?"

She wasn't at all uncertain about the shake of her head. "No."

He gave a funny little shrug. "Good. I didn't think so, but I'm not sure why."

But Gen couldn't put it into words. "That scar along your side," she said. "Can you tell me where you got it?"

He looked down at it, fingered it with uncertain hands. "No."

She just nodded, not really surprised. So instead, she turned back to the trunk and reverently lifted out the coat. Beneath it were other clothes, a man's clothes, all pressed and preserved as if waiting for the man to come back and wear them. Well, she thought wildly, he has.

Before Rafe could ask or comment, she reached over and slipped the coat on him. It fit in a way that spoke not simply of good tailoring, but long communion, molding to him from memory even more than dimension. He looked startled. He looked even more startled when Gen slid her fingers in through the blackened gash in the coat to expose the scar directly beneath.

"That's why," she said simply.

This time, when Rafe faced her, there was more than confusion in his eyes, and Gen could understand for the first time how he had survived such a terrible war for so long.

"Don't you think it's about time you told me your story?" he asked.

Gen sighed. "Yes, I do. Let's get you dressed first, and I'll explain over breakfast."

By rights, none of those clothes should have survived. Not the linen shirts or the woolen or cotton trousers. Not the old house slippers and robe that spoke of a certain amount of financial comfort in an age when there had been little. But the sword said the same thing. The man who had owned these clothes had been an officer and a gentleman. Undoubtedly a landowner, if the workmanship of his wardrobe was any measure.

Gen pulled out enough to get Rafe through the next few days, even long johns and undershirts, and then moved to close the lid again. She didn't want to. Suddenly she wanted to do nothing but sit and sift through every piece of memorabilia up here, as if she were a detective unearthing clues to a murder. But there was a storm coming. She had to protect the house. She had to figure out a way to get in touch with Annie. She had to try to explain what was going on to her guest when

she was still waiting for someone to explain it all to
her.

She'd already begun to turn away when Rafe
stopped her. Already dressed in a slightly yellowed
linen shirt, gray slacks and suspenders, he looked as if
he'd stepped out of an old daguerreotype, especially
with those dark Irish looks and ghostly pale eyes. Gen
admitted that she was distracted by him. Which was
why she missed his intent.

She didn't realize that the light in his eyes had
changed.

"Gen..."

His hands cupped her face and lifted it to his. His
brow gathered, as if he wasn't any more sure than she
what was going on. His mouth...

Gen didn't know when she closed her eyes. It simply seemed the most natural thing to do. She lifted her
own hands to his chest. She felt the flush of exhilaration take hold of her. She succumbed, for the first time
in her life, to madness, and met his kiss.

Gen swore she smelled bay rum. She felt the stub-
ble of new beard against her cheek. She heard the low
moan of a hungry man even over the wind and rain.
She answered, never understanding. Never believing.
Not knowing why the taste of Rafe's lips should spark
such a flood of joy in her. Why the caress of his callused fingertips along her throat should melt her. Why
the simple contact of his quirky, wise mouth should
electrify her. Center her, spin her about, wake her up,

every question and dream and bit and piece of inexplicable memory answered by the sweet, simple kiss of a stranger.

But he was real. Whatever else she'd believed or wondered or questioned, Rafe was flesh and blood, and every emotion she'd felt for him in her dreams was alive in her, tenfold, in his arms.

As if she had always been there, and had only been waiting all these years to find her way back. As if his were the only arms that mattered, the only mouth that gentled her to silence. The only eyes that awoke wonder in her.

It took Gen a second to realize that Rafe had finally pulled away. Her body thrummed with sudden life. Her chest was on fire, and her head was reeling, and she didn't even question it. She simply knew that she would never know this kind of communion again.

"I'm sorry," he was murmuring. "I shouldn't have."

"You had to," she answered, finally opening her eyes to see the trenchant light in his eyes.

He didn't question her. He simply pulled her into his arms, and she went. She didn't close her eyes this time, though. She just rested against his chest and listened to the steady cadence of his heart, felt the rise and fall of his breathing, soaked in the vitality that had slipped inexorably from her hands in a terrible dream.

She soaked in it like a first sun and shuddered at the thought that it would be taken away again.

But it would. Whatever it was, whoever had given her this impossible gift, could not have given it to her without cost. It was a loan of some celestial kind that she shouldn't question, only savor. Minute by minute, hour by hour, until she woke with the clothing back in the trunk and the bed down the hall unslept-in.

The thought truly terrified her, in ways she would have never known until she'd had the temerity to reclaim an old house her mother had wanted to rot away.

Had her mother known? Had she had a visitor like this, and never shared the miracle with her daughter? Or had she simply felt the tremor of memory in this house and been afraid?

Gen had to know. She had to ask, the minute she called Annie.

"Annie," she whispered, and the sound of the wind came back to her. The rain battering at her walls, the surf lashing angrily at the beaches. The storm. And an entire continent away, her daughter would be watching the weather channel and fearing for her mother's return.

The bubble of insulation vanished, and the world rushed back in. Gen couldn't simply pretend that nothing mattered but the man who had come to her in the night. She had to protect her daughter. She had to deflect that terrible, abiding fear before it festered in her little heart as it had in her mother's. Before it took root and grew into a beast that couldn't be tamed.

Rafe pulled gently away. "Your girl?" he asked.

Gen satisfied herself with another long gaze up at his strong, beautiful features. All shadows and angles in this dim place, with that wild hair tumbling over the swath of white, and his eyes like hot fires in the dark. Gen heard the small warnings, the stubborn voices of reason and logic that told her to pay more attention to the shadows and less to the fire. She felt the disquiet take hold in her belly, and tried for once to ignore it. Tried and failed.

She looked down again, pulled away as easily as she could. Took a breath to cover the sharp loss of dislocation, the feeling that she should be bleeding from the movement. She used her daughter to dredge up some latent sense of coherence.

"She's terrified of being left alone," Gen admitted. "Something I'm afraid she picked up from me. Right after we batten down hatches, I need to get hold of her somehow. She's probably heard about the hurricane already, and she'll be terrified."

Rafe nodded and smiled. "A good mother."

Gen couldn't help an answering grin. "Well, the only one she's got."

Gen wasn't sure she trusted the new ease between them. It was as if that kiss had unlocked some new level of understanding, some common recollection of easy camaraderie, familiarity, friendship. They climbed back down into the bedroom and descended the stairs in silence, as if they had done so together a hundred times. It was only when they made it into the kitchen that the disparity once again became apparent.

"Nothing?" she asked.

Rafe looked around and shook his head. "Not a thing. I know it's a place to prepare food, but I'm not sure how."

Gen just snorted. "That's only because you're a man."

"I think that's an insult."

"You think right. Michael wouldn't go near a kitchen unless there was a board meeting in it."

They sat at the butcher-block table and ate, and Gen tried to probe Rafe for recall of any kind. She pointed out items, mentioned popular icons, historical dates. He was like a slate that had been faultily wiped.

He couldn't remember any more about himself than he'd told her—except for the growing feeling that she was somehow in danger.

Gen quashed that idea. "Don't be silly," she said. "I'm not an impulsive person." Except now. "I'm not going to try and go sailing in the storm."

"What if the hurricane's bad?"

She shook her head. "Not the way it looks now. These houses have withstood worse. My only problem is getting hold of Annie. I think one of the fuses has blown in my old radio, and I don't think I have any more. If not, I have to try plan B."

When Rafe heard that plan B entailed a jaunt across an unpredictable landscape in a raging storm, he immediately vetoed it.

Gen lifted her eyebrows in amusement. "I don't think I asked."

His expression grew rather stormy. "And if I am here to save you, what good is it if you don't listen to me?"

Gen waved him off and stood to put the dishes in the sink. "Which reminds me," Rafe said evenly behind her. "You were going to tell me how you knew who I was."

That brought Gen to a sick halt. "This is all so bizarre," she admitted miserably to the refrigerator.

"Can I be the judge of that?"

She turned around, leaned back against the closed door for support. "I guess you might as well," she said. "I sure can't come up with a decent answer." She took a deep breath, but it didn't help. So she launched into her explanation cold. "I met you for the first time five years ago when I first stayed in this house. I saw you periodically over the years—more frequently as time went by, I think. But since I've been here this time, I've seen you every night for the last five nights."

"Seen me?"

"You've died in my arms."

That silenced him.

Gen tried to smile. "I know. It doesn't sound any better to me. I really wish I knew where you got that scar from, because in my dream it's from a miniball."

"Your dream?"

She nodded, that awful feeling of inevitability overpowering her again. The terrifying knowledge that every night, no matter what, she would lose him again and scream and scream with a grief she'd never known. Gen wiped her palms against her legs and struggled for control. She drew in a ragged breath to calm her.

If only the dream hadn't been so vivid. If only it wasn't Rafe she was explaining this to.

"My dream. Every night. I know I'm working in a hospital in Richmond, that it is the middle of May and we've been receiving a flood of wounded from the Wilderness. A charnel house, a slaughter like the world has never known. And then I hear that you have managed to get to my hospital, all the way from Spotsylvania. A miserable little corner of hell there they nicknamed the Bloody Angle, where you were cut down. But you made it to me, when you should have died out there with your men. You made it to my hospital, where I find you, where I gather you into my arms. Where you promise you'll never leave me. And then you die."

Gen didn't even feel the tears that coursed down her face. She didn't hear the funny little sob that caught in her throat. She couldn't take her eyes from Rafe as he climbed to his feet.

"What year was that again?" he asked.

"1864."

"And what year is this?"

"1993."

He stood there a moment, disconcerted and uncertain. Looking so much like the Rafe of her dreams, dressed in those old clothes. Reminding her vividly of just what she'd lost.

"I can't do it again," she insisted in a small voice. "I just . . . can't."

Rafe came closer. Gen tried to back away and couldn't. "What do you mean?" he asked.

She shook her head, the words overwhelming her. "All my life, people have left me. Died. I . . . thought that was what I was so afraid of all these years, but it wasn't. It was you. You terrify me."

"Why, Gen?"

"Because you're not real!" she snapped, wiping at her tears. "You can't be!"

He shrugged, stepping closer. "Why not? I feel real enough."

"You're only real in my dream. You're a figment of my neurosis, kind of like I'm trying to prove to myself that what I've been through isn't so bad after all. Because when you die in my dream . . . when you . . ."

"When I what?"

She did sob now, unable to stop the pain she'd been suppressing. "You promise me!" she shrilled, wanting to hurt him. Wanting to hurt him for hurting her, even if it was only in her subconscious. "You promise you'll always be there, and it's a lie!"

Gen didn't realize how close Rafe had gotten. Suddenly his arms were around her, and she couldn't battle her way back out.

"Maybe it isn't," he offered gently.

Gen pushed at him, furious, frightened. "No," she insisted. "No, that's not possible, damn it! Don't you see? I'm buying right back into that damn dream where I love you more than life itself, and then you're just going to leave again, and this time it's going to kill me. I can't do it. I just can't."

But his voice, when it came, confused her even more. "You love me?"

Gen didn't know what to do. She was wrapped in his arms, in his solid, warm arms, where she would be safe. The arms she'd always run to, for comfort, for support, for celebration. She knew it. She tasted it, caressed it with her memories, as if she were running her fingers over fine silk. Certainty. Impossibility.

She couldn't have felt those things before. She couldn't have these things already imprinted on her subconscious, except through the miracle of dreams. She couldn't love him.

But she did. She always had, with a passion that confounded her, a loyalty that withstood the worst of times, a deep, abiding respect that cast him above everyone else in her life. Even above General Lee, whom she'd met at the—

Gen abruptly yanked away.

He was like a divining rod, an antenna for cosmic coincidence. She seemed to have been tuned into The Oldest Living Confederate Widow for a minute there. General Lee, indeed.

Gen couldn't breathe at all. She couldn't hold still. She thought she could just walk away. But Rafe caught her hand.

"You love me?" he asked.

She looked up, ready to deny it. After all, how could she?

But her heart sang at the mere sight of him. She knew him. She knew him better than he did himself, his strengths and weaknesses, his habits and haunts. And she knew that each one endeared him to her more than the one before.

"You are a crack shot with a long rifle," she said simply. "A born rider, who built your farm with your own two hands." She smiled abruptly. "And mine. Cotton and peach groves. A beautiful little place called Seven Sisters, in honor of your aunts, who raised you. You hate strong liquor, but love a good hard cider, and get squeamish at the sight of blood."

His smile grew. "You do love me."

But Gen couldn't give him that, even though she suddenly wanted nothing more. "I can't afford to."

But Rafe just shook his head, reached over to winnow his fingers through her shoulder-length hair. "It doesn't matter. You do. It's enough."

"For what?" she demanded, trying yet again to pull away.

Rafe sighed, let go. Smiled. "For me. You see, when I woke up, I couldn't understand what was wrong. I knew I loved you. I didn't understand why you didn't love me back."

Gen couldn't move. "What?"

His smile grew, deepened, enticed with its frank delight. "Maybe I am that person from the War Between the States," he said. "Maybe I did die, and came back. Maybe I never really died at all. I don't care. All I care about is that I'm here now, and whatever it takes, I'm going to keep you safe."

"And then you'll leave," Gen insisted.

He shook his head. "I'm not sure I ever left at all."

Gen instinctively held out a hand, as if protecting herself from him. "Don't say things like that."

"Why?" he countered. "Would you rather I not be real? Maybe a ghost or something? Well, I don't think I am, Gen. I feel suspiciously corporeal, and I'm glad. You're here, and I'm even more glad. All I can think is to take the rest step by step."

Gen should have been reassured. Instead, she battled tears again. "Easy for you to say," she scoffed. "You know you're real. I don't."

"The question is," he said, "what difference does it make?"

Gen sighed. "All the difference in the world."

CHAPTER SIX

They got the shutters closed. They checked the generator not five minutes before the electricity from the mainland kicked out for good. They fought with the radio, which was simply too old and cranky to accept help. And all the while they worked in near silence.

Gen couldn't allow herself the luxury of getting too used to Rafe. She couldn't rely on him. Even so, she couldn't ignore the swell of delight every time she turned around to find him close by. She couldn't deny the fact that he filled her house with a music that harmonized beautifully with her own. She couldn't avoid the way her body reacted to his proximity, anticipated his touch, ached for more.

So she concentrated on the storm, the house, and getting in touch with Annie, which was becoming a more complicated problem by the minute.

"I can't disappoint her," Gen insisted yet again as she listened to the wind climb another notch in pitch.

"It's dark out," Rafe reminded her. "You wouldn't make it ten feet without ending up on a reef somewhere."

"Not reefs," she corrected wearily. "Marshes."

"Whatever. You can't go."

She paced the living room, her eyes on the solid expanse of black where the windows had been. The shutters were holding off the storm with no problems, but the weather service had indicated that the worst might be yet to come. Gen couldn't hold still. Maybe it was Rafe's continued warnings, maybe it was her inability to get hold of Annie, but something was very wrong. Something hung in the air like a faint chill, and she couldn't escape it. Something that gnawed mercilessly at her propelled her back again across the hardwood floor until Rafe escaped into the kitchen at the back of the house.

"It only takes ten minutes to get across the island on the moped," she insisted again, pitching her voice over the constant howl of the storm.

Rafe leaned his head out, obviously having figured out the intricacies of sandwiches. "The what?"

"My bike."

He shook his head. "You're going to take a bicycle out in a hurricane. No wonder I'm here."

"It's not...oh, forget it. I'll just go back into the shed and get it."

He stepped all the way out now. "No, you won't. You know better, Gen. We'll try again in the morning."

"But what if it's worse out then?"

"Annie's with her grandmother," he reminded her.

Gen only laughed. "Her grandmother doesn't believe in little girls' fears," she informed him.

"Please, Gen," he pleaded. "Just wait till morning. She'll make it through one night all right. I promise."

Gen bit her tongue to keep from telling him about the kind of promises he made.

She was starting to believe it. To just assume that somehow Rafe had jumped right from a battlefield hospital in the 1800s to her front lawn, that she was caught in some kind of bizarre time loop caused by the electric disturbance of the storm and her emotional instability. That she was not just Genevieve O'Shea Mallory, but whoever that shadowy woman was who walked through the Confederate hospital in Richmond.

There had to be a better explanation. There had to be some kind of proof that this was all just a silly mixup of some kind.

Finally Gen came to a stop, right in the middle of the room. Instinctively she lifted her head, as if she could see through two floors and into that dusty, claustrophobic little room at the top of the house.

It would give her something to do. Something to keep her mind off Annie.

She didn't move for a very long time.

"Go on," Rafe said, as if he were privy to her thoughts. "I think I'd like to know, too."

She glared over at him for a moment. Around them the house shook from sudden thunder. The trees screamed in protest at the wind's mauling. The world was a maelstrom of energies, all unleashed on her little house. Well, maybe this was the proper time to dig up ghosts, or to put ghosts to rest. With one last sigh of protest, Gen headed back upstairs.

The trunks were still there, hunched in the shadows like somnolent beasts. The generator didn't power the dim bulb up here, so Gen brought candles and flashlights and set them out, which formed shadows to climb the walls and swayed in tune to the wind. She fought those same shivers she'd had before, whether of dread or portent, she couldn't tell. Gen had never set much store by prescience before. After the past few days, she might just have to change her mind.

The first trunk must have belonged to the dead Confederate soldier. Gen didn't have the nerve to name him amid these shadows, as if she would call up yet another just by chanting his name enough. His clothes were all there, his shaving razor and strop, his boots way at the bottom. She pulled them out, still fairly supple after all these years, to give to Rafe. Two ledger books with careful, exact script in them, and a packet of letters. Gen set them aside.

She closed everything else back in, amazed at the wealth of artifacts she'd already found. Wondering why they had been hidden rather than honored. The War of Northern Aggression, as her neighbor in Atlanta still called it, was a matter not just of pride in the South, but of deep reverence. People defined themselves still by what regiment their great-granddaddies had ridden in, what fierce battles they had survived, and which they had finally died in. Sabers were hung over fireplaces and souvenirs brought out with amazing regularity to be shared and mourned over.

And yet, hers had certainly been the only family in Atlanta without a story to share, a plantation to grieve for, at least a dozen family members to memorialize. The Civil War had simply never been a topic of conversation in the house. In fact, the only inheritance that had even been acknowledged was the island. And that had come with the unspoken understanding that the only treasures there were the sea and the salt marshes.

Gen wondered why. She wondered now more than ever.

Then she opened the next trunk, and the questions became more important. Because she found clothing she somehow recognized.

Practical dresses, frilly gowns, fans, slippers. Jewelry, some of it exquisitely delicate. Gen pulled it out, held it in her hands and felt an odd heat from stones unworn in over a century. A small fortune in precious and semiprecious stones, which had been callously shut away in a moldering attic rather than handed down with fond stories of their owner.

It made Gen angry. She should have known something about this woman, her great-great-grandmother, if she was right, and she didn't even know her name.

She found her answer beneath nightdresses that still held their starched form, as if waiting for their owner to return for them any minute. It was a journal, of the sort all ladies and gentlemen kept in the last century. A small, careworn book with a leather cover and a faded ribbon for place marker. Gen's hands shook as she reached for it.

Was that a noise?

Gen whipped around without the book, almost expecting to see her ancestor materialize out of the dark. She could feel her here, could feel that old, old grief, the joy that had shattered into a million sorrows. The lost soul of a woman who had loved too much. Gen wanted to speak to her. She wanted to hear her voice and know what terrible legacy she had passed to her unknowing great-great-granddaughter.

Evidently it wasn't to be. Gen heard another scraping sound, but this was from the floor below.

"Is it all right if I come up?" asked a voice.

Gen instinctively drew her hand away from her find. She wasn't sure she could share this with anybody. It was, after all, only hers. Her family, her history, her dreams.

Rafe's memory.

"Thank you for asking," Gen answered, reaching for the little journal again. "Considering how eerie it is up here, I would have had a heart attack if you'd popped up out of nowhere."

He looked even more unreal in this light, just an impression of life. Towering, gleaming oddly in the half-light with that shirt on that opened at the throat.

Gen wanted to look. She wanted to enjoy. She was afraid to.

"Are you okay?" he asked, crouching beside her. "You've been up here forever."

Startled, Gen looked around as if she'd find verification in the clutter. "I'm sorry. I've just been... reacquainting myself with my past. There are some boots over there you might like. Try 'em."

Rafe obliged. Gen went back to the trunk.

"They fit perfectly."

Gen didn't even smile. "What a surprise." She carefully set the journal atop the things she was saving from the other trunk. Procrastinating. Putting off the inevitable as long as she could. Instead, she lifted out the little box of jewelry again.

"He must have loved her very much," Rafe unaccountably said behind her.

Gen couldn't keep herself from jumping. This place just wasn't good for her health. Her heart was stumbling around again, as if trying to hold her life and another's at the same time. As if the memories that had been confined in this trunk were too much for one person to survive.

"Why do you say that?" she asked, still looking down at the filigreed-gold-and-garnet necklace.

"Those. They're breathtaking."

Gen nodded. They were. Not only that, they were individual, not the usual kind of jewelry one saw from the Civil War. Someone had designed these to fit perfectly around one neck, to slip onto one well-loved finger....

She hadn't even thought about it, but there it was. Her wedding ring. A gold band with a unique design—a heart held on each side by hands.

"A claddagh ring," Gen whispered, awed. Amazed by the delicate workmanship, the emotion expressed in its giving.

"A what?" Rafe asked, crouching next to her.

Gen had trouble holding still. He was too near, especially now, with her holding Rafe's most sincere expression of love for her in her hand.... She meant the other man's.... She didn't know what she meant. Because suddenly, inexplicably, she was overcome by the certainty that this ring had been forged for her.

It belonged in her hand, on her finger. It should never have been taken off, no matter what anybody thought. She could have wept with the feeling of relief at finding it again.

"Gen?"

Gen shuddered. Snapped the box closed so that the gold would never wink at her again, the garnets and emeralds would lose their silky fire. So she wouldn't remember.

"The, uh...claddagh ring," she explained, her voice strained. "It's an expression of affection and devotion, traditional in Ireland. It's only become popular here in the States in the past twenty years or so. I'm surprised."

"It's beautiful," he agreed. "What else did you find?"

Gen looked back into the shadowy recesses of that trunk. "My dress," she admitted.

Rafe looked over. "The one in the nightmare?"

She nodded. "I wish I understood any of this."

"No letters, no pictures, nothing else?"

"Journals."

"Good. Maybe we can find something out after all."

Gen finally couldn't help it. She looked up at Rafe, needing his support, needing the gentle strength in those beautiful eyes. "I'm not sure I want to."

His smile was as sweet as sunrise. "I know," he said, reaching out to gentle her with a touch. "But I think you're meant to. I think that may be what this is all about."

Gen fought the urge to simply rest in the comfort of his hand and challenged him. "And what about you?" she demanded. "What's your part supposed to be?"

His expression saddened. "I don't know, my love. I just know that I have to be here."

Gen sighed, struggled against tears. The storm raged outside, but it was more perilous here. She wasn't at all sure she was going to survive this.

"There's another box in that trunk," Rafe said simply. "Have you gone through it?"

She stared at him. At the trunk. "What box?" she demanded.

He reached past her and dug thorough the dresses and cloaks and button-top boots. When he withdrew his hand, it held a small box.

Gen found herself shivering again. How had he known? What was she going to find inside? Because she knew there was something important there, something she needed to see. Something she didn't want to see.

Without a word, Rafe handed her the little box. Gen looked at it, worn cardboard banded in faded satin. She drew a shaky breath and pulled the once-gold hair ribbon away. Pried open the lid. Looked inside.

She should at least have been surprised. She wasn't. It wasn't just that Rafe had known where the photos were. It was that he'd somehow known who they were of.

A bright young lady in her best watered-silk dress, the garnets winking darkly at her throat, her heavy hair captured in a snood. Standing, as was the fashion of the day, behind the chair that held the handsome officer in his gray uniform and plumed hat, the old carved sword hanging by his side, a sash of office bisecting his chest.

His boots were polished to a gleam, his uniform sharp and wickedly handsome on him, his hat rakish, his gloves creased over his belt. The young woman had been caught looking over at him, and the light in her eyes was passionate, the smile on her lips proud. The man looked appropriately solemn and martial. The cream of the South's fighting men. Probably the last picture they had taken together before he went off to save his land. The last time their eyes had reflected their pride and happiness and anticipation. After this, there had just been the war.

"I always was partial to red hair in a woman," Rafe said beside her as he looked at Gen's mirror image in the photo.

Gen nodded. "I know." And couldn't say how.

But she knew she would. Because someone had had the forethought to inscribe not only the date—April 14, 1861, two days after the taking of Fort Sumter—but the names of the handsome, happy couple. In swirling, spiderish script on the white cardboard at the bottom. Genevieve Anne Stanton O'Shea and Rafael Edmund O'Shea.

Beneath that lay the picture of the little girl.

CHAPTER SEVEN

I met him at the cotillion. Such a dashing young man, with his blue eyes and black, black hair. He was the very devil, complimenting all the ladies in that wonderfully wicked Irish accent....

"I don't think that's a good idea."

Gen looked up from the first page of her great-great-grandmother's journal to see Rafe's curious frown. "I thought this was the whole idea."

He shoved his hands into his pockets and paced the other way. "I know. But those pictures..."

Gen set the book down in her lap. "Exactly. Those pictures. Not just you and me, but finding out that my great-grandmother was named Anne. Just like my mother. Just like my daughter. I never knew, Rafe. Not any of it. Heck, I still don't even know my grandmother's name. I think that one of those trunks contains her life, though, and I have the most horrible feeling that her name was Genevieve. I think it all happened for a reason, and I think the answers are in this book."

"I don't think you want the answers," he insisted.

That brought her to her feet. "Why not? What do you think I'm going to find? That I am that woman in my dream? That my dead great-great-grandmother has some kind of unnatural sway over my life?"

"I don't know," he retorted, dragging a hand through his hair. Truly upset now, agitated enough to finally get through to Gen.

She set down the journal and walked over to him. Caught him midflight and held on to him. "Rafe," she said, "what is it?"

His eyes were unnaturally bright, brittle. He couldn't seem to look at her, as if the sight of her might somehow hurt him. "I . . ."

"What?"

But he could only shake his head. Finally, though, he focused his gaze on her, only making her even more unsettled. "I don't know," he said, enunciating each word carefully. "Just like I didn't know why that box was there, or why I knew I liked red hair, especially yours. Why I know so clearly that you're the only woman I'll ever love, and that you're in some terrible danger."

"And this has something to do with it?"

It took him a second, but he nodded. "It's crazy, isn't it? I mean, I'm the one who's been urging you to find out more. Now I think you could find out too much."

How did she tell him it was too late? That there wasn't anything in this world, even him, that could keep her from finding out the truth? Somewhere in these words lay the clues to why the women in her family had tried so hard to hide from their past. Why, maybe, she was so terrified of being abandoned. Could this woman, this phantom through whose eyes Gen had been able to look, have had such power that she had been able to infect Gen with her own tragedy? Rafael and Genevieve O'Shea had had one child, a daughter named Anne. From the only information Gen had, Anne had had one child, a girl. That girl had had Gen's mother. And Gen's mother had had her. And something of those women hovered in this old house like a sorrowing ghost that Gen suddenly needed to exorcise.

She had to know.

"You're here with me," she offered as excuse. "We can't be surprised." Still he wouldn't bend. Gen straightened in self-defense. "I'm not the one who opened the door on the past, Rafe."

"It doesn't feel right."

"What about you?" she asked. "Don't you want to know? My God, you can't remember anything. You know me, you know this place—which is called O'Shea's Seven Oaks, by the way—but nothing else rings a bell. What if somehow you *are* that Rafe, the one my great-great-grandmother lost?"

"What if I am?" he demanded. "Would that change anything? Would that give her her husband back? Would that mean that I love the wrong woman?"

"Do you know me?" Gen asked.

"I told you I did."

"I mean, do you *really* know me? Not just recognize my hair and my eyes and name?"

"Yes! That was never a question, damn it. I know how you laugh and how you cry and how gentle you are with children. I know that I've never felt anything more delicious than your hair, and that when you make love you sing...."

Gen gasped. No one in the universe knew that but Michael. No one.

She felt the tears collect in her throat.

"Then what does it matter?" she asked, her voice hushed, her hands trembling where they held on to him.

"It matters," he said softly, his eyes dark with turmoil, "because I can't lose you again."

Gen felt Rafe's arms wrap around her waist. She knew he'd eased closer somehow. She understood that he was going to make love to her. And she never questioned it.

She simply lifted herself into his embrace. She met his mouth with her own, as if words simply weren't enough anymore, as if their hunger was, indeed, a hundred years old. As if the woman in her dreams had been given one more chance to hold her husband in her arms and feel joy.

Gen felt joy. She felt dizzying delight, a pleasure she'd never known at a man's hands before. She heard Rafe's soft, guttural moan of satisfaction as he dug his hands into her hair and pulled her hard against his body, and she knew that she had spent her entire life waiting for such a sound. Such a feeling. Such a singular sweetness in a man's eyes.

Outside, the wind shrieked and moaned like a terrified woman. The trees clattered, and the rain pounded almost as loudly as the thunder. The house literally seemed to shake before the attack, adding its own small noises of protest.

But in Gen's bedroom, there was a curious bubble of quiet. The hushed silence of rediscovery, of careful attention, of long-remembered desire. Gen sought Rafe with instinctive movements, and he answered. They moved in a dance both well learned and well loved, smiling, laughing, humming with a united passion few are privileged to enjoy. A passion heightened by the love of two people who drew their strength from each other, who woke each morning impatient to share their day with their love, their friend, their anchor.

In those moments, as her body awakened to a shattering life and her heart swelled with a love she had only remembered in a dream, Gen knew why that other Genevieve had loved so completely and lost so much. She knew why that other Rafe had promised never to leave. Because his memory would be so strong, so interwoven with Genevieve's very being, that he would always be with her.

Gen thought she knew her great-great-grand-mother's terrible secret. And she knew it was for the love of a man. For the love of this man.

Gen knew it was very late. Rafe lay quiet in her arms, his hair tumbled over his forehead, those terrible lines of strain eased. She looked down on him and wondered what would happen when the storm blew over. She wondered if he would return to wherever he'd come from. Whether she, too, would be left to mourn him, when she'd only been given a day. After what had just happened, she couldn't think of that.

Carefully she eased out of bed and threw on a robe. And, while Rafe slept, sneaked back down to the living room to pick up Genevieve O'Shea's journal again.

Gen didn't feel the time pass during that long, stormy night. She didn't hear the wind that refused to ease or the rain that must surely have turned the rare freshwater stream on the island into a raging torrent. She didn't hear the surf, except as a counterpoint to the terrible scenes Genevieve described as the war approached, as it first threatened and finally destroyed the idyllic life she had known with her husband and child.

Genevieve had been the daughter of a prominent planter near Atlanta. She had grown up amid the South's aristocracy, never questioning her place in it, or its place in history. She had been pampered and loved and given every benefit, not only of money, but of well-educated parents. And then, one night in the spring of 1854, the seventeen-year-old girl had thrown everything away for the love of a stranger.

He'd appeared at the spring cotillion, a guest of one of the other planters. Standing there in a room swirling with the brightest and most elegant peacocks of the South, this man in his simply tailored broadcloth coat and fawn-colored slacks had stood out like a sun amid orbiting planets. Genevieve had been intrigued, then enchanted, and finally compelled. Rafael Edmund O'Shea, a sea captain who had decided it was time to find himself some land, had stolen her heart.

Her parents disowned her. Not only was her husband a Catholic, he was a man with no place in their world. No status, no family, no tradition. Genevieve knew all along, though, that he had potential. She recognized his power, his intelligence, his determination. She ran away with him no more than four weeks after the cotillion, sacrificing everything for a man with a flashing smile and big dreams.

She worked as hard as he, surprised at how much she enjoyed it. Together they built Seven Sisters, their farm near Savannah, into a place that gained respect and acclaim. Their daughter, Anne Genevieve, was born there, and thrived. And then Rafe won Little Cyril Island from another planter in a horse race, and the young family fell in love all over again.

Gen read the tender descriptions of the isolated little island where the family had built the first O'Shea's Seven Oaks. She could almost hear the laughter of those days, the excited plans and quiet reposes. The sea that had lulled her so many nights was the same one that had embraced the couple. The old trees were the ones they had planted together to celebrate anniversaries.

Gen read it all with a growing feeling of trepidation, knowing already what had happened. She paged through the entries of those terrible war years when Genevieve had battled single-handedly to save her land while her husband fought, how she'd taken her child with her to Richmond because the war effort had needed her so much. How she'd worked there until she couldn't stand, couldn't sleep, couldn't eat.

How she'd heard the news that her husband had come in search of her.

My hands are soaked with his blood. They have tried to take him away from me. I will not let them. I cannot. He is my life, and now that he is gone, all is over.

The one thing Gen couldn't understand was how Genevieve could have sacrificed her own daughter. But she had, delivering her to her parents, who had managed to somehow escape the worst of the Yankee fury, and survived in trade in Atlanta. Seven Sisters had been lost, but no one seemed to have any use for Little Cyril Island. It was there that Genevieve finally retired in the summer of 1865.

And there, the last entry was written.

I have tried so hard to go on living. I know he would want it. But even for the sake of my darling Annie, I cannot. I simply do not have the strength anymore.

Genevieve O'Shea's last words.

Gen sat for a long time, looking into the mottled shadows of her home, listening to the wind keening for that poor, lost woman, for the child she had abandoned and the love that had changed her life. Gen had no tears for her, only a terrible heaviness. Only an odd sense of relief.

"Thank you, Genevieve," she said quietly. "At least now I know why."

There were still other questions to be answered. Another woman whose mystery Gen needed to decipher. She felt so very tired, as if Genevieve had saved up all that sorrow these long years to finally share its burden with another person. Gen wasn't sure she was strong enough. She wasn't sure she really understood what magic had been wrought in this old house to finally bring Genevieve home again. But she knew that the door was truly open. She had to find out the rest, and then she had to bring it back to her mother...and her daughter.

Briefly Gen looked up toward the front windows. The noise was abating. Maybe Rafe was right. Maybe she'd actually be able to get to that other radio today.

She hoped so. It was more important now than ever that she get in touch with Annie. Because somehow this psychic memory had been passed down to her own daughter. This certainty that she would be left behind, just as the other Annie had been.

Gen had to make sure that her Annie never had to think that again.

But first she had another life to look into.

She checked her bedroom on her way past, just to make sure. The sight of Rafe sprawled across the mattress made her smile. Good thing she didn't mean to sneak out in the storm. Her protector would have slept right through it.

It was becoming a ritual in the attic now. First Gen laid aside the trapdoor. Then she placed the flashlight and lit the candles one by one, as if preparing for a solemn rite. Finally she turned to her history and chose which puzzle to unlock. She could have picked Annie's trunk. It was here, full of bustled dresses and feathered hats from the 1880s. Annie's turn would come. First Gen needed to find out about the third Genevieve. She had to know if there was really a pattern here.

She pulled open the steamer trunk, hoping to find the flapper dresses and rope pearls so popular in the twenties. Instead, she found a briefcase.

"What the...?"

"I was hoping you wouldn't come looking till I was gone."

Gen almost knocked over one of the candles in her scramble to her feet. "No," she breathed, paralyzed by the figure that was detaching itself from the far shadows. "No, you're dead!"

"Those rumors have been greatly exaggerated," Michael said, smiling quietly. Still Gen couldn't move. She couldn't think. "Why—"

He shrugged, stepping closer. "They were getting too close. That last time I was here, I hid away some necessary papers. I figured after a mourning period I'd pop up and get them and be off for good. I slipped in while you were busy on the beach last night, but I didn't realize you were bringing company home for the night." He shrugged. "I also underestimated the storm."

Gen had claimed in the end that she didn't know him anymore. It was a fight they'd had all the time. She'd had no idea how right she was.

It took a minute, but Gen instinctively guessed the rest of the story. She found herself gaping at her own husband.

"The whole thing was a setup," she accused. "The accident at sea, the identification so we'd think the body had simply been lost to the currents..." Her brain tumbled fast and furious as she began to understand the magnitude of the deceptions her husband had been practicing. "The records ... You were embezzling money from the bank."

"Lots of it." He came close, close enough that Gen could smell the Aramis on him. "I considered asking if you wanted to come along when I left, but you just aren't any fun anymore, Gen."

Tears clouded her vision. Betrayal crowded her chest like a hot balloon. Too much. This was simply too much. She wanted to strangle him on the spot, the rage was so strong in her. She wanted to curl into a corner in shame.

"So you've been hiding out in my house."

"I'm afraid so. Which means I've heard everything." His gaze briefly flicked toward the floor below. "I presume the obligatory forty-eight-hour mourning period is over, my love?"

"Don't call me that."

His hands went up. Gen was appalled to see that one held a small gun. "No offense." He smiled. "But then, he is a complication I hadn't planned on."

Gen couldn't take her eyes off that pistol. "You'd planned for me?"

Michael shrugged. "Well, I'd kind of hoped I could get in and out without you knowing. But after being forced to spend all this time with your venerated ancestors, I came up with an alternate plan."

Gen was sure she didn't like the tenor of this conversation. "What do you mean?"

He was casually pointing the gun now, which was making Gen feel even more uneasy. And he was laughing.

"It's probably a good idea I left anyway," he was saying. "If you're anything like the other women in your family, I'd say you had about another five years before you went right off the deep end. They were all obsessed with the guy who named the house. The Confederate captain. No wonder your mother wouldn't have anything to do with 'em. I guess she figured the only place for skeletons this unique was in the attic. Or maybe she was afraid that if you found out about the dear old family traditions, you might get ideas, y'know?"

Surreptitiously Gen began to edge backward, hoping to get to the end of the trunk. "I appreciate the history lesson, Michael . . ."

Michael stepped closer, the gun steadier now. "It really is interesting. Your grandmother looked just like you. In fact, she had your name, Genevieve. Your mother never talked about her, either, did she? Wanna know why? Guess how she died?" He made another step, punctuating his news with a bob of the gun. "Which was how I came up with my plan, by the way."

Gen knew, even before he told her. Her heart sank. Her breath caught in her throat. Not her, too.

"Suicide," Michael said with a nod, as if verifying her suspicion. "The big *s*. Seems that when her husband died, she decided it was kind of the family thing to do. Couldn't go on without the love of her life, and all. From what I could see from all the paperwork up here, that kind of behavior skips a generation." He smiled now, a manic light in his eyes. "Kind of sets an interesting precedent, don't you think?"

"But you're not the love of my life," Gen retorted instinctively.

He laughed again. "And I suppose the stud muffin in the towel is?"

Gen struggled for air, for sanity, losing hope of either. She kept her silence, measured her distance. Fought the shakes that threatened, and prayed that Rafe would stay where he was until she figured something out.

"No," Michael said with another blithe sweep of the gun, "I don't think anybody who finds this stuff up here is going to question for a minute the fact that you sent Annie off, just like your grandma sent your mom off, so you could do yourself in in dramatic fashion. Sad, but predictable, y'know?"

"I'm not the same."

Michael's smile was brilliant. "Who's gonna know? Especially after I sprinkle those journals all over the house. Sorry, Gen. I mean it. But five million tax-free is a much prettier dream than growing gray with you."

Now Michael was really smiling. He was also pointing the gun right at her. "Come on. Let's go."

"I'm not going anywhere with you. You're going to have to shoot me right here."

"So that whoever finds you will know it wasn't self-inflicted? All I have to do is follow through with one of those old shotguns from your grandpa over there. Don't fight it, Gen. I win one way or another." He aimed the gun, which couldn't miss at this range. "You might as well cooperate."

Gen didn't do anything of the kind. "No, Michael!" she screamed. "Please!"

But he pulled the trigger anyway.

CHAPTER EIGHT

He would have shot Gen square in the center of the forehead if she hadn't dived behind the trunk. Gen hit the floor. The gunshot echoed in the raftered room as the bullet thumped into the wood directly above her.

"Damn it," Michael snapped, moving forward again. "Don't make me chase you. I don't want to hurt you any more than I have to."

That actually made Gen laugh. "You're an ass, you know it?"

She scuttled away again, trying her best to reach one of those old rifles along the wall. She couldn't fire any of them, but she could damn well swing them.

She never got that far. Her head was still down, so she could gauge Michael's progress only by the sound of his footsteps. He'd just made it past the trapdoor. Suddenly he let out a surprised oath. Gen stole a peek around a corner to see him wide-eyed with astonishment. She saw the gun hand go up and the rest of him topple forward.

Then she saw the hands around his ankles.

"Hit him!" Rafe yelled, clambering through the gaping square as Michael hit the floor with a flat thud.

Gen scrambled for one of the guns. Michael was already twisting toward the new threat, the gun coming around. Rafe let out a roar of aggression, and Gen knew he was going to throw himself between that gun and Gen. She couldn't let him.

She got her hands around an old Richmond musket. The thing probably hadn't fired in a century, but it was good and heavy. She clambered to her feet with it.

Michael fired again, and Rafe grunted in pain. Gen turned, the rifle in her hands, and saw Rafe's shoulder blossom scarlet. She cried out, the fear as old as this place, the desperation too deep for words. Still Rafe fought, trying to pin Michael to the floor. Michael bucked and kicked, the gun held firmly in his hand.

"Back away!" Gen screamed at Rafe, ready to swing. "Get away from him!"

But he wouldn't. If he let go, Michael would bring the gun to bear again. So Gen did the only thing she could do. She swung the rifle butt down on the pistol.

Both Michael and Rafe yelled and pulled away. The gun clattered across the floor. Gen dived for it before Michael could get hold of it again. As she turned back, she saw that Michael was still fighting. She saw that Rafe was losing. And she saw Michael come up off the ground. There was no time for the pistol. Winding up like a long-ball hitter, she swung the rifle at Michael's head.

The old rifle butt cracked in half as it hit Michael with a sickening *thunk*. Michael gave no more than a grunt of surprise and then crumpled, unconscious.

"Rafe?" Gen cried, dropping the rifle without a thought. "Are you all right?"

Rafe never moved from where he was crouched before her, his astonished gaze on the inert man stretched out in front of him.

"What if I say no?" he asked, finally turning one of the most wicked smiles Gen had ever seen on her. "You gonna hit me, too?"

He made her laugh. How could he make her laugh at a time like this? She was shaking like a tree in a windstorm and crying like an infant. Her husband, whom she'd buried no more than five months ago, lay unconscious on the floor, and her lover, whom she'd buried over a hundred years ago, sat smiling at her, bare chested and bleeding. This was going to take a lot of working out.

"We need to get you to a doctor," Gen insisted.

Rafe looked down at the fresh blood on his skin. "I'm not going to die, girl. But let's make sure he doesn't cause us any more trouble." He reached over into a pile of furnishings and came away with a curtain tie. "Did I hear you say he was supposed to be dead?"

Gen found herself sighing as she went about tying ankles while Rafe tied wrists. "That's kind of getting to be a common theme around here, isn't it? I'd like you to meet my husband, Michael, who I thought had died in a private-plane crash over the Caribbean.''

''What do you think this means?''

She gave in to a stunned shiver. ''I think it means I'm going to be getting myself a divorce.''

Rafe just nodded. ''He wasn't worth dying over.''

That brought Gen to an uncertain halt. ''Do you think this was it? This was what you were protecting me from?''

He seemed to consider the question for a moment. ''Considering the fact that you mostly protected me, I guess I probably wasted a lot of the celestial effort it took to bring me here.''

Gen nodded, numb and shaky, her equilibrium forever shattered by the events in this house.

This house.

There was one other thing Gen needed to do before she left this attic. Stepping gingerly over a now-moaning Michael, she returned to her grandmother's trunk. She lifted out the briefcase, which was embossed with the initials *MPM*, and set it aside. She'd have to take it to the police when they handed over her husband. Until then, she wanted no part of what was inside. Duplicity had no place here. Gen was looking for something much older, much more important.

She found it where Michael had looked first. The wedding picture, old, faded, black-and-white, with the same smiles, the same joy and anticipation. And the answers Gen still didn't understand.

On April 24, 1926, Genevieve O'Shea O'Carroll had married Edmund R. Burke. Her grandparents. Her own face looking back from yet another year.

Gen wondered how long she'd had him. How long her joy and contentment had lasted before being shattered on the stones of loss.

She wondered, even knowing what these women had come to lose when their husbands died in their arms, how they could have left behind their children.

Maybe that was why their memories had been so embedded in this old house that they had seeped into Gen's life. Maybe it wasn't their loss she'd been meant to experience, but their failing. She did understand, finally, why her mother had locked this all away where she wouldn't have to face it. Where she could protect her own daughter and granddaughter from it.

Why, maybe she'd never completely destroyed it.

"It still doesn't make sense," she said out loud, looking down on this woman she finally knew.

Gen hadn't realized how quiet Rafe was until he answered. "What doesn't?"

And she turned to see him in the candlelight, ephemeral and faint, as if painted in faded watercolors. Unreal, unwhole, like a memory that had been worn away by too much retelling. It frightened her. He frightened her, because just the sense that he wasn't real enough to last into the sunlight terrified her.

"If you're this man—" she lifted the picture "—these men, why weren't you here for me? Why isn't

Annie your daughter? Isn't that the way it's supposed to play out?''

But she was looking for answers from a dream, and he didn't have them.

Gen began to shake as she wrapped Rafe's shoulder in the kitchen. Around her the wind moaned and sighed. The rain and surf sang the same song. Trees clattered and shutters rattled with the probing fingers of the storm. Gen figured that the sun was probably up somewhere out there above the clouds. Beyond her island, the world went on.

But here she struggled as mightily as the storm to hold on to her reality.

It was beginning to sink in. All of it, from the first chords of that terrible nightmare to the terrible mystery of her devotion to a man she couldn't have rationally known, yet had made love to as if she'd known him forever—to the shattering discovery that her husband, whom she'd only just buried, had come back from the dead to betray her. He hadn't just deserted her—whether by accident or intent—callously disregarding her very real fears. He had coldly and deliberately taken advantage of her. He had calmly made his plans knowing full well what it would do not only to his wife, but also to his daughter.

Gen's hold on reality had been shaky enough before. She was really afraid that it had been dealt a fatal blow.

She thought of what she'd been through in the past two days. She thought of what she suspected, what she knew, what she'd been told and given and robbed of. And even with the warm, vibrant touch of Rafe's skin beneath her fingers, she wondered whether he was real. Whether any of this was real, or whether she was simply living out some terrifying dream that would leave her spent and silent when she woke.

If she ever did wake.

She didn't even notice Rafe's surprised reaction when she walked away.

"Gen?"

His voice brought tears to her eyes as she paced to the shuttered front windows. Couldn't he be real? Couldn't she know what those women had known? Couldn't, once in her life, she be given a gift that wasn't taken back? She heard him follow her and fought the twin demons of delight and despair.

She turned on him, her voice accusing. "Who are you?" she demanded, hand to chest, eyes wide, heart battering her ribs. She was shaking and pale, trying so very hard to put into words the impact of what she'd been through. Trying to sort out what couldn't be sorted out. "Why are you here?"

Rafe stood still, never once taking his eyes off her. "To love you."

But Gen shook her head. "That's what Michael told me. Over and over again. Why should I believe you?"

"Because you know me."

"I thought I knew him. I thought I knew myself, but I didn't realize that I'd been carrying these memories in me all these years. I didn't know I could love a man the way—" She stopped, her hand at her mouth, as if she could hold in the truth. As if it would make a difference.

Rafe stepped carefully toward her, and Gen fought the urge to run. He was so sweetly familiar to her, when he shouldn't have been—his hair, his eyes, that sly dimple in his left cheek when he smiled. The pride he took in his land and his work.

She knew she couldn't be remembering any of this, feeling any of it. And yet she was. So strongly that she thought she would burst with it. And yet, before she'd come to this house, she had known none of it. She'd lived her life in comfortable anonymity, never once expecting to be consumed by a passion of any kind. Never suspecting her own capacity for life.

She had grown, loved, married and given birth, not for a moment believing that life could be more than it was.

She'd been wrong. She'd never believed in a timeless passion, and yet that same passion was what had awakened her night after night. A depth of love and understanding and communion that a woman should never be cursed with, because after holding Rafe in her arms, Gen knew that there would be no one else who could fit there again.

And it was that devotion, that singular delight simply in the sight of him, that made her question it. Question her own sanity for feeling it.

"I don't have the answers yet," Rafe insisted gently, his eyes so sharp in the frail morning light, so intent. "I just know that this is where I have to be."

Gen's shrill laugh startled even her. She shook her head, as if she could rid herself of the panic that bubbled. She loved him. Dear, sweet God, she loved him so much, and that was impossible. It was all impossible, and yet she couldn't offer any explanation that would make more sense.

"I have to call Annie," she said and turned away to get her raincoat.

He followed. "No, Gen. You're too upset."

She spun around to face him, wishing she could explain. He had no memory, so he didn't realize how completely wrong all this was. How Gen knew that only Annie would be able to pin her to the ground, where she could sort all this out again.

"He's trussed up like a Christmas goose," Gen insisted with a wild wave of her hand that took in the attic. "He can't hurt me. Besides, the storm's easing up."

"It's eased," Rafe retorted, grabbing her arm. "Not over. Why don't you wait a bit?"

Gen begged for understanding with her eyes, panic escaping into her voice. "I don't think I can. I need to hear her voice, Rafe. I need her to know I'm all right. Don't you understand?''

For the longest moment, he simply watched her. Considered her words with frowning eyes. Gen felt his gaze as if it were a caress, slow and warm and familiar. The soft probing of sunlight against closed lids. But, finally, he nodded.

''I'll come with you.''

Gen was already stuffing breaking-and-entering tools in her pockets. ''I'll be fine.''

Was she afraid that he would carry the unreality of this place with him if he came? She didn't know. She just knew she needed space right now, and this was the only way.

Rafe was still struggling to get into his boots when Gen walked out the back door. She refused to listen to his protests, couldn't wait for him to join her.

The surf was still violent. Rain slanted hard against debris-strewn sand. The wind was like a living thing as it tormented plant and water alike, and the station was two miles away. Gen didn't consider it. She just turned north and walked. She didn't hear anything but the wind and the crashing of the rain and surf. She didn't see anything but the next few steps in front of her. She didn't hear the door slam as Rafe ran out of the house, or his sudden, frantic call to her that he'd remembered.

She had to get to that radio. She had to find the rest of the world—the rest of her world. Gen had never felt so panicked, not even that day when she'd searched in vain for her father, when she'd known deep inside that he wasn't coming back. People had petted her and held her and telephoned her mother. They had sent the police after Jim Carson and found him dead of a heart attack, right there in the parking lot.

It was even worse than Eddie, worse than watching her friend dip under the water and never resurface.

It hadn't been as bad as this. Gen couldn't explain it, couldn't defend it. She just knew that if she didn't get to that radio, whatever gift she'd been given by a capricious past would be taken back. She knew that if she didn't make sure it was all real, it wouldn't have been.

She had to call Annie.

Gen reached what had once been the stream after fifteen minutes of walking. She looked into the torrent the storm had produced, at the deadly whirlpool it created with the raging surf, and turned inland, hoping for a better crossing. Her head down to protect her from the worst of the rain, she didn't notice that she was walking toward a thick stand of trees. She didn't see how the wind tortured them, bending and twisting the age-old limbs like string. She didn't see the danger. She didn't hear the frantic sound of Rafe's voice as he ran toward her out of the rain.

"Genevieve, no! Stop! Michael didn't kill you! You drowned!"

Just then, one of the limbs tore loose and hurtled toward her.

CHAPTER NINE

The force of the blow was stunning. One minute Gen was pushing against the wind, the next she was reeling backward, her feet slipping in the crumbling streambed. She saw the water surging beneath her, knew that once she was in it she'd never make it out before she was sucked into the surf. Before she drowned, because Gen, who lived on an island, couldn't swim a stroke.

"Rafe!" she screamed without thinking.

And he was there. Bare chested and barefoot, his hair plastered to his skin, the bandages soaked away. A terrifying vision of fury, charging through the storm.

A savior with strong hands and perfect balance.

Gen was fighting for her life, her arms pinwheeling and her feet scrabbling for solid ground, her mouth open in terror. She thought she heard a terrible roar. She closed her eyes and held her breath. She felt her hand being caught in a vise, and suddenly she was completely airborne.

He literally yanked her away from the edge of the bank just before it crumbled completely away and washed down toward the seething ocean. Gen landed on her bottom in an ignominious heap, stunned and shaking. She tried to wipe her hair out of her eyes to get a look at her magic savior, only to have him do it for her.

He sat right down next to her on the ground, the rain soaking them both and the wind tearing at their hair.

"How did you do that?" she demanded with a breathless smile. "I thought I was going to die."

He simply shook his head. "Not this time, my love. Not this time."

"But how did you know to come find me?"

His answer was simple, his smile quiet. "I remembered."

Gen opened her mouth to say something. She couldn't. Suddenly she wasn't sure she wanted to know. There were so many secrets behind those crystal blue eyes, so many memories she wasn't sure she shared. So many answers she wasn't sure she should want.

"Remembered what?" she demanded, her voice just as oddly quiet as his. She didn't wonder how it was that they could hear each other so well in the open like this. The storm still tortured the trees not a hundred feet away, and in the other direction the surf pounded the beach with unabated fury. But here, in this little shallow, the wind seemed to miss them.

Rafe motioned toward the raging river beyond them. "What kind of danger you were in."

Gen took a look over at the seething water she'd considered from much closer just moments before, and then returned her consideration to the man seated alongside her. "But I thought . . ."

He shook his head. "I wasn't here to save you from Michael. Evidently you did that all by yourself, even without my help. I was here to save you from you."

"You were— But how did you know?"

She saw the smile then, that dimple that bespoke such impish delight, and was so distracted by it that she didn't anticipate his answer.

"Because I'm not from your past. I'm from your future."

"My future," Gen said yet again as she sat in the bentwood rocker in her living room.

Warm and dry in one of the old dressing gowns and bent over the phone in his lap, Rafe simply nodded. "It's kind of a long story."

Gen scowled. "It's going to be a long storm. Humor me."

That smile again, a bit sheepish now, as if he'd been caught at a prank. He looked up at her. "Don't you want me to fix the phone so you can call Annie?"

Gen caught her breath. "How did you know the line was cut?"

He shrugged a little. "It's part of what I remembered. It was the one thing nobody could explain when they found you. The phone lines in the house had been cut. I imagine Michael did it to keep you from getting help. You're just lucky I enjoy playing with antique gadgets."

She made a vague motion. "You don't have—"

Rafe shook his head. "Fiber optics and satellites. I think I can have it working again in about fifteen minutes."

"I think I need to know what to tell Annie before I talk to her."

Rafe put the phone back down on the table. Then he stood and invited Gen from the rocker to the couch, where he could hold her hand as he talked.

"I know it sounds bizarre...." he finally began.

"No more bizarre than anything else that's happened this weekend."

He shrugged. "Don't be so sure. I'm pretty sure I ended up on your beach because I tried to save your life."

Gen was getting impatient. "We already established that point."

But Rafe was already shaking his head. "Not now," he disagreed. "Then."

"Then."

Another nod. "The year 2120. There's another Genevieve...."

If Gen hadn't been sitting, she would have had to. In fact, she thought of crumpling into a little pile on the floor. "My descendant?"

"Your great-great granddaughter."

She'd thought she couldn't be more surprised. More moved. She was wrong. Tears pushed up the back of her throat and stung her eyes. Her child's child's child's child. Dear God, what a concept! To know before your thirtieth birthday that your name, your memories, would be carried on so far.

"And she's . . . like me?"

Rafe's smile this time was bittersweet. "I always thought she might have been. She has such talent, such passion."

"But is she all right?" Gen demanded. "Did you save her?"

Rafe leaned forward, took Gen's hand in his. "*Will* I save her, you mean. I tried my very best, but she was so despondent."

Once again Gen was left behind. "Despondent? What are you talking about?"

Rafe took a careful breath. Had the courage to look Gen right in the eye, even though he must know she could see and understand every emotion in his expression. She did, and her heart stumbled with a terrible grief.

"Oh, no, Rafe. She didn't."

He held on even more tightly. Gen could barely feel his touch. She could only think of those other women, those faded, hopeful photographs her mother had locked away to keep her safe.

But Rafe wasn't telling her about hope. "You see," he said, "by the time I was born, your suicide has become something of a legend among the O'Shea women."

"My suicide?" Gen demanded. "But I'd never—"

Rafe's smile was gentle, sad. "They didn't know that. None of them. You were found after the storm, fully clothed. Washed ashore. The journals were all out, the trunks gone through. Your mother had locked everything away to try and keep you from being obsessed by the legacy of the O'Shea women, but she found everything and reached the same conclusion as the coroner's inquest. Suicide. It didn't just renew the interest. Your daughter invested it with a kind of cult status. After your death, I'm afraid she never really recovered."

Gen couldn't breathe. She couldn't imagine such a thing, such a terrible impact on her baby, and her baby's children down to the fourth generation.

"But what about your... Gen?"

Rafe shrugged uncomfortably. "I was pulling a gun out of her hands," he said simply, and held on tightly as Gen moaned with distress.

"Gen," he insisted. "I don't think you understand. You've changed all that. *We've* changed all that. We've stopped Michael and shorted out his plan to disappear. We've prevented you from dying, and stopped the O'Shea legend, just like your mother tried to do.''

''Annie...'' Gen murmured, her eyes on the phone.

Rafe nodded. ''You'll have the chance now to teach her about the mistakes her ancestors made, and how you'd never make that same mistake again. And maybe she can teach her children and grandchildren, so they don't go through it all.''

Gen couldn't stop shaking her head. ''To think that she would have ended up believing I'd deserted her, when I would have died trying to prevent her thinking that very same thing. It would have been a horrible mistake.''

''It was, Gen. And I think that that was why it was so important I come back. That I be here for you.''

''But there's still something I don't understand,'' she insisted. ''If this is all part of some cosmic karma kind of thing, where we keep being reincarnated so we can find each other, why didn't I have a Rafe in my life? Wasn't there every other time?''

She wasn't prepared for his smile. ''You did,'' Rafe assured her gently. ''I researched it all myself while I was trying to help Genny. You had a friend when you were a little girl, a very close friend.''

It only took a second before Gen's eyes grew very wide. ''Oh, my God. Eddie. Edmund R. McCalpin.'' Her eyes did fill this time, as she faced the man she'd loved for so long. Would evidently love throughout time. ''We were only seven. I never even asked what the *R* stood for in his name." She couldn't do much more than shake her head in wonder. "So, you saved me twice in one lifetime."

"My pleasure," he said with a smile. And a kiss. A soft, slow meeting of reacquaintance, of recommitment. Gen sank into his embrace and thought about the kind of love that transcended time, the smoke of a passion that rose life after life, never extinguished. She thought of the joy she'd known, even briefly, in this man's arms, and could no longer question how he had come there.

For a long few minutes, they simply rested in each other's arms, savoring the cadence of matched heartbeats, greedily clinging to a love too many times lost.

Gen had so many questions she wanted to ask, about Rafe, about his life and the ones before. So many things she wanted to know about the Rafe she was lucky enough to hold in her arms.

But there were other questions that had to be raised, and Gen wanted no part of those. Even though she knew there wasn't any way around them.

"You're a farmer," she said instead, her eyes closed, her heart beginning to race.

"Kind of," he agreed. "I raise horses."

She nodded against him, suddenly hearing those old echoes, the voices of other women who had held their future in their arms and not known its power.

"Do you remember the other times?"

She knew she didn't have to explain. Rafe lifted a hand to her hair. "Bits and pieces. It began the same way it did with you, the dreams about Richmond, about the island, about drowning, memories of other Genevieves—except I always had a Gen to love. But I guess when I was trying to find something out that might help her, I became kind of obsessed with you. I simply couldn't believe the story that was handed down."

"Rafe."

He lifted her hands to his mouth and kissed them. "Yes, my love."

The tears that had threatened spilled over onto his hands as Gen fought for the courage to give back her gift. "You'll have to go back now," she said, her voice hushed with misery. "Now that you've saved her."

She hadn't wanted an answer, so Gen didn't know what to make of the sweet delight in Rafe's eyes. "I'm not sure what happens now," he admitted. "I'm still not sure how I landed here, but I certainly don't have to go back."

"But, Rafe," Gen insisted instinctively, "you belong there, with that Genevieve. In your own time."

His smile was mischievous. "You're that anxious to get rid of me?"

"But you have a life there. Your work, your Genevieve."

"I've never really been in touch with my own time, Gen. Horse raising isn't exactly a growth industry in my day and age."

Gen couldn't understand. "Life isn't better then?"

He smiled down at her. "Some better, some worse. But I've spent the last five years of my life learning about you, learning about the twentieth century, and I think I want to raise my horses here, with you and Annie. I think I've belonged here all along."

"But what about your Genevieve?"

His eyes glinted with wry delight. "You're my Genevieve. It's what I've been trying to tell you. The Gen in my life is my cousin. I love her, but I've never been in love with her. I've been in love with you since the first picture I saw of you."

"Your—"

He nodded, gave her a delighted smile. "Yes."

Gen felt her heart stumble and right itself again. She couldn't quite breathe. Emotions pitched and swirled in her like the surf outside, stunning her into silence, lifting her to a soaring exhilaration that sang in her like a high wind.

Stay. He wanted to stay. With her.

"It's that easy?" she asked.

Rafe held on tightly, with his hands and arms and eyes, his attention as fierce as his protection. "Don't you think it's about time the O'Shea women had a little good luck in the love department?" he demanded. "Not to mention the men they keep falling in love with. Think of it. We'll marry and have more babies while I raise horses and you head your own business, and we'll grow very old together, so the cosmos will be forced into getting two other poor suckers to pop into our grandkids. And we'll be able to raise them all right this time.''

Gen couldn't decide whether to laugh, sing or cry. "Can we do that?"

He shrugged, the dimple deep, his eyes glittering with anticipation. "I don't know. But two weeks ago, would you have said we could have done this?"

Gen did laugh now. "Good point." She took a shuddering breath, ignored the pounding from two floors up that heralded Michael's impatient request for attention. She curled her fingers around Rafe's and let herself fall headfirst into his mad enthusiasm, and knew for the first time in her life what it truly meant to find happiness.

And that was just counting this life.

Gen smiled and let herself fall back in love. "Let's call Annie."

And when she did, she realized that for the first time in her life, there was nothing to fear. Not the past or the future or the unknown, because they all held the same amount of joy and grief. Gen knew that the next few months weren't going to be easy. She had to get past Michael's crime, the divorce, the financial implications of what had happened. She had to help a man from another time fit into her life, and she had to explain to her mother, who had tried so hard to protect her from this very man for so long, why it would be right.

But now, for Annie and Gen, the future held something indescribably precious, for which they had waited a long time. And Gen couldn't wait to share it with her.

"One more thing," she said, the receiver already in her hand. "Your scar."

He shrugged. "Another war. The fight wasn't as fierce, and the medical care was much better."

She turned yet again to dial, and then stopped. "Your clothes..."

That produced the most wicked grin of all. "Simple," he acknowledged. "It's summer. We don't wear much in summer anymore."

Gen blushed. Rafe was still smiling.

"A custom I think we might begin a little early," he suggested. "You think?"

Gen went ahead and dialed. "Right after the wedding," she said. "In private."

Yes, she thought with a very satisfied smile as she heard the phone ringing on the other end. The future was looking better and better all the time. She was very glad she was going to be around to enjoy it.

* * * * *

KATHLEEN KORBEL

I can vividly remember the first time I put pen to paper to write my own story. I was ten years old, the oldest daughter in a family of seven children who all tried to squeeze into a tiny, two-bedroom home with my parents and grandfather. I had spent my entire life in St. Louis, with summer trips to Michigan, never having seen a mountain, much less an ocean. I lived in a comfortable, safe, predictable universe.

And then I was introduced to possibility. When I wrote, even more than when I read, anything became possible. *Anything.* Just with the magic of words and my own imagination, I could be whomever I wanted, live wherever and whenever I wanted, do things that no mortal human could do. In that little bedroom with the pink ballerina wallpaper, I suddenly discovered the magic of imagination.

Today, my imagination rules. It transcends physical bounds and takes wing where I can't. In my books, I can be a pilot or an alien. I can swing a golf club or a broadsword with equal ease. And now, with the invitation to write for the Silhouette Shadows anthology, I can imagine a love so deep, so compelling, so dangerous, that it indeed breaks all the rules we humans now hold true.

It is a popular belief that there is a veil between this world and the next. That somewhere, just out of sight, are the answers to ancient mysteries. The Irish claim that on their island the veil is at its thinnest. Having visited there, I believe them. There is an air of ancient power there, a quiet communion with other voices we simply don't seem to hear in the more practical places of the world. There is a palpable sense of possibility.

I believe that there are other places like this. Special places where it is somehow easier to touch the things we can't quite see. Places where the whisper of the trees seems like something more, where the earth seems heavy from the passing of other feet, where because the veil is so thin, anything is possible. A place where the love of a man and a woman can gain such power that nothing can quench it, not time, not distance, not even death. I hope you can find that place, too, in "Timeless," because, ultimately, that is what we most hope love is.

Kathleen Korbel

Devil and the Deep Blue Sea

CARLA CASSIDY

To my own Darlene, may you always
repel the darkness and embrace the light

CHAPTER ONE

Darlene Taylor leaned over the stone retaining wall, fascinated by the frothing fury of the water below. The ocean waves thundered in, foaming up in whitecaps that momentarily swallowed the rocky shoreline. The sound roared in her ears, like that of an approaching storm, rising and falling with the shifting tide.

She took a deep breath, intrigued, yet slightly repulsed by the scent of salt and the underlying odor of decaying kelp.

Intrigued, yet slightly repulsed... That pretty much summed up the way she'd felt since arriving at the Raven's Nest Inn two days earlier. Something about the ancient inn on the Maine coast unsettled her.

Since the moment she arrived, she'd felt a strange sense of déjà vu. There was something vaguely familiar, distantly haunting, about the place, like the refrain of some long-forgotten song whose words lingered just out of reach in the subconscious.

There was an energy here, a rather unpleasant energy. It seemed not to focus on any one person or area, but rather to engulf the entire inn, as well as the couple who owned it. She'd tried and tried to dismiss it, but her unease refused to go away.

"Darlene?"

She turned to see Wilma Swanson, one of the owners of the inn, approaching. Darlene swallowed a small groan. The gray-haired, birdlike woman had been positively maternal from the moment Darlene arrived.

"There you are, my dear. I've been looking everywhere for you." She linked her arm with Darlene's and patted it fondly, the wrinkles in her sun-browned face deepening as she smiled. "I've got somebody I want you to meet...another guest. He just arrived a little while ago."

The little woman positively vibrated with suppressed excitement, and again Darlene found herself choking back a moan as she realized that the old woman had matchmaking on her mind. "Oh, I was just enjoying the view, and I'm really not dressed to meet anyone." She ran a hand self-consciously down the sides of her worn jeans, then reached up and finger-combed her breeze-tangled hair.

"Nonsense," Mrs. Swanson said, her head bobbing up and down on her long, thin neck. "You look just fine, and it's getting much too cold out here. You'll catch a chill. Besides—" she smiled again "—I think you'll like him very much."

Darlene's protests were like the flutterings of a moth's wings against a screen. With a fatalistic nod she followed Mrs. Swanson across the large stone patio.

The inn hovered above them, a large three-story structure weathered to the color of shadows. It rose as if defying the rocky ledge where it sat, as if refusing to surrender to the water or be swallowed up by the forest that crowded in nearby.

Instead of seeming to welcome her as a guest, the inn somehow made her feel like an intruder. It offered no warmth, no invitation. Once again Darlene found herself wondering why her uncle Donald had chosen this particular place for her to spend her three-week vacation.

As they entered the inn's back door, which led into a long hallway, Darlene steeled herself to meet Mrs. Swanson's "friend."

I'll be nice and polite, but I'll make it clear that I'm here to rest and relax, not to socialize, she thought firmly. She drew a deep breath as they entered the parlor.

As usual, a fire was blazing in the stone fireplace, warding off the damp chill of the early-autumn evening. The room was filled with dancing shadows, and for a moment Darlene thought there was nobody else in the room. She turned around to look questioningly at Wilma, but the old woman had disappeared.

Then she saw him. He was sitting in a wing-backed chair, and he seemed to blend into the deep darkness that surrounded him.

As usual, Wilma had turned on no lights against the encroaching shades of night. What Darlene had found charming before, irritated her now as she perused the stranger in the semidarkness of the room.

He apparently hadn't heard her enter, for he didn't move a muscle. He was staring into the flames, as if transfixed by the dancing fire and the visions he found there.

Darlene could see only part of his profile, but it was enough for her to tell that his face was constructed of harsh lines and strong angles. There was no softness in his face, no hint of compassion or humility. He didn't look as if he would welcome company. Something about the arrogant tilt of his head, an aura of power and control that invited no intrusion.

I could back out of the room right now and he would never even know I was here, she thought, contemplating doing just that. But before she had a chance to move, he turned and looked at her.

For a moment, his eyes retained the glow of the fire, the darkness of their pupils reflecting a red glow that made Darlene unconsciously utter a small gasp and stumble backward several steps.

"Ah, you must be the charming new guest Wilma has been raving about," he said, standing and rising to an impressive height. His voice was as smooth as a silken cape.

The profile that had promised a strong face had not lied. Dark, heavy eyebrows arched boldly above his ebony eyes. High cheekbones slashed across his tanned countenance, emphasizing his straight nose and sensuous mouth. He possessed a handsome face, one that compelled, yet held an intensity that made her want to turn and run. "I'm Quintin Marshall."

He held out his hand, and for a brief moment Darlene hesitated, not wanting to place her hand in his. Something about him bothered her . . . something inexplicable. . . . She flushed when one of his dark brows rose questioningly and quickly stuck out her hand to meet his.

"Darlene Taylor," she murmured, coaxing her facial muscles into what she hoped was a pleasant smile. As his hand enfolded hers, ripples of pleasure danced through her at the unexpected warmth of his skin . . . a warmth that swept up her arm and suffused her entire body.

She broke the contact with a nervous laugh. "You startled me for a moment. I didn't see you sitting there." Wilma hadn't warned her that the man was handsome as sin, with a magnetic presence to match.

"I'm sorry," he said, although he didn't sound the least bit regretful. "I was just getting ready to indulge in a glass of sherry. Would you join me?"

Her first impulse was to decline. There was something about the man that had her on edge. He was far too attractive, and she realized she was spending too much energy wondering what his wonderfully sensuous lips would feel like against her own. "I'd love a glass of sherry,'' she heard herself responding, as if from a distance.

Why not? she rationalized. For the past two nights, ever since she'd arrived, she'd enjoyed a glass of sherry in front of the fire before retiring to her room for the night. Why should she change her habit just because tonight there was another guest?

She sat in the wing-backed chair opposite his, observing him as he walked over to the portable bar in the corner of the room.

He had a physique to match the strength of his face. His black slacks attested to the fact that his legs and buttocks possessed not an ounce of spare flesh. The charcoal-colored dress shirt displayed his broad shoulders and flat abdomen.

Before he'd turned to the bar, she'd noticed that the top two buttons of the shirt were open, allowing a thatch of dark hair to peek out provocatively. She flushed as he turned around suddenly, catching her in her frank appraisal of him. He smiled. It was a smile of cynical knowledge, and it unnerved her.

She murmured her thanks, careful not to touch his hand as she took the wineglass full of amber liquid that he held out for her. He settled back in his chair and gazed at her, his dark eyes mysterious, yet not unfriendly. ''So, Darlene Taylor. What brings you to the Raven's Nest Inn?''

''I'm here on vacation.''

"Indeed?" Again one of his dark eyebrows rose quizzically. "Raven's Nest is rather off the beaten vacation track. I'd think a woman as lovely as you would have preferred a beach in Florida, or the excitement of New York City."

She sipped the sherry and shook her head. She began to relax, with the fire warming her exterior and the sherry's smoothness hitting the pit of her stomach. "Actually, it was my uncle Donald who encouraged me to come here. He's a frequent visitor here at the inn, and he thought the isolation and quiet would be good for me." Again she saw his curiosity, and she continued. "You see, for the past year I've been taking care of my grandmother." Darlene's stomach tightened convulsively at the thought of the woman who had raised her from childhood. "She was quite ill, and... she passed away last month. Uncle Donald thought it would be a good idea for me to take some time for myself and just relax before I get on with the rest of my life..." She broke off, realizing she was rattling on, telling this man far more than he needed to know. "Anyway, here I am," she finished with a shrug.

"So you are." His smile didn't quite reach his enigmatic eyes. "And what do you think of Raven's Nest?"

Darlene got up, uncomfortable with the intensity of his dark gaze and walked over to the large window that overlooked the rocky ledge and the thundering waters below. She stared out to where the light of dusk cast shimmering illusions upon the turbulent waters. "The inn is quite nice," she said noncommittally. "It's older than I expected, more isolated." She looked out the window once again, thinking of the strange disquiet that had plagued her since her arrival.

She sensed, rather than heard, him rising from his chair, and a moment later she felt his presence directly behind her. She could smell the scent of him, a wildness that invaded her senses. She could feel the heat of his body, even though he didn't touch her at all.

"The land was called Raven's Nest long before the inn was ever built. Ravens make their nests among the crevices of the rocky cliff, but the wind and the water usually destroy the nests before the eggs can ever hatch."

Again she was struck by the melodious depth of his voice. But the image that his words painted was less than pleasant. "How tragic," she said after a moment's hesitation. The shimmering illumination of twilight suddenly stopped, leaving behind only night-darkened waves. "There's something very savage about the scenery," she said after another moment.

"Yes, but there can be beauty in savagery," he observed. His breath stroked the back of her neck with heat, and he moved closer, pushing the heavy draperies aside to allow them a wider view of the scenery. Although he still didn't touch her, she felt his closeness as if he were pressing intimately against her back. She was suddenly afraid he would touch her, and she didn't want him to.

Darlene's mouth was suddenly uncomfortably dry, and she wished he'd move away from her. His nearness overwhelmed her, making it difficult to think.

In sudden desperation, she stepped away from him, going back to the chair and sitting down. She sipped her sherry to ease the dryness of her throat and directed her gaze away from him and into the flames of the fire.

She pushed a shining pale strand of hair behind her ear and watched the flickering fire, surprised at the intensity of her emotions concerning this virtual stranger. She raised the wineglass once again to her lips and finished the sherry.

She was suddenly anxious to be away from this man with the dark, opaque eyes and the sensuous lips that made her insides quiver strangely. "I think I'll call it a night," she said, standing up and offering him another pleasant but forced smile.

He looked at his watch and offered a protest. "Ah, but the night is just beginning." His eyes once again captured the glow of the fire, sparking with red glints that unnerved her. "The hours of darkness are usually the most interesting ones."

Darlene flushed. Something about the man, and everything he said, was too evocative, too sensual. "I was raised with the adage 'Early to bed, early to rise...'"

"A most boring bit of wisdom," he observed.

"Yes, but one I adhere to just the same." She set her empty glass on the coffee table, not looking directly at him. "Thank you for the sherry and good night, Mr. Marshall. It was nice meeting you." She moved quickly out of the room, suppressing the impulse to turn and look at him one last time.

As she left the room, taking with her the sweet scent of her floral perfume, Quintin Marshall settled back in the high-backed chair again. He returned his gaze to the depths of the fire, his mind still filled with a picture of her face.

Darlene Taylor. She was quite beautiful. Her oval face, ivory complexion and wide blue eyes lent her an aura of undisturbed innocence. Yet there was an inherent sensuality about her that had instantly drawn him to her. Even in faded jeans and an oversize sweatshirt, it had been obvious that she had a pleasing figure, one that had instantly made his blood race hot and thick through his veins.

He took another sip of his sherry, enjoying the warmth of the alcohol. He leaned his head back, trying to imagine the taste and texture of her lips beneath his, the weight and warmth of her breasts against his palms. Yes, she was really quite perfect. He could understand why she'd been chosen. She would make a beautiful bride for Satan.

CHAPTER TWO

Darlene knew something was different the moment she descended the stairs to the dining room the next morning. The sound of laughter drifted toward her, an alien sound in this inn of shadows. Until the arrival of Quintin Marshall the night before, she had been the inn's only guest. But now the ring of merriment from the dining room spoke of new people, and a strange sense of anticipation seethed in the air.

"Ah, Darlene, there you are." Harold Swanson, Wilma's husband, greeted her as she hesitated on the threshold of the dining room. If Wilma Swanson reminded Darlene of a bird, then Harold was a farm cow. He had huge brown eyes and a lumbering gait, and his face wore an expression of perpetual bewilderment.

"Good morning, Mr. Swanson," she replied, noting the sudden silence of the other people in the room. She lingered just inside the doorway, feeling as if she'd interrupted something private among the others.

"Come...come and join us." Harold beamed her a smile of encouragement. "These are special guests, and I've just been telling them all about you."

Darlene smiled in confusion. Why would he be telling other guests about her? He's just being nice, she thought, trying to include me.

"So this is Darlene." An attractive, sophisticated-looking brunette walked over to where Darlene stood. "I'm Susan Bennet, and the bald one over there is my husband, Dr. Will Bennet." She pointed across the room, where a chubby bald man waved a greeting. "The others are Mildred Walker and her husband, Jerry, and Ken Beacham and his wife, Sara."

Darlene nodded to all of them. "Did you all arrive together?"

"We arrived last night, but not all at the same exact time," Susan explained. "The bunch of us get together and stay here at the inn once a month."

"How nice...sort of like a social club," Darlene commented, murmuring a thank-you when Harold brought her a cup of coffee from the buffet.

"Exactly...although we're missing three more of our group. They should be arriving later this evening."

"Are you all from the same town...or in the same profession?" Darlene asked curiously. They certainly looked like a diverse bunch. Mildred and Jerry Walker were at least fifteen years younger than the others.

"Oh, heavens, no. We're just people who have common interests and goals."

"Here we are, folks." Wilma entered the dining room carrying a tray of food, interrupting any further conversation. "Get settled at the table and I'll bring in the rest of this feast."

Breakfast was delicious, and the others were extremely friendly, but Darlene felt a discordant presence in the room, surrounding her like a cloak of gray, gauzy material. It was nothing she could put her finger on, nothing said or done by anyone else...just a feeling that something was amiss...something that made her want to be away from these people.

In particular, there was something about Dr. Will Bennet that disturbed her. His florid face seemed vaguely familiar, touched off the strange sense of déjà vu she'd experienced for the past three days.

Quintin sat down the table from her, quiet, somehow set apart from the others. Although he didn't speak to her directly, every time she looked up his gaze was on her, making her more and more uncomfortable as breakfast progressed. She was aware of his strange eyes on her even when she wasn't looking at him. She tried desperately to keep her attention focused on her plate, but again and again she found her gaze locked with his.

She'd tossed and turned all night long, plagued by erotic, sensual dreams. Dreams in which she and Quintin had been the principal players...dreams that even now had the power to pull heat into her cheeks.

She looked up at him now, and blushed when he smiled with secret mystery, as if he knew about her dreams, had shared them with her. She quickly looked down at her plate again, feeling the blush in her cheeks intensify.

After breakfast, she excused herself from the group, needing to be away from the other guests, and Quintin in particular. The veil of grayness that had seemed to surround her lifted as she breathed in the fresh, salty air on the patio.

She hopped up and sat on the stone retaining wall, staring at the waves of water that rose and fell, shouting their roar in a voice that somehow soothed with its consistency.

For the first time since her grandmother's death, she realized how very alone she was in the world. Her uncle Donald was her only other relative, and she'd never been very close to him. While she had cared for her grandmother, her friends had moved on with their own lives, and she'd lost touch with most of them.

Still, despite a core of loneliness, she was content at the moment. It was impossible not to be, with all the wild beauty that surrounded her. She released a deep sigh. Overhead, a bird cawed loudly, as if greeting her, and the sound added to her sense of relaxation.

"Darlene!" Wilma's voice exploded Darlene's tenuous peace. She opened her eyes to see Wilma hurrying over to her, her face blanched of color. "Please get down! Don't sit on the wall!" she exclaimed, her hands waving wildly in the air.

Darlene unfolded her legs and quickly stepped down onto the concrete patio. "I'm sorry. I didn't mean to frighten you."

Wilma grabbed her hand and squeezed it fiercely. "You could accidentally fall to the rocks below and be badly hurt...even killed." Wilma shivered, as if horrified by the very thought. "If something happened to you, they'd never forgive me...." She flushed. "I mean, your uncle...and, well, I'd never forgive myself."

Once again Darlene felt a dark cloud of disquiet swoop down around her. Wilma's concern for her safety was too fierce, too intense, and far too personal, for comfort. "I'm fine, Wilma, really," she replied, hoping her voice didn't reflect the irritation she felt. A little maternal fussing was acceptable, but this overwhelming protective urge was too much. "In fact, I had just decided to go for a walk."

Without waiting for Wilma to reply, she walked across the patio and down the path that would lead her to the water's edge. She took deep breaths, trying to regain the momentary peace she'd felt before Wilma's intrusion.

At the end of the path, she stepped cautiously onto the rocks, knowing they were not only slippery but dangerously sharp, as well. She made her way to a large stone perched just above the foaming water and sat down.

At moments like these, she was grateful to her uncle Donald for suggesting this place. She had always enjoyed the outdoors, and here, with the ocean at her feet, the horizon painted in the pinks and golds of approaching sunset, nature was at its best. She closed her eyes, giving in to the moment of relaxation.

"May I join you?"

She instantly tensed. She didn't have to turn around to know who stood just behind her. His deep voice washed over her, strong and assured above the pounding waves. Her heart stepped up its pace in response, and although she knew her peace would be shattered if he joined her, she suddenly wanted him sitting next to her. She nodded.

Quintin eased himself down beside her. His thigh was pressed intimately against hers as they shared the small space on the rock.

For a moment, he didn't speak. Darlene could feel the energy that pulsated around him, could smell the evocative wildness of his scent as it engulfed her. She offered him a hesitant smile, trying to dispel her own unease.

"Your smile is as beautiful as the scenery," he observed, reaching out with his index finger to sweep a strand of her hair away from her face.

"Your flattery is as polished as the rocks at the water's edge," she returned, refusing to meet his gaze, knowing the power that was contained there.

He laughed. It was a low burst of sound, as potent as a caress. "Not only beautiful, but direct, as well." There was a moment of silence. "Why aren't you inside with the others?" he asked.

"I don't know.... They were all having a good time, and they seem to be close friends. I didn't want to intrude." She wrapped her arms around her knees and rested her chin atop them. "Besides, it's nice out here."

He nodded. "If you think it's nice now, you should be out here standing on the rocks at night, with a full moon overhead, lighting the water."

She had a sudden mental image of him standing on the rocks, like some ancient, primitive warrior praying to the god of the moon. It was an evocative picture, and she quickly shoved it from her mind. "I think we had a full moon last night," she observed, remembering the moonlight that had spilled into her bedroom window the night before, as she tried to sleep.

"Not quite. It might have looked full, but it won't be a true full moon for another four nights."

She looked at him, for the first time curious. Again she was struck, not only by his utter handsomeness, but also by the aura of power that clung to him. It was as if he owned the very air that surrounded him and allowed others to breathe it by choice.

He smiled and although the gesture curved his lips sensually, she realized the smile didn't reach the dark abyss of his eyes. "I find the moon fascinating," he explained. "Did you know that there was a time when it was thought that to sleep in the moonlight made you crazy?"

She nodded. "Lunar...lunatic...that's where we got that word." She smiled again. "Sorry, I sound like a schoolteacher."

He laughed again, and the sound affected her like a bass drum booming rhythmically in the pit of her stomach. "Ah, throughout history the moon has supposedly possessed both white and black magic."

"I don't know anything about magic. I just think it's something pretty to look at," she returned, refocusing her gaze on the distant waters of the ocean.

For a moment neither of them spoke, and the silence grew thick as it lingered. "Are you from around here?" she asked, desperate to dispel the growing tension.

"I'm from Portland."

"Do you have any family, Quintin?" she asked, his name feeling strange on her lips. She wanted to know more about him. Perhaps if she heard he had a normal family, a normal life, it would abolish the bewitching spell that drew her to him.

His facial features tightened, and his eyes narrowed. "My parents were killed when I was eight years old. I was raised in a series of foster homes."

"Oh, I'm so sorry." Instinctively she reached out and took his hand in hers. "I lost my parents, too, when I was really young. I was only four years old when they were killed in a car accident."

He turned her hand so that he now held it in a clasp that was both harsh and caressing. "So I guess that means we have a lot in common." His gaze captured hers, and once again she was trapped by those dark depths that seemed to speak some unknown language. "You're so beautiful, so innocent...." He spoke the words with regret, as if in some way her innocence would soon be tainted or destroyed, and Darlene felt an all-encompassing dread fill her. Yet at the same time she caught herself unconsciously leaning toward him, hungry to taste the dark fires that burned in his soul, eager to experience a plunge into the flames of hell's fires. She wanted him to kiss her, and he seemed to read her desire for a taste of his lips.

As his mouth covered hers, she felt his darkness swirling around her, enclosing her in a mist of sensual pleasure that pulled every rational thought out of her mind.

His lips plied hers with heat and she knew that somehow his kiss had touched her soul, branded her, made it impossible for her to go back to what she'd been before the kiss.

As he slowly withdrew his lips from hers, she once again gazed into his eyes...eyes that were somehow both familiar and terrifying. The curve of the brows, the shape of the eyes themselves, called to something in her, reminded her of something... She just couldn't quite put a finger on it. She only knew that somehow, in some way, he'd made a connection with her, forged a bond that would be difficult to forget.

She moved away from him, breaking the hypnotic eye contact. "I should get inside. It must be time for lunch."

"We still have an hour before lunch," he protested.

Darlene flushed, feeling as if time had stood still while he kissed her. She needed to get away from him, needed to take a moment to settle the quivering of her nerves. She smiled uncertainly. "I guess I didn't eat enough at breakfast, because I'm famished."

He stood up and held his hand out to help her up. She took his hand, but released it the moment she stood up, not wanting any kind of physical contact to linger between them. "I'm hungry, too," he said.

She looked up at him, flushing, as it was obvious that he wasn't talking about a hunger for food. His gaze traveled boldly over the length of her, letting her know exactly what he was hungry for.

They walked back to the inn in silence, the sun skittering behind a cloud and casting shadows on the hollows of his face like a lover finding a familiar position. Again Darlene felt a shiver of apprehension streak through her.

Despite her intense attraction to him, there was a darkness in him that frightened her. She felt no real physical threat from him but rather a deeper, more pervasive fear—a fear for her spirit.

She'd never really believed in the concept of evil before, but she suddenly realized that was what she feared. Since the moment she had arrived at the inn, she had felt surrounded by evil and had not known from where it emanated. She looked up at Quintin. Who was this handsome man, and what bewildering power did he have over her? Was he the source of the blackness that imbued the inn and its inhabitants?

As she stared up at him, the shadows on his face spread, swallowing his features in complete darkness.

CHAPTER THREE

Eyes... Black eyes, radiating madness... They stared at her, emitting an unspoken threat that filled her with terror. She couldn't discern any other feature on the face, and that only made it more frightening. The eyes demanded attention, commanded something... something she didn't understand.

Darlene sat straight up, releasing a choked sob of fear. For a long moment she stared around her, finding nothing familiar that could help her chase away her nightmare bogeyman and the swirling mist that surrounded her. As the mist receded, she realized she was in her room at the inn, surrounded by darkness that was deepest in the corners. She reached for the light on the bedside stand and uttered a sigh of relief as the soft illumination pierced through the veil of darkness.

Although she was now fully awake, she knew from experience that it would be some time before the dream faded enough from her mind to allow her to return to a more pleasant sleep.

For a long moment she lay there, taking deep breaths, waiting for her heart to beat at a less frantic pace. Still trembling from the horror of the familiar nightmare, she unwound her legs from the tangled sheets and swung them over the side of the bed. Still trembling, she stood up, reaching for the silky light blue robe that was at the foot of the bed.

As she put on the robe, she drew a deep breath and thought again about her nightmare. It was not an unfamiliar visitor. It had haunted her for as long as she could remember, filled with darkness, dancing shadows, and a pair of black eyes that instantly evoked intense fear. She had no idea where it came from or how to make it go away. She only knew that sleep was next to impossible following one of the dreams. She wrapped her arms around herself, shivering slightly in the damp chill of the room.

A nice hot cup of tea is what I need, she thought as she grabbed her flashlight from the nightstand, opened the bedroom door and peered out into the hallway. The beam of the small flashlight valiantly attempted to penetrate the blackness of the hall, but its attempt was ineffectual.

As she moved cautiously down the two narrow staircases that led to the ground floor of the inn, she thought again of the unsettling feeling she'd had since arriving at this place.

From the moment the taxi approached and she caught her first glimpse of the inn, perched precariously on the rocky cliffs, she'd had a sense of familiarity. *I've been here before,* she'd thought as she climbed out of the cab and stood staring at the forbidding place. But, of course, she knew that was impossible. She had no memories from before the age of four, when she'd come to live with her grandmother in the small town of Gloville, Missouri.

And as far as she knew, she'd never before been to Maine. Still, she couldn't shake a strange feeling of familiarity. She had the feeling of ancient memories floating in the air around her, the feeling that if she could just pluck one out of the air and examine it, she would understand why there were certain things in the house, certain rooms, that strummed a distant chord of forgotten memory.

She entered through the swinging doors that led into the kitchen and turned on the dim light over the sink, relieved at the resulting soft glow.

Wilma had told her to feel free to use the kitchen at any time. "We don't stand on ceremony here at Raven's Nest," the old woman had said, and she'd then laughed, as if enjoying a private joke only she understood.

Private joke or no private joke, Darlene was grateful for access to the kitchen. There was nothing more soothing than a nice hot cup of tea and a nibble of something sinfully sweet to chase away the lingering foul taste of one of her nightmares.

She put a kettle of water on to boil. Then, discovering the remains of the killer chocolate cake that had been served at dinner, she cut herself off a generous slice. She turned to carry it to the table, but froze.

One of the shadows in the corner of the room co-alesced into a manlike shape that moved toward her. The plate crashed to the floor as she stifled a scream.

Quintin Marshall stepped out of the shadows and into the dim light. "I'm sorry. I didn't mean to frighten you."

Her hands flew up to her mouth. "You . . . you just startled me. I didn't know anyone else was in here." Her heart still pounded with a frantic rhythm. She bent down and quickly scooped up the ruined slice of cake, grateful that at least the plate hadn't broken. She kept her gaze carefully averted from him, once again feeling a strange, magnetic force emanating from his presence.

"Is there any more of that? I'll cut you another piece," he offered, his voice deep and darkly sensual.

"There's more in there, but I, uh . . . changed my mind. I'm really not hungry." Her appetite was gone, lost to the stronger sensation of disquiet. What was it about this man that so put her on edge? She dumped the cake in the garbage, then set the plate in the sink.

"I think I'll get a piece," he said as the teakettle sputtered its first whistle.

As he cut off a piece of the cake, Darlene fixed herself a cup of tea and sat at the table. She hoped he was a fast eater. She drew her robe more tightly around her and tied it firmly at her waist.

Since he was clad in a pair of dark jogging pants and nothing else, not even shoes, it was obvious he hadn't been expecting company, either. And she definitely hadn't anticipated drinking her tea with a darkly handsome man with devil eyes and a bare chest that made her want to reach out and tangle her fingers through the tuft of hair there. Her cheeks flamed with heat as she remembered the kiss they'd shared that afternoon.

He joined her at the table, bringing with him the evocative scent of the night and the ocean breeze. He looked at her, his eyes so dark it was impossible to tell pupil from iris. "Couldn't sleep?" he asked.

"I, uh . . . had a bad dream," she answered, stirring sugar into her tea.

"This inn was built on bad dreams," he replied, his black eyes flashing with intensity.

"What do you mean?"

He studied her for a moment, and then his lips formed an enigmatic half smile. "It doesn't matter." He cut into his cake and took a bite.

Darlene wanted to pursue the topic, but something about his facial expression kept her from pressing the subject. "That's the most decadent cake I've ever tasted," she finally observed after a moment's hesitation. "I had a huge piece right after dinner."

"There are rewards for being decadent."

"And usually a price," Darlene returned, wondering how they had ever gotten onto such a strange subject. Yet Quintin Marshall looked like a hedonist, a man who sought pleasure as some people looked for religion. He was a man who would take pleasure and leave it with equal ease. "Are you here on vacation, as well?" she asked, shoving dangerous thoughts aside, yet needing to know more about him.

"I'm on a sort of working vacation. I'm a salesman, and I'm trying to sell some updated equipment to Wilma."

Darlene stared at him, startled by his choice of occupation. A salesman? It seemed too benign, too safe, for this man. "Will you be staying here at the inn for long?"

"As long as it takes."

She sipped her tea, fascinated yet frightened by the dark aura that seemed to surround the man. Secrets lived in his black eyes . . . secrets that compelled discovery, yet warned that perhaps they would not all be pleasant.

She mentally shook herself, wondering what it was about this man that evoked a warmth that coiled through her insides, yet raised goose bumps on her skin. She watched surreptitiously as he ate his dessert.

His dark hair shone with a midnight blue luster, and she wondered what it would be like to tangle her hands in it, to use its thick richness to pull his sensuous lips down to claim hers. His chest was well muscled. Beneath the mat of dark hair, it was tanned the color of smooth maple. Darlene wondered if his flesh would be hot. But how could it be, when all his heat seemed to be centered in his eyes?

His dark eyebrows rose, and his lips curved upward, as if he knew the direction her thoughts were taking, and was enjoying it. Fever flamed in her cheeks, and she studied the inside of her teacup, wishing she knew how to read her future in the dark brew.

"You mentioned earlier this evening that you're here to relax before you get on with the rest of your life. What do you intend to do when you leave here? You said something earlier about sounding like a teacher. Is that what you do?"

Darlene shrugged and looked at him again. "I have a teaching degree, and that's something I've always wanted to do, but so far it hasn't worked out that way. My career was sidetracked by nursing my grandmother. I've got an application in at an elementary school back home. I'm hoping to be hired there next fall."

"Where's home?"

"Gloville, Missouri. It's a small farming community about sixty miles outside of Kansas City." Although the conversation was banal, Darlene had the feeling that he was assessing and weighing her every word with an unwarranted intensity. His strange fervor frightened her almost as much as his physical attractiveness overwhelmed her.

There was a surreal fog that seemed to appear around them each time they were together, making everything fade away except the two of them.

"So you're a farm girl. Any farm boys back home waiting for your return?"

Darlene shook her head. "No. Taking care of my grandmother was a full-time job this past year. I lost touch with friends...and didn't have time to cultivate any new personal relationships."

He nodded, as if satisfied with her answer. His eyes glittered, dark and mysterious. Darlene had a feeling it wouldn't have mattered if she'd told him she had a husband and ten children waiting for her back in Gloville. If Quintin decided he wanted her, nothing and nobody would stand in the way of his desire.

She shivered, suddenly needing to escape from his oppressive presence. She didn't want to look into his eyes anymore. She had the feeling that if she did she would be lost forever, captive to the hypnotic quality that lingered in their depths.

"I think I should probably call it a night," she said, rising from the table and taking her cup to the sink. "I'm sure I'll be able to sleep just fine now."

"I'd hate to think of you suffering more nightmares." He, too, stood up, moving to fill the doorway she had to pass through to go back to her room. "You forgot this." He held out her flashlight.

"Thanks." She reached for the flashlight at the same moment a clock chimed nearby. She jumped in surprise, and he placed his hands on her shoulders to steady her.

For a moment they stood face-to-face, counting the chimes that rang, their sound slightly distorted and discordant.

"Twelve o'clock. Midnight." His deep voice filled the silence when the chimes finally stilled. "The witching hour."

"Yes," Darlene breathed softly, unable to move away from him. As she stared up into his eyes, she felt as if she were surrounded by an enormous, thick energy that made it impossible to move, difficult even to breathe.

His hands burned through the silky material of the robe, and his eyes glowed with the fires of hell. She was losing herself in his eyes, could feel her free will flying away like dust in a high wind. His hands began to move, lightly caressing her shoulders.

She knew he was going to kiss her, and she was afraid... afraid that if his lips touched hers again he would possess a part of her soul that she would never be able to regain.

But there was a small part of her that wanted his kiss, that ached to feel those sinfully sensuous lips against hers once again. There was magic at work... a black kind of magic that sucked all rational thought, stole reason and whirled it into an insane vortex of passion.

One of his hands moved from her shoulders to the back of her head at the same time his lips descended toward hers. His kiss was bold, invasive, more a possession than a caress. His lips were demanding, leaving no room for denial or protest. He stole the breath from her body, engulfed her in a fever that created both a flush and a chill.

She responded with a wantonness that frightened her. It was as if he somehow beckoned to some inner element she hadn't known she possessed.

She dropped the flashlight to the floor and allowed her hands to touch the smooth muscles of his back.

Hot...yes, his body was hot, like a flaming torch held against her skin. Pressing closer, she allowed the kiss to linger for an indecently long time.

His hand on the back of her head held her captive as effectively as if she were bound to him by chains. She couldn't move, and she didn't want to. She could only accept the heat, the sensual pleasure his lips offered.

When he finally broke the kiss, the dark magic evaporated, leaving Darlene confused, horrified and more than a little bit frightened by her uninhibited response to the kiss.

"You...you shouldn't have done that...." she gasped as she backed away from him. She reached up and touched her lips. They felt swollen and fevered.

He reached out and caressed a strand of her shining blond hair, wrapping it around his fist like a bond of silk. "Powers far greater than us are at work here, Darlene." Again he stood so close to her that she felt the need to run, felt as if by merely staring into his eyes he could steal away her free will.

He allowed her hair to fall free once again, and his fingers moved to trail down the side of her face, his index finger pausing to rub sensually across her lower lip. "I like kissing you." His voice was a shadowed whisper. "And I intend to do it again . . . often."

I just might have something to say about that, Darlene wanted to protest. But when she stared into his eyes, when she felt the mesmerizing power there, she wasn't so sure she had any say at all about what he would or would not do to her.

She stepped back, away from him. "Good night, Quintin."

"Sweet dreams, Darlene," she heard him say as she picked up the flashlight, then turned and ran. She took the stairs two at a time, feeling as if the devil himself were nipping at her heels.

Once safely inside her room, she took off her robe, her hands shaking, and crawled beneath the blankets.

Despite the fact that he'd frightened her, despite the fact that she felt she'd just had a close encounter with Lucifer himself, her body burned for his hot touch, and her lips ached with wanting.

She smiled to herself. The devil had no horns, no pitchfork—he merely had black eyes and a body made for loving.

There was no way she would believe he was a traveling salesman. No way. He'd lied about his job, and she wondered why. And his talk about powers at work—what had it all meant? He'd made it sound as if fate were responsible for bringing the two of them together here, as if they were both helpless to fight against the inevitable end fate had chosen.

Ridiculous...the whole thing was completely ridiculous! There was no fate at work here. There was nothing mysterious about any of it. The man was no mystical being. He was no devil in disguise. He merely had a practiced line and a smooth delivery.

Although for the past couple of years Darlene's time and energies had been devoted exclusively to her grandmother, there had been a time in college when she had dated frequently. She'd even entertained the idea of marrying one particular college mate who'd shared her dreams and ideals. That relationship had been unable to withstand the strain when she'd taken over the care of her grandmother.

However, nothing in her past dating experience had prepared her for Quintin Marshall, and his own particular brand of dangerous sensuality and powerful magnetism. Dangerous...Yes, she had an immediate feeling of danger when she gazed into his eyes. It had nothing to do with a physical threat, but it was a danger just the same.

She knew she was an innocent when it came to the realm of sexuality. There hadn't been time in her life to explore that part of herself. The relationship she'd had in college had never progressed to the point of physical intimacy. It was no wonder a man as smooth and practiced as Quintin Marshall had such a profound effect on her.

She punched her pillow and snuggled down, wondering what her dreams would bring for the rest of the night. She was tired. She didn't want any more nightmares. She also hoped she didn't dream of him. Her body was hot enough without the further complication of erotic dreams and sensual images.

She closed her eyes, willing her body to relax, her mind to drift free. She concentrated on making her breath come evenly, in an imitation of the rhythm of sleep.

Eyes...dark eyes... The vision filled her mind. Black eyes that commanded...demanded. Her nightmare visions filled her head, causing her to tremble once again.

She gasped and sat up, suddenly realizing what it was about Quintin Marshall that so unnerved her. His eyes...those black, intense eyes...they were the exact same ones that had haunted her nightmares for as long as she could remember....

CHAPTER FOUR

Quintin stood at his second-story window, staring down at the woman walking on the patio below. Darlene Taylor. She didn't know it yet, but their destinies were as intrinsically bound as those of two leaves on the same tree. Their fates had been proclaimed long ago, their futures promised in blood to a greater cause.

She was a helpless pawn in a game she wouldn't understand. But what a beautiful pawn she is, he thought to himself. Each and every moment he spent with her, he was more drawn to her. It had been a long time since he'd wanted a woman as much as he wanted her, and he was accustomed to getting what he wanted.

He turned when a knock came on his bedroom door. "Yes?"

The door creaked open and Wilma entered, carrying a tray of coffee and toast. With a hesitant smile that was tinged with awe, she set the tray down on the table near the window.

Quintin's gaze was once again captured by Darlene's movements below, and Wilma moved to look out the window, as well. "You're pleased with her?" she asked, holding her breath in anticipation.

"Exceedingly," he answered, not taking his eyes from the slender blond woman on the patio below.

"Then we can continue preparations for the ceremonies?" Wilma asked breathlessly.

Quintin turned and stared at the old woman, who tried unsuccessfully to control a shiver as she stood beneath the power of his intense gaze. "Even had I not been pleased, we would have continued preparations for the ceremony. Is this not what we've been waiting for, working toward for years?"

Wilma bobbed her head emphatically. "Of course. I'll tell the others to proceed as planned."

Quintin nodded curtly, and the old woman scurried out of the room. Old fool, he thought scornfully. He returned his gaze to Darlene. The sunlight caressed her blond hair, making it sparkle with brilliant highlights. He remembered the feel of it in his hands, its soft silkiness. It had been two nights since he'd tasted the sweetness of her kiss, her hungry response to him. He wanted to taste her lips again.

He wondered if she had any idea of the importance of her role in the devil's dance of desire to take place on the night of the full moon? Probably not.

It didn't matter.... The game would be played to its end. He couldn't stop it, and neither could she. But then, he didn't want to stop the game.

Darlene sat in the corner of the parlor, watching the other guests dancing to the tinny sounds of the radio and laughing and mingling among themselves.

She watched Quintin move from group to group, and she noticed how each and every person treated him with a distant respect. He seemed to hold himself apart from the others, but they listened to what little he had to say as if the wisdom of the world was hidden in his words.

She'd spent much of the day out on the patio, thinking about this man who had taken command of her dreams and filled her with a deep, burning desire. His eyes... how was it possible that his eyes had haunted her dreams for as long as she could remember? How was it possible that a virtual stranger had existed in her subconscious years before she'd actually met him?

Surely I'm mistaken, she thought, looking at him now, across the room. *It's impossible that those are his eyes in my dreams... impossible. They just happen to look like the ones that frighten me in my nightmares. It's a mistake, or just a weird coincidence,* she concluded firmly.

She turned her attention back to the guests and their activities. Including Wilma and Harold, the inn now held twelve people, and all of them were in the small parlor. One thing Darlene had noticed about the new guests was that they liked to party. She'd fallen asleep the night before to the sounds of merriment drifting up the stairs. The noise had lasted long into the night, making Darlene toss and turn and wake up feeling as if the night had been far too short.

She now stifled a yawn with the back of her hand, deciding she would linger down here for just a few more minutes, pretend sociability, then go upstairs to her room and try to catch up on her sleep. Maybe the others would make it an early night.

"Dance?"

She looked up to see Quintin standing in front of her, his hand stretched out in invitation. His eyes beckoned to her, summoning her to join him as slow, strangely haunting music drifted upward from the radio.

She didn't even think about declining. She had no power against the commanding darkness of his eyes. She reached out her hand and placed it in his, allowing herself to be drawn up into the strength of his arms.

He was summer heat assuaging winter's chill. His body pressed hot and intimate against hers, and his gaze possessed her as they began to move to the music.

Darlene's sense of reality shifted. Everything in the room faded away as she lost herself in the blackness of his eyes, in the intimacy of the dance. She felt as if they were dancing on the edge of the earth and if she released her hold on him she'd spin off into a black hole of nothingness.

He's bewitched me, she thought, realizing there was a hypnotic power in his gaze that she couldn't fight. He was in complete control, and she had no will, no desire to protest.

She was aware of his heart throbbing with a pulsing beat that spoke to her own. She knew her heart answered, like a primitive drum communicating through a mysterious jungle. She was intensely conscious of his body pressed tightly against hers, her soft curves molding to the muscular planes and angles of his.

He was a wonderful dancer, moving with a smoothness and agility that somehow didn't surprise her. There was no hesitation, no awkwardness, and she realized he would probably make love with the same confident assurance. The thought caused a flame to flicker in the pit of her stomach and she realized that she wanted to make love with him, wanted him more than she had ever wanted a man in her life. She wanted his total possession, not only of her spirit, but of her body, as well. And in the intimacy of their embrace she knew he wanted her, too.

She was acutely aware of his hand at the small of her back, spreading an all-consuming heat. His breath was hot and wild on her face, and his lips were curved in a small smile of promise that stole her breath away. She closed her eyes, knowing that if he wanted to, he could take her now, on the faded carpeting, and she wouldn't have the strength to protest.

"Ah, that was beautiful ... simply splendid." Susan Bennet's voice broke the spell, and Darlene opened her eyes, realizing that the music had ended and she and Quintin were surrounded by the other guests, who were clapping and smiling their approval.

With an embarrassed blush she moved out of Quintin's arms, reality clashing with the spell she'd been in. "I ... I think I'll go on up to my room," she murmured, starting for the parlor door.

"Oh, you can't go yet," Wilma protested, shoving a glass of liquor into her hands. "We're going to drink a toast."

"I don't think—"

"But you must," Wilma insisted, overriding her protests.

Darlene shrugged, too tired to argue about such an inconsequential matter. The glass was small—she could down the entire contents in one gulp. Besides, it might relax her enough that she could sleep, no matter how loud or how long they continued to party tonight. It might give her sleep without heated images of Quintin.

It took only moments for everyone to obtain a glass, and once they had them raised, Will Bennet cleared his throat. "To Raven's Nest," he said solemnly. "May there be many future generations to carry on our traditions and ceremonies."

"Hear! Hear!" Susan added as they all downed their drinks.

Darlene drank hers in one swallow, shivering at the strong, nutty flavor and the lingering bitter aftertaste. "And now, I really must say good night," she said, as she handed her empty glass back to Wilma.

For a moment, her gaze caught Quintin's, and she read something in his eyes, something she couldn't understand. It was as if his eyes were trying to tell her something that his lips couldn't say. She broke the eye contact, confused by the emotions he stirred in her.

"If you insist, dear. Sleep well." Wilma patted Darlene's shoulder affectionately.

Darlene said good-night to everyone, refusing to allow herself to gaze into Quintin's eyes for more than an instant. She didn't want to dream about him tonight. She wanted a peaceful, dreamless sleep.

As she started up the stairs, a wave of dizziness swept over her. It seemed to come from nowhere, and she clung to the banister, waiting for the attack of vertigo to pass. But it didn't pass. Instead, as she gripped the wooden railing, it seemed to intensify, bringing with it an overwhelming lethargy that made it difficult for her to move.

She forced herself up the stairs, dragging herself each step of the way, fighting the overwhelming urge to curl up on the worn carpeting and not move another muscle.

What's wrong with me? she wondered. She'd been tired before, but never like this. Each step she took forced a breath of exhaustion from her lips, and she wondered if perhaps she was on the verge of getting sick.

She finally made it to her room, where she collapsed on the bed, too tired to change clothes, too tired even to unbraid her hair. The whirling in her head made her afraid to move, afraid she would be sick.

She closed her eyes, grateful that the spinning in her head seemed somewhat better. She was just bone tired. That little bit of alcohol had apparently pushed her over the edge.

With a heavy sigh, she gave in to the darkness that called to her in sweet, serene whispers.

She was floating outside in the chilled night air, floating like a leaf plucked from a breeze-whipped tree. She could smell the pine forest that deepened the shadows of the night that surrounded her.

She was in a dream. She knew it was a dream because she knew that in reality people couldn't float. But it was so real...so vivid. How could a dream wind raise goose bumps on her arms? How could dream trees smell so alive?

"She's awake," a voice whispered nearby, startling her as she suddenly realized she was not in the dream alone.

"No, she's not," another voice answered. "She can't be. I put enough stuff in her drink to keep her out all night long."

Darlene's brain raced, trying to reach beyond the gauzy veil that seemed to surround her, trying to figure out what the voice meant, who the people were. They sounded familiar, but she couldn't quite put names to the voices.

She tried to sit up, willing herself to leave behind the dream state she was in, but she couldn't move. She was trapped, unable to do anything but follow in whatever direction her dream would take her.

It wasn't until she realized that she wasn't floating but rather was being carried through the forest on a canvas stretcher, that the acrid taste of fear first crept up her throat.

If she wasn't floating, then it was possible this wasn't a dream.... Her heartbeat accelerated and her mouth grew dry at this new thought. If it wasn't a dream ... then what was happening to her, and why couldn't she move? Who were these people, and what did they want with her?

She saw stars above her, a blanket of darkness sprinkled with distant fiery lights amid the tree branches that danced overhead. Again the pine-scented, salt-flavored night air summoned goose bumps to dance across her skin, and a new realization struck her. She no longer wore the jeans and sweatshirt she'd had on before. She was clad in a long, thin white cotton nightgown that provided little defense against the phantom night wind's breath.

She now saw the people who carried her, three on each side... figures cloaked in black robes, cowls concealing their faces from her view. She sought to see the faces hidden behind the voluminous material, but the darkness of the night was too thick and the folds of the cowls effectively hid the features of the robed people.

How strange... Why are they dressed like that? Her mind worked and groped to discover the meaning of it all. Frustration gnawed at her as she once again sought to see beneath the cowls. Who were these people? Where were they taking her, and why was she being carried?

Get up, her brain commanded her, but there seemed to be a short circuit between brain and muscle, a lack of follow-through between desire and physical ability. Again icy fingers of fear licked at her insides as she fought against the paralysis that kept her immobile.

This is real, her mind screamed in silent terror. *This is not a dream. This is really happening.* The knowledge made her heart pound in a frantic rhythm.

Danger... The scent of evil surrounded her, encompassed her, and her brain flashed warning signals. But she was helpless and the shadows of unconsciousness teased at her, threatening to plunge her into darkness once again.

She fought against it, afraid to embrace unconsciousness, afraid of what would happen to her. Although she couldn't move, she wanted to see what happened. She had to make sense of what was going on.

They were now in a clearing where the moon shone overhead, a big, full ball of light. No, not full, she thought irrationally, remembering Quintin's observation. The moon wouldn't be full for another night or two. But it was full enough to cast down an eerie light that only added to her confusion.

The clearing was lit with torches thrust into the ground at varied intervals, their light illuminating a large flat stone that was in the center of the area.

She was placed on the stone, and the people moved back, forming a circle around her. She could feel the cold of the stone seeping through the canvas stretcher she lay upon, through the gown she wore, crawling into her insides like something dead and evil.

The clearing filled with a strange chanting that rose and fell, words that were indecipherable by her foggy brain. Although she couldn't understand the words, which sounded foreign, the chanting itself made her fear swell. She remembered something... The chanting... it was both alien, yet frighteningly familiar.

What was wrong with her? Why couldn't she move? Why couldn't she think? Why couldn't she peel away the layers of fog that seemed to wrap around her brain?

At the foot of the stone where she lay, two people stood apart from the rest. One was clad in red robes, the other in white. Both of their faces were hidden in the shadows of deep cowls. But the shape of their bodies were vaguely familiar. The red-clad figure was tall, enormously barrel chested beneath the folds of the robe. The other one was equally tall. Darlene knew she should recognize them both, but she couldn't quite think of who they were. She was out of the realm of reality as she knew it.

As the red-robed person raised his hands over her, swirling terror gripped her, enfolding her in cold hands and she gave in to the mist of darkness that welcomed her.

She awoke with a start, early-morning sunshine streaming through the window—a strange contradiction to the darkness she'd just left behind. For a moment she lay there, afraid to move, afraid to trust in the sunlight that filled the room with light and warmth.

A dream. She sobbed in relief, realizing she still wore the jeans and sweatshirt she'd fallen asleep in. A nightmare. It had all been a vivid, crazy, horrifying nightmare.

She stood up, her legs still trembling with the lingering horror of her dreams. It had been so real.... She'd been able to smell the pines, see the winking stars overhead...hear the eerie chanting of the strangely robed people who surrounded her.

"Just a dream..." She spoke aloud to break the spell of mystery that still teased her with haunting fingers. "You silly woman, it was just a dream." She laughed unsteadily.

She moved on wooden legs to the mirror of the dresser. *Reality check,* she thought as she stared at her reflection, somehow relieved to see herself unchanged. Apart from her tousled hair, pale complexion and wide eyes, she was the same as she'd been when she fell asleep on the bed. There was nothing to be afraid of.... It had been a crazy dream.

She released a sigh and laughed at her own fears. She stuck her tongue out at her reflection in the mirror and mentally shook off the last vestige of lingering terror. The sun was shining and she felt surprisingly rested. It had been nothing more than a crazy dream, chased away by morning light.

With another small laugh, she picked up her hairbrush and ran it through her tangled mass of hair. The first stroke dislodged something that drifted down to the floor.

She stared, her body tensing, fear washing over her again in sickening waves. A pine needle. How had a pine needle gotten into her hair?

CHAPTER FIVE

It could have blown into my hair yesterday, when I was outside, Darlene told herself, picking up the pine needle and twirling it around between her fingers. She threw it in the trash can, then sat back down on the edge of the bed.

Yes, it must have blown into her hair. That had to be the answer, because any other thought, any other explanation, was totally insane. It was crazy to think that somehow someone had changed her clothes and carried her out into the forest while she slept.

She frowned, remembering the strange, bitter aftertaste of the alcohol she'd drank the night before. Drugs? She shoved the thought aside, finding it too terrifying even to consider.

The only rational explanation was that the pine needle had lodged itself in her hair sometime when she'd been out on the patio the day before. The wind had been blowing. It seemed a rational explanation.

After showering and changing her clothes, Darlene had relegated the entire episode to where it belonged... as a crazy, unusually vivid nightmare, and nothing more.

She had a quiet breakfast alone, served by Wilma, who was distracted and unusually quiet. In fact, the whole house was silent. The other quests must have been up very late, Darlene thought as she wandered into the parlor and sat down before the empty stone fireplace.

She leaned her head back and realized that she had not missed having a television set until this moment. She was in the mood to watch some mindless sitcom reruns, felt the need for canned laughter and slapstick comedy. Despite the fact that she'd written off her night experience as nothing more than a very bad dream, she still felt an alien apprehensiveness that she couldn't seem to shake.

After a mere week of her three-week vacation she was ready to leave, go back to the familiarity of her grandmother's house, get on with her life. She fought an overwhelming desire to leave this place and its strange occupants behind.

Still, there was one particular occupant she wasn't ready to leave. Quintin. Even his name brought a flush of warmth to her. There was unfinished business between them. Something was happening, something she was reluctant to leave incomplete. She felt as if she were a meteor spinning out of control and he was on the same course and her spinning couldn't stop until they collided.

She got up out of her chair, her restless energy refusing to allow her just to sit and do nothing. Maybe she would take a walk. Her decision made, she started for the door. "Oh!" she exclaimed, as Quintin filled the doorway, his lips curving into a smile at the sight of her.

"Good morning."

"Good morning," she returned, as always fighting off a breathless panic at the mesmerizing sight of him.

"Did you sleep well?" His dark gaze studied her intently, as if he were privy to every dream she'd ever had, might ever have.

"Yes..." She flushed. She'd never been a very good liar. "Well, actually, no. I had strange nightmares all night."

"Many people believe nightmares hold the secrets of the future...that they should be viewed as warnings."

"Warnings? Am I in danger?" she asked softly, her heart pounding an unsteady beat of anxiety.

"Oh, here you two are." Wilma spoke from behind Quintin, interrupting whatever it was Quintin had been about to say. "The others are awake now and were wondering if you two were going to join them for coffee."

"I was just on my way out for a walk," Darlene explained.

"And I'm going with her," Quintin said. His words both pleased Darlene and filled her with a new anxiety.

"Oh, well, then...that's fine," Wilma assured them, beaming one of her brilliant—almost too brilliant—smiles. "Enjoy your walk, and we'll all see you two later." She smiled at them like a mother hen viewing two of her favorite chicks.

"Shall we go?" Quintin looked at Darlene expectantly. She nodded and followed him past Wilma and down the long hallway to the door that led outside.

The air was thick with the fragrance of the dying summer, and despite the brilliant sun overhead, there was a nip in the air that whispered of winter's approach.

Quintin started down the path that led to the water's edge, but Darlene stopped him.

"Let's walk this way," she suggested, pointing to the opposite path, which would carry them into the nearby forest. "I've never gone this way before."

For just a moment, a brief single instant, he hesitated, but then he shrugged and joined her, making her wonder if she had only imagined the moment of hesitation.

As they entered the thick trees the chill deepened, making Darlene grateful for the cardigan sweater she'd thrown over her shoulders.

She gazed over at Quintin, noting how his midnight blue cable-knit sweater pulled tight across his broad shoulders and relaxed its hold around the flatness of his abdomen. Again she felt the magnetism of his overwhelming physical presence.

She hadn't explored the forest before, and so she consciously turned her attention to their surroundings. The leaves on the trees had just begun to change colors. There was a hushed silence surrounding them, a silence that gave her the impression of time standing still. It was darker here, as the sun was unable to fully penetrate through the trees that surrounded them.

She wrapped her arms around herself and offered Quintin a tentative smile. "I love autumn," she said, taking a deep breath of the fresh air. A hint of pine scent reminded her of her nightmare, and she consciously shoved the thought away. "When I was little, my grandmother and I would gather red and gold leaves and press them between the pages of a book. Once they were dried, we'd decorate the whole house with them."

"Autumn's not me. I prefer the heat of summer," he replied.

She nodded, unsurprised by his comment. Her mind filled with a sudden image of them in a bed amid tangled sheets, their bodies shining and slick with the warmth of a summer night and the heat of their passion. His smile widened, and she jerked her gaze away from his, feeling again as if he were privy to her every thought, her every dream.

"When I was a little boy, I used to love to explore the woods," he said after a moment of silence.

She relaxed at his words. It was such a normal thing for a young boy to enjoy. "I think all kids like the mystery of a forest," she agreed.

"When I was twelve, I decided I'd live in the woods." He paused a moment, then continued. "Anything was better than the home I was living in at the time. So I packed up some food and a blanket, took a knife and an old skillet from the kitchen and headed out." For the first time since she had met him, Quintin's facial muscles were relaxed, and his eyes were warm with memories. She felt herself as dangerously drawn to this new dimension of him as she had been drawn to his intense mystery.

"It was great for the first day or two. I felt like Davy Crockett exploring new territory. I found a place to make camp near a little creek and felt I'd found a little piece of heaven on earth. I managed to stay out there for three days. Then my food ran out, my blanket wasn't thick enough to ward off the night air, and I realized I wasn't the man Davy Crockett was."

Darlene laughed in sympathy, then sobered. "Did you get into trouble when you went back?"

His eyes darkened once again, and his jaw clenched tightly. "I got strapped for taking the things I took with me. They told me I'd come with nothing, and when I left I'd go with nothing."

Darlene wanted to reach out and hold him, to soothe the wounds that had healed over but left scars she knew he would never forget. "It just doesn't seem fair," she said softly. "We both lost our parents at an early age, and it doesn't seem fair that your child-hood was horrid but mine was filled with love, thanks to my grandmother."

He smiled at her, the black intensity back in his eyes. "Yes, but often we get an opportunity to rectify that which we were powerless over as children."

Darlene stopped walking and looked at him. "What do you mean?"

He stopped also and faced her. "Just that fate has a way of giving people opportunities to settle old scores." The tension left his face and a new emotion played on his features. She recognized it—desire.

His desire reached across the space that separated them and snaked around her, wrapping her from head to toe.

His gaze was dark, a deep abyss that summoned her to jump in, to lose herself in the murky depths. She answered the call, stepping toward him.

This is madness, she thought dazedly, *madness or destiny.* It didn't matter which, for no matter what it was, she was helpless against the force that propelled her toward him.

Like a magician conjuring fire at his fingertips, he reached out and stroked her cheek, creating an in-ferno of desire within her. His touch trailed down the side of her face, coming to rest on her lips. With a trembling hand, she reached up and captured his, taking his index finger into her mouth, wanting to taste him. She was vaguely aware of the fact that it was the most blatantly sensual thing she had ever done, and she knew it was because of him. He stirred the sexuality that had been dormant inside her all her life.

Naked hunger consumed his features, and with a groan he pulled his hand away and took her mouth with his.

His mouth covered hers, hungry, demanding, as his arms pulled her against the hard length of his body. Enfolded in his embrace, she felt surrounded by him, fused to him. *I am his,* she thought with a curious mixture of joy and despair. His possession of her was complete.

As his hand moved upward, caressing her beneath her blouse, a moan caught in her throat. The cardigan fell off her shoulders as, with an expert's ease, he captured her breast beneath the lace of her bra. She felt her nipple blossom and swell beneath his touch, and a moan escaped her lips.

He deepened the kiss and she felt herself being carried on a hot wind of passion, hurtling toward the dark and mysterious place that existed inside him. She wasn't afraid—rather, she welcomed the journey, knowing he was beside her, a part of her, his soul entwined with her own.

As one of his hands teased and tormented her breast, his other pressed more firmly against her back, making her aware of his own intense arousal. She arched against him, wanting to wrap herself around him, within him. His breaths came more rapidly, and his heart thunderously echoed the frantic beating of her own.

She cried out when he gently withdrew his lips from hers, removed his hands and stepped away. Instantly bereft, confused by his sudden withdrawal, she gazed up at him.

"This is neither the time nor the place," he explained with a look of regret. She realized then that his eyes couldn't be the ones from her nightmares. For at that moment, his shone with a humanity that was absent from those that haunted her dreams. She blinked, still dazed by her tumultuous emotions.

"Come on, let's go back." He gently touched her arm, but she stepped away from him, needing space from his overpowering sensuality.

"No... I think I'll walk a little bit farther." She needed to think, to blow out the cobwebs that always seemed to enshroud her brain when he was near her.

He hesitated, as if reluctant to leave her out here alone. "Darlene?" He looked as if he had begun to say something, then changed his mind. "This forest can be dangerous to those who don't know it. Don't walk too far, and don't stay out long."

"I won't go much farther...." A heated blush swept into her cheeks. She liked the way his concern made her feel. "I just need to walk a little bit more," she finished.

He nodded slowly, reluctantly. "Then I'll see you back at the inn." He turned and disappeared down the path they had taken to come here.

Darlene watched him go, then turned with a tremulous sigh and began to walk. As she moved down the path, her mind played and replayed each and every moment she'd spent with Quintin. He was as much a mystery now as he had been that first moment she'd seen him sitting in the deep shadows of the parlor. Yet she felt safe with him, trusted that he would never harm her.

Her body filled with heat as she thought of his kisses, his caresses.... She was definitely unsafe with him in that area. The man had bewitched her completely. She stumbled over a tree root as a sudden thought struck her. Despite his mystery, despite the fact that she didn't believe he was a simple salesman...despite the dangerous power he seemed to command over her...she was on the verge of falling in love with him.

It was insane. But the rational world she knew had tilted askew the moment she'd arrived at the inn. She was falling in love with Quintin Marshall.

She slid down to the ground at the foot of a tree, letting her new knowledge wash over her. Her thoughts of Quintin were interrupted when she suddenly realized that the pine scent now surrounding her was much more pungent than before. It reminded her of the terrifying dream she'd had the night before.

She stood up, frowning, as she studied the tree branches overhead, finding a horrifying similarity between her present surroundings and her nighttime terrors.

As she slowly moved farther down the path, her breathing became shallower, as if the air surrounding her had thickened. The trees seemed to bear down on her, enclosing her in a cocoon of uncomfortable claustrophobia. Panic lodged in her throat, and she swallowed thickly as she realized that she'd been down this path before . . . last night, in her dream.

Her feet moved her forward woodenly, as if she were a marionette being manipulated by something other than her own will. Her heart beat a rapid tattoo in her chest as she went deeper and deeper into the forest, driven by a knowledge that she knew she could not possibly possess.

The scent of pine was cloying now, and her footsteps slowed as she realized that, if she was right, the clearing should be just ahead.

She wanted to stop, didn't want to go any farther. But she couldn't stop. She had to know if the clearing with the slab of stone was just ahead. She couldn't bear the uncertainty of turning around, going back to the inn and never knowing for certain. She had to move forward.

A moan escaped her lips as she broke out of the thicket. She stood in the middle of the clearing from her dream. Like a huge horizontal gravestone, the flat slab of stone lay there in the center of the clearing, mocking her with its very existence. "No..." The protest escaped her lips on a whisper of despair. Yet to deny the stone's existence was to proclaim herself utterly mad.

For a long moment, she simply stared at it, as if expecting it to disappear in a puff of smoke. Then she moved forward toward it, thrust back into her nightmare. Her hand trembled as she reached out and touched the cold hardness of its surface. She gasped, feeling its solidness beneath her fingertips. It was real... Dear God, it was real.... She could remember the feel of it against her back.

And if the stone was real, then what about the other images? What about the people in their black robes and concealing cowls? She was vaguely aware of the sound of waves. Eyes dulled, she noticed that on the other side of the stone was a cliff with a sheer, rocky drop into the ocean below. She suddenly remembered that the noise of the waves had been in her dream.

She whirled around, her eyes darting around the clearing in pure panic. Had it been a nightmare, or had she been drugged and brought here? The question screamed in her head, causing her to stumble backward, away from the stone. It could just be another one of her crazy feelings of déjà vu...the strange, haunting feeling that had occurred to her from the moment she'd come to the inn.

She froze, as a shaft of sunlight danced through the deep shadows and glinted on something gold on the ground next to the rock. Dread overwhelming her, she moved to the object and leaned down and picked it up.

A gold-plated barrette. The same barrette that had held her braid when she'd fallen asleep on her bed the night before. It burned in her hand, indisputable proof that she had been here before. She gasped and threw it to the ground.

The terrifying nightmare had been real. She'd been drugged and carried through the forest. She'd been placed on the stone…and darkly robed people had all chanted over her.

The inn and its guests no longer seemed simply strange. They were now malevolent. The scent of evil burned in her nose and a sob tore from her throat as she realized that she had in some way become part of their sinister intentions.

Escape. The word screamed through her veins. She had to get out of here, had to leave this place. She was in danger—mortal danger.

She turned and ran blindly down the path. The underbrush and the tree limbs seemed alive with intent, reaching out to scratch at her, sending thorny fingers out to impede her as she ran. She felt as if the nature that surrounded her were making a direct effort to keep her here forever. Hysterical sobs choked in her throat as she fought her way down the path.

Tears blurred her vision as she raced through the forest. She'd get back to the inn, pack her bags and get the hell out of here. She didn't know what exactly was going on, but she sure wasn't going to stick around to find out.

She slowed her pace as she suddenly thought about Quintin. Was he a part of this vile madness? Did he have a role in whatever was going on?

She swiped at her tears impatiently, willing her breathing to return to normal. Surely not...surely Quintin was as innocent in all of this as she was. Surely her heart would know if he was evil. Yet, no matter what protests her heart made in his defense, she couldn't ignore his dark magnetism, the way she felt bewitched whenever he was near.

Bewitched...Witches...Dear God, was that what was going on? Had she stumbled unknowingly into a coven of witches? A group of Satan-worshipers? She thought of the dark robes, the glowing candles, the strange chanting, and her blood ran cold.

Everything suddenly made a horrifying kind of sense, and she realized she had to escape before tonight, when a full moon would shine down on the earth. She thought again of the stone slab and realized that it was no wonder Wilma and Harold had treated her as an honored guest. She was to be their unholy sacrifice.

CHAPTER SIX

She encountered nobody as she entered the inn, and for that she was grateful. For a moment she hesitated in the darkened hallway, unsure what should be her first step in making her escape.

The inn was isolated, a thirty-minute car ride to the nearest town. She was reluctant to take off on foot, and she didn't have a car.

"I'll call for a taxi," she murmured aloud, but then she froze as another thought struck her. She'd been here nearly a week, and not once had she heard the ring of a telephone.

But there has to be one, she thought, choking back a sense of despair that threatened to immobilize her. *This is an inn,* she reasoned. *There has to be a way for guests to make reservations. There has to be a phone.* All she had to do was find it.

As she moved stealthily down the hallway, she heard the murmur of conversation and muted laughter drifting out of the dining room. She looked at her watch and realized it was lunchtime. Good, she thought with a first hint of optimism. Perhaps while they were all busy eating she could locate a telephone.

She began her search in the parlor, looking in drawers, behind knickknacks, searching for telltale wires that would indicate the presence of a telephone. Nothing. Tears of frustration burned in her eyes. She had to find a phone. She *had* to.

Frantic with fear, she moved into the next room, a small sitting room she hadn't entered before. Hope swelled in her chest when she saw a small desk in the corner. Surely she would find a phone here. Her gaze skittered across the desk top, looking only for the object she so desperately needed. The desk top held an array of items: a reservation book, an account ledger, a strange-looking paperweight. But she didn't find what she sought.

She stared around the room, eyeing shelves of books, the small coffee table next to an antique love seat, anywhere a sane person might keep a phone. But these people were not sane, and there was no phone to be found.

Impotent frustration welled up inside her, and with a sigh of defeat she sank into the love seat. Her foot accidentally kicked a large black book off the coffee table. The book slid to the floor, spewing photographs onto the faded carpeting. A photo album.

Curiously she dropped to her knees, gathering the loose photos in her hands. They were old black-and-white shots of people standing on the patio of the inn.

She thumbed through them rapidly and gasped when she saw one particular picture. The woman in the photo had short, curly blond hair. Dimples danced on either side of her pretty smile. The man with her was tall and handsome, and his front teeth overlapped slightly in his boyish grin.

Darlene knew these people, although their memory had faded somewhat with time. Still, a silver-framed photograph of them had sat on her bedroom dresser since the time of their death. These were her parents.

Cold fear washed over her, engulfing her in icy waves. Why was there a photo of her parents here? Without conscious thought, she continued to flip through the stack of pictures. She didn't recognize the other people, but she found another picture of her parents. A little girl with solemn eyes and pale hair was sitting on her mother's lap. She knew the little girl was her, and her mind reeled with the implications.

The vague sense of familiarity that had haunted her from the moment she had arrived here, the sense of déjà vu that had unsettled her...it all made a crazy kind of sense now.

She had been here before, as a child, and what she'd been experiencing was the stirring of vague memories, memories half forgotten with time, perhaps unconsciously suppressed so that she could maintain her sanity.

She gasped when she flipped over another picture and the eyes from her nightmares glared back at her from the black-and-white photo. The sepia tones of the photograph only intensified the effect of harshness.

Her hand trembled as she stared at the man in the old picture. It was Quintin, and yet it wasn't. The features were the same, but they had been painted with a much harsher brush. The light that burned in this man's eyes was corrupt with evil. These were her nightmare eyes, and what filled her with retching horror was the fact that they were not crazy images conjured up by a frightened child. They were real, and the man was real.

She flipped the picture over, unable to stand looking at those eyes another minute. On the back of the photo, written in ink, was a name.

Devon Marshall.

Devon Marshall. Quintin Marshall. Her heart stopped in her chest. Dear God, the man was Quintin's father. She knew it with a certainty. And that meant Quintin was probably part of the madness that surrounded her.

"No!" She thrust her hand against her mouth to stifle a sob. *Please, not Quintin,* she begged. *Please don't let him be a part of this.* A headache thundered at her temples as her nightmare visions swept back to haunt her. She had to get away.

She shoved the pictures back in the album and set it back on the coffee table. She didn't want to see anymore . . . she didn't need to see anymore.

Thoughts of finding a phone disappeared as the need for escape overwhelmed everything else. She left the room and ran for the stairs, wanting only to gather her things together and get out. She didn't care if she had to walk a hundred miles . . . a thousand miles. She couldn't stay in this place another minute.

Once in her room, she dragged her suitcase out of the closet and flipped it open on the bed. Frantically she grabbed her clothes out of the closet and drawers, throwing them in the suitcase without bothering to fold them.

Her headache increased its rhythmic pounding as a sense of urgency pressed down on her. Each minute that ticked by filled her with a more powerful sense of imminent peril.

She froze when a knock sounded on the door. Her breath caught in her throat, she stood motionless. She closed her eyes, willing whoever it was to go away and leave her alone.

"Darlene? Darlene, are you all right?" Wilma's worried-sounding voice drifted through the door. "I saw you come up here, and you looked upset. Are you ill? Is there something I can do for you?"

Darlene cursed the old woman and her maternal concern. She knew she had to answer, and her legs trembled as she moved toward the door and cracked it open a fraction of an inch. "I, uh . . . I have a headache and thought I'd lie down for a little while. I'm sure it will be better after a rest."

Like a miniature bulldozer, Wilma pushed her way through the door, concern furrowing her wrinkled brow. "Shall I bring you some aspirin? I have some of those coated ones that don't upset your—" She stopped speaking when she spied the opened suitcase on the bed, and her concern was usurped by surprise. "Oh, it looks like you're packing." She said the words flatly, without emotion, her gaze regarding Darlene intently. "Surely you aren't thinking of leaving us? You still have two weeks of your vacation left."

"Well, I, uh...was just going through my clothes." Darlene knew it sounded weak. She'd never been able to lie convincingly.

"Oh, dear!" Wilma backed out of the room and closed the door.

Darlene flew into a flurry of packing, realizing time was running out. If she was going to leave, she had to do it immediately. She closed the suitcase and headed for the door.

Grabbing the knob, she tried to open it, but it wouldn't budge. It had apparently been locked from the outside. She was too late. She was trapped like a fly caught in a spider's web.

A sob of despair choked in her throat as she tried once again to open the door. No luck. With a groan of impotent rage, she beat on the door with her fists until she was panting from her efforts. She leaned against it, gazing frantically around the room, looking for another way out.

She ran to the window and looked down at the three-story drop to the concrete patio below. There was no escape here. There was no escape anywhere.

On wooden legs, she moved over to the bed and sank down on the edge. She was in her worst nightmare, surrounded by people who meant her harm, and this time there was no waking up to the safety of morning's light. She closed her eyes, wishing that when she opened them again she would be back in her grandmother's kitchen, the scent of lavender sachet and fresh-baked gingerbread filling her with a sense of security and love. But she knew that when she opened her eyes she would still be locked in the room, evil surrounding her.

She had no idea how long she sat there before she heard the rattle of keys outside her door. She jumped up off the bed and backed against the wall, afraid of who or what might enter.

With a sob of relief, she threw herself at the burly man who entered the room. "Uncle Donald!" she cried, wrapping her arms around his huge chest, clinging to the only thing that was familiar in her nightmare world. "Please, you've got to get me out of here. We've got to leave here right now."

"Here, here, now…" He patted her on the back and untangled himself from her frantic hug. "Wilma tells me you aren't feeling well." Wilma and Harold stood just outside the door.

Darlene stepped back from her uncle, opening her mouth to answer, but before she could, a wave of nauseating horror filled her. She was struck with a vision. The barrel-chested man in the bloodred robes—he'd seemed familiar to her.

She now realized it had been her uncle Donald.

She reeled back from him, hitting the wall behind her with a thud. "You—you're in on this," she gasped. "You're part of this evilness. You all want to kill me."

Donald laughed—it was a deep rumble, like thunder. "Don't be melodramatic, Darlene. Nobody wishes to harm you. In fact, it's just the opposite. You, my dear, are our hope for the future."

Darlene frowned, curious despite her fear. "What do you mean?"

He reached out and took her hands in his. She fought her impulse to jerk away, repulsed by the coldness of his hands as they wrapped around hers. The coldness of death. "You were born here, in this house. In the bedroom down the hall."

"I knew it," she murmured. "I knew this place felt familiar."

He nodded. "You were conceived in a special ceremony for a very special purpose, an honor of the highest order. Your parents gave you to the Master of Darkness. You and Quintin have a destiny to fulfill, a destiny that will bring us all the power and glory of the earth." His voice rang with a religious fervor.

She yanked her hands from his. "Quintin?" She breathed his name in torment, closing her eyes against the pain that wrapped around her heart. "He knows about all this?"

She heard somebody enter the room, and she opened her eyes to see Quintin, his face utterly expressionless, his gaze not meeting hers. She stared at him, willing him to look at her, wanting him to tell her he wasn't a part of this, that there was some sort of a mistake.

But he didn't look at her. His gaze remained firmly fixed on some point on the wall behind her.

Donald clapped Quintin on the back and smiled benignly. "Like you, Quintin was also conceived for a special purpose. His father was one of our most obedient followers, and Quintin was given to the Master in a ceremony of blood." He smiled first at Quintin, then, once again, at Darlene. "We've waited years for this night, this moment. On this night of the full moon, you will each fulfill the destinies chosen for you."

"What will happen to us?" Darlene whispered the question, her heart pounding in her throat.

Donald's smile widened. "Tonight at midnight, with the full moon overhead, Quintin will be filled with the spirit of the Master, and in a special ceremony he will make love to you on the sacrificial altar. And you, my dear—" he grinned at her like a proud father "—will conceive and deliver the child of Satan."

The world tilted and swayed, and Darlene felt she was slipping off the edge of sanity. "You're crazy," she blurted, backing away from them all. "You're all crazy."

"Now, now, no need for that," Donald said patiently. "You can make this easy, or you can make it difficult on yourself. Accept your fate. Enjoy your fate. Enjoy your dalliance with the devil."

She stared at Donald, then looked at Quintin once again, her gaze playing over his features, looking for a sign, a hint, of mercy. "You...you would rape me?"

Still his gaze didn't meet hers. "I'll do whatever is necessary." His voice was as emotionless as his features. With a groan, Darlene slid down onto the edge of the bed, her legs no longer able to hold her up.

"That's it, dear. Rest." Donald motioned for the others to leave the room. For just a moment, Quintin's dark eyes found hers, and in them she saw an urgent message that she couldn't understand. It was gone as quickly as it appeared, swallowed up by blackness. He said nothing as he left the room.

"You must be prepared for this special night of ceremony and magic," Donald continued. "Tonight we receive the blessings of the Master, and none of us will be the same again." With that, he turned and left the room.

Darlene heard the click of a lock turning, and knew she was once again trapped, locked in a room with no escape.

She didn't know how long she sat unmoving on the bed, her brain frantically trying to sort out what she had learned. Quintin's parents, and her own parents, had obviously been a part of this coven of wickedness. Had her grandmother known? Why hadn't Darlene been warned? No wonder she had never felt comfortable around Uncle Donald. She shivered as she remembered the way he had looked in his crimson robes.

Visions danced through her head, visions she knew now were memories. Through a child's mind, she remembered being in the clearing, watching as the robed adults around her raised their arms in supplication to the demons of hell. She remembered seeing Dr. Bennet there and now understood why he made her uncomfortable.

She relived the fear that had raced through her as a tall, dark-haired man with black eyes had called upon the powers of darkness to fill him, consume him. It was no wonder she had repressed the memories for years.... They were vile, full of despair and horror. Living through the horror of the ceremonies as a child had forced her memory to block out the experience.

And finally she remembered meeting the eyes of another child across the dimly lit clearing, and she realized with a certainty that the child had been Quintin.

She moaned again, her heart struggling with what her brain already knew. Quintin was part of this. He was as evil as the rest of them. Why hadn't her heart told her? Why was there still a small part of her that wanted to cling to the belief that his being here was all a mistake, that he was as much a helpless victim as she? *Fool,* she chided herself for her hope, for the love that still existed in her stupid heart.

She finally roused herself from the bed, realizing she'd been there for hours, struggling to comprehend the betrayals that surrounded her. Her parents'... her uncle's... Quintin's... She had never had a chance against all their machinations.

Walking over to the window, she saw the first finger of dusk reaching over the horizon, bringing with it a darkness that filled her soul with despair. Soon it would be dark. Soon it would be midnight and the ceremonies would begin. The child of Satan... She would rather die.

The concrete patio beckoned to her, and she thought of how easy it would be to leap out the window. She would die, but she would die with the knowledge that she had protected herself from being raped on an altar of blood, used by people whose desires were perverse and vile.

Still, despite the beckoning call of death, a part of her clung to the idea of escape. Her gaze lingered on the large drainpipe that ran down the corner of the building. It was fastened to the side of the building with large metal brackets—brackets that could be used for footholds and handholds. It would be dangerous. There were no guarantees, but the alternative was abhorrent, and not to be considered.

With a grunt of effort, she raised the window and stared at the screen that covered the opening. With a whimper of panic, she tore at it with her fingertips, unmindful of the scratching and tearing of her flesh. She wanted out, and the screen stood between her and freedom.

Unable to remove it with bare hands, she hurried over to her suitcase and fumbled in her cosmetics bag. With a triumphant cry, she removed the scissors from her traveling mending kit and ran back to the screen. Hands trembling, fear giving her new strength, she cut through the screen.

It took her only minutes to gouge out the mesh. Gasping in relief, she quickly removed the screen and once again eyed the drainpipe.

It looked tinier now, not as substantial as it had moments before. She wondered if it could hold her weight or if the brackets would snap off the wood, sending her to the concrete below.

If only there were another way... But as she looked at the darkening skies, she knew time was running out. This was her only way out.

She crawled up on the windowsill and crouched there. It was still a jump to grasp the pipe. If she missed, she would plunge to her death. But either way, she would escape. Taking a deep breath, she hurled herself out the window.

CHAPTER SEVEN

She felt herself flying through the air. The breath whooshed out of her as she hit the side of the house. She grasped the pipe, and the sharp metal of the bracket dug painfully into her fingers.

For a moment, she simply hung there, afraid that any movement would send her rocketing to the concrete below.

Gazing down, she clung more tightly to the pipe, fighting off a wave of dizziness. Beads of perspiration broke out on her upper lip. She closed her eyes. *Don't look down,* she instructed herself. Slowly, her eyes still closed, she began to inch down the pipe, her hands and feet blindly seeking each bracket for support.

Shades of evening whirled around her, and she was enfolded in the misty fog that rolled off the water. She was grateful for the fog, hoping that once she got down from the pipe she could hide in its veil of gray.

Inch by painful inch, she moved down, hope causing her heartbeat to pound in her temples. If she could just get away from the inn, she could walk as long as it took to safety.

She had nearly reached the bottom when she heard a sound above her. Looking up, she saw Wilma's startled face poking out the screenless window. "She's getting away!" The old woman's cry filled Darlene with pure, unadulterated panic.

Choking back a sob, she scurried down another yard of pipe, then jumped the remaining couple of feet to the patio, her legs absorbing the jolt painfully.

Without any conscious choice, knowing only that she had to get away, she took off down the path just ahead.

The wind blowing off the nearby ocean waves whistled in her ears and whipped her hair around her head, but even so, she could hear the cries of people behind her. She turned to see dark figures in the swirling fog, chasing her, gaining ground as she stumbled off the path and onto the slippery rocks of the shoreline.

Darkness fell abruptly, as if night were a menacing creature that had swallowed the day whole. There was only a faint illumination coming from the nearby waves, and above their thundering roar she heard her name being called, over and over again.

She didn't stop, didn't think. She was in survival mode, all thought swept away as she picked her way over the sharp, slippery rocks. Tears further impeded her progress, blurring her vision as she tried to outrun the devil.

She cried out as she slipped, falling to one knee, the rocks tearing through the material of her jeans and into her flesh. She stood up, feeling the trickling of blood from the wound.

"Darlene." The deep, achingly familiar voice came from just behind her, so close that she knew its owner could reach out a hand and touch her.

She suddenly realized the futility of her attempt at escape. Standing on the rocky shoreline that just ahead disappeared into the water, she was trapped—trapped between the devil and the deep blue sea.

Hysterical laughter bubbled to her lips, and she shoved the back of her fist against her mouth, knowing that if she gave in to the laughter she truly would lose her mind.

She turned and faced him. At that moment, the full moon pierced the layer of fog, caressing his bold, strong features with a lover's touch. His raven hair whipped around his head, giving her the impression of a warlock come to claim her soul. Yet his eyes held a tenderness that made her laugh turn into a sob. God, she loved him. She must surely be mad.

There was an intense urgency in his expression as he reached out his hand to her. Once again she was aware that his eyes were speaking to her...saying things she wanted to hear, needed to hear. "I'll help you, Darlene, but you have to trust me."

She realized the words had been spoken aloud.

Her head told her not to be a fool, that it would be better to throw herself into the ocean than to trust this man with the burning gaze and the black soul. But her heart surged with renewed hope. Had she been right all along? Was he, too, merely a helpless victim? Was it possible that he had come to help her, that he knew a way out, a path of escape?

She stared deep into his eyes, seeing not the fires of hell, but something very different. Something that made her trust her instincts, believe in her heart.

Relinquishing herself to him, she placed her heart before him, her life at his feet. She reached out her hand to him.

He grasped her hand in a strong, sure grip, and for a long moment their gazes remained locked. Again she felt as if he were trying to communicate something to her... something he couldn't say with his mouth but wanted her to know. Then, tightening his grip on her hand, he turned and shouted to the people who stood at the edge of the path. "It's all right, I've got her."

Darlene gasped breathlessly. She eyed him accusingly, his shout to the others ringing in her ears. The brunt of his betrayal caused her to sway dizzily. With a moan of utter despair, she closed her eyes, giving in to the swirling darkness that rushed up to claim her.

With a strong, sure movement, Quintin swept her up in his arms and started back where the others waited. He was grateful for the fact that he had managed to catch up with her, to capture her before she'd done something stupid, like throwing herself into the water.

She was a necessary ingredient in what they had all worked to attain for years. All would have been lost had she perished in the sea.

He tightened his grip on her still, lifeless body, noting the way the moonlight caressed her features. He would not allow anything to stop the chain of events set to unfurl on this night of the full moon. He had worked too hard, they had all planned too long, come too far, to allow anything to stop what was written in destiny's book for this night.

When she awakened, she was lying on the stone altar, clad in the wispy white gown she remembered from before. The gown did little to prevent the seeping of cold into her body from the stone beneath her.

The only difference between this and her dream was that this time she wasn't drugged. She had no blessed confusion to muddy her mind.

Her hands were bound tightly to a stake behind her head, and her legs were tied to posts an opposite sides of the stone. Dear God, she was helpless, like a sacrificial lamb on an altar of death.

For a moment she was dazed, and she searched for the darkness that had cushioned her in peaceful oblivion. But the oblivion was gone, leaving her to stark, terrifying reality.

The clearing was full of flickering lights and dancing shadows. She was aware of the crashing of water against the nearby cliffs. She turned her head and eyed the sheer drop of the cliff, wishing she could free herself from her bonds and leap to her death. Anything to escape the horror of what she was about to endure.

She closed her eyes, and the acrid odor of burning torches filled her nose. She heard the distant, mournful cry of some night bird. A cool breeze molded the gown to her body, raising goose bumps on her skin. She was completely alone—alone with her terror....

She twisted, trying to break the bonds that held her, but the ropes merely tightened their grip. As the rough-hewn rope bit into her flesh, she reluctantly stopped her movements, her wrists and ankles burning painfully.

As she thought of Quintin's ultimate betrayal, tears scorched her eyes. She swallowed convulsively, not willing to shed tears for him. He was part of this coven of evil. He was a devil, a demon cloaked in the disguise of masculine beauty.

How else to explain the power he possessed over her? He wielded a black magic that had stolen her soul. His power over her had been profound, all-consuming, and she now realized it came from the blackness of his soul. It was no wonder she'd been helpless to the sensual pull he had. It was no wonder she hadn't been able to fight against his magnetic presence. He was using a dark power not of this world.

And now he was prepared to take by force what she would have freely given to him in love. The thought made her eyes burn once again with repressed tears.

Her blood raced coldly through her veins as she heard the distant sound of voices chanting. She tensed, unmindful of the ropes gnawing into her skin, as the sound came closer and closer.

They came into the clearing. They were robed in the darkness, but this time no cowls covered their faces. There was no longer any need for them to hide their faces. Their features glowed in the torchlight, reflecting their unholy reverence and fervor, their pride in having chosen the darkness over the light. Every guest of the inn moved into the clearing, forming a circle around the stone where she lay like a helpless butterfly trapped by the sharp sting of a hat pin.

Following the black-robed people came her uncle Donald, his robe gleaming the color of spilled blood. His chubby, florid features were twisted with madness as he came to stand near her head. And behind him, in a robe of ghostly white, was Quintin. Darlene's heart cried out in sorrow when she saw the hatred, the bitterness, that hardened his face and flamed in his eyes.

He was a lost soul, lost to her and all she believed in. He was damned to hell for embracing this blasphemous travesty of a religion.

As he came to stand at her feet, she closed her eyes, unable to look at him, to think of what he was about to participate in. He was about to make a mockery of the act of love.

The chanting rose and fell like the waves that pounded the distant cliffs, and Darlene felt a ripple of raw energy pulsating in the air. A gust of wind—hot, as if it had been belched from the bowels of hell— swept over her, and a crackle of lightning split the night sky. It was as if the very atmosphere surrounding them were reacting to their chant.

Their voices reached a crescendo, and Darlene ached to shove her hands against her ears to still the eerie sound. Then...silence, a silence so profound it seemed unnatural.

"Children . . . the power and the glory of the great Lucifer is ours tonight." Donald's booming voice filled the silence. "We are the chosen. We have served the Master well, and he is pleased. All we have worked for, all we have waited for, will become reality tonight as our two children join together." He threw back his head, his mouth spewing gibberish. Then words came once again. "We are the blessed. . . . After tonight the world will be ours." His eyes glowed with unadulterated madness.

"You're insane!" Darlene exclaimed, unable to remain silent any longer. "You're all crazy!" she screamed, her fear venting itself in cries of anger. "Don't you see that what you are doing is wrong? It's . . . insane!"

"Oh, no, my dear. We aren't the crazy ones," Donald replied, his voice a rhythmic monotone of reason. "I'll tell you who the crazy ones were—your parents and Quintin's parents." He leaned over her, so close that she could smell his rancid breath on her face. "They promised their children to Satan, then sought to renege on their promise. They tried to get away from us, take you away from us. And that is a crime punishable by death." The fire in his eyes burned brighter, scorching her with their glowing intent. "They tried to get away, they wanted to leave the bosom of the family. But traitors don't live."

Darlene gasped. "You killed them. You killed my mother and father."

"And Quintin's," he agreed. "I did what the Master of Darkness bade me do. I had to destroy the betrayers."

"Destroy the betrayers," the others echoed, their eyes glazed as if they were in some sort of hypnotic trance.

Darlene looked at Quintin, whose facial expression had not changed. It was as if he'd been cast in stone.

Once again lightning rent the sky, and the hair on Darlene's arms danced upward in response. "You're a murderer!" she screamed at her uncle, her eyes darting around, looking for help from somebody, anybody.

"I killed to protect our covenant with the Master. And now the time grows near." Donald ignored her cries and raised his hands to the turbulent sky. "Our beloved Master is near. I feel his power. I feel his very presence surrounding us." Once again his head rolled back and unintelligible mutterings came from his mouth. The crowd began to chant once again, their voices bordering on hysteria.

As the sky exploded in crackling lighting, Donald snapped his head upright and looked at his wrist-watch. "At midnight the Master will take his place in Quintin and impregnate the bitch that was promised to him. Tonight we conceive the child of Satan." The others screamed their joy. Insane rapture twisted their features in ugliness. "Quintin, my child...prepare yourself for the power of Satan."

Quintin moved closer toward the stone, positioned himself between her legs like a lover. His white robe surrounded her like a bridal veil, and although he didn't touch her, his heat engulfed her.

"Please..." she whispered as he hovered over her. She gazed deep into his eyes, searching... pleading... "Please don't... I...I love you." The words slipped out of her as if a final appeal to what-ever humanity might still exist in his soul.

He froze above her, his face twisted with a rage so intense that it stole her breath away. She watched in horror as he threw back his head and released a hoarse cry of torment. She tensed, closed her eyes and waited.

CHAPTER EIGHT

Thunder boomed overhead, and somebody screamed. It was a cry of outrage and fear. The weight of Quintin's body suddenly disappeared from on top of her, and Darlene opened her eyes.

For a moment she didn't understand what she saw. There were new people in the clearing, men carrying flashlights and handcuffs. The lightning flashed through the sky, illuminating the activity surrounding her. Men were rounding up the members of the coven, handcuffing them. Police... Where had they come from? Who had summoned them? She moaned, not caring about the hows or whys, the realization that she was safe sweeping over her in waves.

She searched the clearing, seeking the dark man who owned her heart. Quintin—where was he? Was he being handcuffed with the others?

Her breath caught in her throat when she saw Donald slowly backing toward the cliff, with its deadly drop. Quintin stood before him.

"It's all over, Donald. Give yourself up," Quintin said, his voice strong and sure. His dark hair blew in the wind, which had suddenly turned frigid, and the white robes whipped around his lean body, billowing like the wings of an avenging angel. But there was no mercy in his dark eyes as he gazed at the man who was responsible for his parents' deaths.

Darlene suddenly realized that Quintin was responsible for the lawmen's miraculous appearance. Her dark demon was actually an angel in disguise.

"I won't go to prison," Donald said, his voice filled with righteous determination. "I had to kill them. They would have ruined us all."

"You ruined yourself," Quintin returned evenly. "Now come along peacefully."

"Peacefully?" Donald threw back his head and laughed uproariously. The sound was like that of the damned hounds of hell. "That's not my way. I want chaos and dissension. I want turmoil and anarchy." The lightning overhead was reflected in his eyes.

Quintin reached out and grabbed Donald's wrist, and the movement carried them both dangerously close to the edge of the precipice. Lightning erupted again, harshly illuminated the faces of the two struggling men.

Darlene's breath caught in her chest as she viewed the faces of good and evil. It was a conflict as old as the forest that surrounded them, as ancient as the earth beneath their feet.

Closer and closer they inched toward the cliff, neither seeming to care that they were perilously close to the edge. Quintin was strong, well muscled and well trained, but Donald was big and burly, with the strength of insanity surging in his veins. The match seemed even.

All other motion in the clearing stopped as everyone watched, breathlessly, the life-and-death struggle taking place between the two men. Even the wind, which had been blowing relentlessly, suddenly halted, as if holding its breath in anticipation.

Darlene stifled a moan, realizing what it was her uncle was attempting to do. Quintin was no longer holding on to Donald's wrist. Donald now had a death grip on Quintin, and he was pulling him closer and closer to the edge of the rocky cliff. He intended to throw himself off the cliff, but he intended to take Quintin with him.

"Uncle Donald! No!" she screamed, her heart echoing the thunder that reverberated through the clearing.

He looked at her, startled, and in that instant Quintin jerked back and stepped away from him. "It's over," Quintin said breathlessly to the older man.

"Over?" Once again Donald laughed. "I embrace the Master's way." With that, he turned and dived off the cliff, his red robes fluttering in the wind and his laughter ringing all the way down.

Then . . . silence, except for the sound of the relentlessly pounding waves.

Darlene didn't realize she was crying until Quintin bent over her, his fingers gentle as he swiped away her tears. "I'm sorry, Darlene. I'm so sorry."

He motioned to one of the other men, who quickly cut the ropes that held her. Once she was free, he gathered her into his arms, his embrace warming her from the inside out.

"Why... why didn't you tell me you weren't one of them?" she asked him, sobbing.

"I couldn't." His voice was as mournful as the wind, which had begun to blow again. "It had to be played out to the end. They had to believe without question that I was with them, one of them." He kissed her forehead, her eyes, stroking her tear-dampened hair away from her face.

She looked up into his eyes and saw that it was not the fires of hell that burned there. It was the glow of love and its illumination spilled inside her, lighting her with a brilliance that filled her soul.

Later—hours later—Darlene and Quintin stood together on the patio of the inn, watching the sunrise chase away the last of the night shadows.

It had rained during the night, and the morning air was rich with the fresh scent of a world washed anew. The storm had passed, and the sun sent brilliant streaks of light across the sky, promising warmth and beauty.

Quintin's arm was strong and tight around her shoulders, and she knew that if she looked up at him his eyes would reflect the love that shone in hers.

They had spent the hours of the night talking. He'd told her about the family he'd gone to live with when he was sixteen years old, a couple he now claimed as his mother and father. The man was a police officer, and when Quintin was old enough to make a career decision, he'd decided to follow in the footsteps of the man he'd come to love.

It was in reinvestigating his own parents' murders that he had been led back to the inn and its coven, and he had decided to go undercover and expose the man responsible for their deaths.

She smiled up at him now. "You know, I never did believe the story that you were a traveling salesman, but there were several moments when I did believe you were the devil."

"I think for a time I was," he admitted softly. "I was all caught up with hate and the need to avenge my parents' deaths. I think I lost a little bit of my soul to this experience."

Her heart moved in her chest, and once again she marveled at the connection she felt with this man. "Your soul is fine. I...I'd somehow know if it wasn't." His arm tightened around her, and she turned to stare up at the inn. Shuddering, she remembered Quintin's words...that it had been built on bad dreams. "They were all crazy...insane."

"Not really. The truly insane one was your uncle. The rest of them were just stupid, lost souls looking for something nobody seemed able to offer them."

"And our parents?" she asked painfully, still finding it difficult to understand why her parents would have been involved in any of this.

He shrugged. "Who knows what possessed them to get involved in the first place? They were all sheep following a charismatic shepherd who promised them the world would be at their feet." He gazed down at her, his eyes still dark, but no longer mysterious. "The important thing to remember is that our parents tried to get away for our sakes. They sacrificed their lives for our safety."

She nodded and looked back at the forbidding inn. "What will happen to this place?" she asked softly.

"It will be up to the courts. Probably nothing. Wilma and Harold's only real sin was being stupid. They knew nothing about the murders. If they get a sentence at all, it will probably be a light one."

"Should I be afraid?"

"You have nothing to fear from any of them. They are nothing without Donald's leadership." His arm once again tightened around her. "Besides, no harm will ever come to you as long as I'm by your side."

She smiled up at him, loving his strength, his beauty of spirit. "Do you intend to spend a lot of time by my side?"

"Only forever," he answered. "That is, if you agree to marry a Portland, Maine, cop who sometimes gets carried away with his work." He gently swept a strand of her hair away from her cheek. "I hear they desperately need good teachers in Portland."

"And I desperately need you," she answered.

His eyes glowed with the look she'd come to savor, and his lips descended to hers, consuming her, engulfing her. This time she wasn't afraid of the depths he swept her away to. She didn't fear the magic of his caress—rather, she reveled in it.

He reluctantly broke the kiss, his fingertips trailing slowly, sensually down her cheek and capturing her chin. "As much as I hate to admit it, Donald was right about one thing."

"What?" she asked, looking up at him curiously, trying to ignore the raging inferno his simple touch created inside her.

"Destiny brought us together here. Perhaps our purpose was to dispel the evil—or perhaps our fate was simply to fall in love. In any case, I know we belong together. I love you, Darlene. And when we have a child, it will be conceived in love, a child of the light."

She smiled up at him tremulously. "Yes," she whispered, and as his lips claimed hers once again she gave in to the hot winds of passion that stirred inside her. She felt their souls touching, then wrapping around each other. She knew he would always be there inside her, their spirits bound for eternity. Yes, he possessed her, but it was the sweetest possession she'd ever known.

* * * * *

CARLA CASSIDY

Perhaps because I was raised in a warm, safe, secure family, I've always been intrigued with the darker side of life. When I was very young, my father used to turn out all the lights in the house and chase my brother and me around like a bogeyman. Although I was terrified, the terror was tempered with the underlying knowledge that even if I was caught, I'd be safe.

When I heard about the new Silhouette Shadows line, I felt the same as when I was being chased by my lovable bogeyman. I saw this line as a chance to explore the dark side, delve into the psychology of fear and evil, yet enjoy the comfort of knowing there would be a satisfying ending. To me there is nothing quite so provocative as a man who embodies qualities of light and dark, the eternal struggle between good and evil, and the ultimate triumph of love over all.

So, join me in a journey as we explore the unknown, indulge vicariously in the powers of darkness that beckon. Hold my hand...try not to be afraid as we travel toward the light at the end of the dark.

Carla Cassidy

The Phantom of Chicago

LORI HERTER

To my husband, Jerry,
whom I met and married in Chicago.
He tolerates my obsessions
with patience and a sense of humor.

CHAPTER ONE

Forty feet beneath State Street in Chicago's Loop, in the murky gloom of an abandoned tunnel, a tall man stood carefully smoothing back his dark hair with his hands. Intent on his work, he peered into a small mirror he'd affixed with glue to the tunnel's concrete wall. The wall domed upward to form a ceiling only a few feet above his head. Behind him, on a square wood table next to a small bed, stood a battery-operated lamp that lit the smooth, curved walls all about him with a cold, eerie light. The invasive light faded into blackness down the far reaches of the tunnel.

Behind the lamp, in the shadows, the back wall at this widened place in the tunnel system was made of brick. An old double doorway interrupted the brick. The door had been the turn-of-the-century subbasement entrance to Winthrop's Department Store, where merchandise, mail and coal had once been delivered by the diminutive electric train system for which this complex maze of tunnels had been built. The rusting, old two-foot-gauge railroad track remained intact in the concrete floor. In recent years, the tunnel system had gotten flooded by a leak from the Chicago River.

The water had been pumped out, but the dampness from that event remained in the atmosphere and lent a dank, mildew odor.

The man peering in the mirror took no notice of the thick air as he concentrated on smoothing back his brown hair with gel. After living down here for weeks, he'd grown accustomed to the atmosphere. By now he knew much of the complicated tunnel system well enough to draw a rough map of it, and he could get anywhere he wanted to in the Loop by traveling underground. He knew how to circumvent most security systems and could enter virtually any of the old Chicago buildings whose subbasements were connected to the abandoned railroad tunnels.

He tossed the tube of gel into a nearby box of newspapers and other odds and ends. Limping to the table, he picked up a thick candle, lit it with a match and brought it back with him to the mirror, hoping it would help him see better in the odd light. He had a good flashlight, but it would have caused a harsh glare in the mirror.

The candle worked much better, he found, as he lifted it to study his altered appearance. His hair, severely combed straight back from his angular face, looked darker in color due to the gel he'd used to keep his thick strands flat. This wasn't a style he particularly liked, but it helped camouflage his identity.

He noticed his white bow tie was crooked and he straightened it, then stepped back to see as much as he could of his formal clothes in the makeshift mirror. His black, swallowtail, cutaway coat, black vest and white, pleated dress shirt all looked immaculate—no small feat considering his surroundings.

He glanced at his wristwatch, squinting to read it in the dim light. Seven forty-five p.m., almost time to be on his way. Quickly he turned from the mirror. As he did so, a sudden pain in his thigh made him wince, and he reminded himself not to move in just that way. His leg was still healing from the deep bullet wound.

Ignoring the pain, he remembered that he still had the last and most important item of his costume to put on: the white mask. After bending to set the candle on the floor, which again made his thigh ache, he limped back to the bed. The blue sheets and pillow had been made up neatly. On top lay the leather mask he'd set aside while he put on the rest of the Phantom of the Opera costume he'd "borrowed" from Winthrop's. The large, distinctive department store had stocked a marvelous assortment of high-quality costumes for Halloween.

He picked up the mask and checked the black elastic band connected to each corner as he walked back to the mirror. Carefully he brought the mask to his face and pulled the elastic over his shining, slicked-back hair, letting go to allow the band to fit snugly around the back of his head. The mask's polished white leather extended from the tip of his narrow nose to just below his hairline. Two almond-shaped holes that tilted slightly upward at the outer corners allowed him to see.

He bent to pick up the candle again and held it near his face. The stark white mask seemed to make his clear green eyes show up brightly in contrast, and his dark lashes gave him a mysterious, even spooky, quality when he moved his eyes. Good, he thought, smiling with satisfaction.

He intended to make a profound impression on Crystal Winthrop, the woman he adored, at the gala charity ball he planned to crash this evening. On this singular occasion, this night he'd planned for revelations and truth, he decided he'd go by his true name, which he'd never used: Eric. This was not only appropriate for the costume he'd chosen, but because tonight's mission was a personal one, invented and instigated by Eric to suit his purposes.

Eric drew in a deep breath, feeling every bit the overpowering male the mirror showed him to be. Perhaps his recurring fevers from his wound, and his long, lonely weeks of isolation had begun to affect his equilibrium, but he felt justified and ready now to go out and capture Crystal for himself, the woman he'd needed and wanted for so long. He knew this was not an orthodox way to win the woman of one's desires. But Eric had good reason: Crystal was planning to make the mistake of her life by marrying the wrong man—a dangerous man.

Eric forgave her for overlooking *him* as a potential mate. Despite her chronic obliviousness to him, Crystal's curiosity and rebellious spirit, her buoyant energy and flair for fun had kept introspective Eric fascinated all his life. Though she came from an influential family, wealth and position were not the features that attracted Crystal to a man. She seemed to want brawn, flash and magnetic sensuality, judging by the assortment of men with whom she'd been linked romantically over the years.

But this evening, Eric intended to make her forget all the others, including her current, ungodly handsome fiancé. Eric *the Phantom* would fulfill all her wild longings tonight, and he would save her from the danger she didn't know awaited her.

This would be a night of destiny.

He picked up a long black cape he'd left lying on a nearby chair and swung it over his shoulders. As the heavy material swished majestically about him, a sure sense of dark eminence settled over him. The heady feeling energized him and heightened his senses. Was he getting too carried away? he wondered as he felt his heart begin to pound with anticipation. Maybe all these weeks spent alone beneath the earth and this costume were making him go slightly crackers. He felt besotted with a mad aura of mystery and power. Even his leg had stopped hurting.

Eric decided he didn't care if he *was* skirting the edge of madness. High time he broke out of his careful mold! He'd become the fantasy figure he needed to be in order to rescue the woman he worshiped from her treacherous suitor, in order to reveal himself to her alone as the sensual man of her desires, whom she'd so carelessly overlooked her whole life.

He took another deep breath, grabbed his gloves, swept his satin cape about him and headed above ground.

"Oh, Dad!" Crystal exclaimed with annoyance as she strode past her father in their elegant lakefront home.

"I'm serious about this!" her father, Laurence Winthrop III, grandson of the man who founded Winthrop's Department Store chain, said in his most pontifical manner. "How can you appear at a charity ball crawling with reporters and gossip columnists wearing a dress like that? Especially when you're the chairperson of the committee that's putting on the ball. You're certain to be photographed. Change into something else!"

Crystal glanced down at her ultra low-cut, antique-gold ball gown and felt a trifle self-conscious. Her dress did push the limits, she supposed. The cinched waistline showed off her tiny waist and the daring neckline was set off with low-slung, puffed little sleeves at her upper arms. She'd had the dress designed for her particularly to frame her breasts and shoulders, superbly molded to feminine perfection from her hours of body-shaping exercises at her weight machines.

"It's a Halloween ball," she argued, regaining her patience. She knew she'd have her way, even if she did still live under her father's roof, so there was no use making a fuss with him. "This is my *costume.*"

"Then put a sheet over it and go as a ghost!" Laurence said, scratching his head of thick, iron gray hair. He wore a tuxedo and was planning to attend the same ball, sans costume, after a business dinner. "Who are you supposed to be, anyway? Mae West? Marilyn Monroe?"

She laughed at him. "Am I wearing a blond wig?" she asked, pointing to her auburn hair gathered up in an elaborate hairdo of old-fashioned ringlets.

"Lady Godiva, then?" he asked, as if puzzling over the matter.

"I don't have a horse and I'm not nude," she answered back.

"Might as well be!"

"I'm going as Beauty, of *Beauty and the Beast,*" she explained. "Tony's going as the Beast."

"Well, *that,* at least, makes perfect sense!"

"Daddy!" Exasperated, she plunked herself down, wide taffeta skirts and all, on the Chippendale couch, where her pedigreed calico Persian cat was lounging. She leaned to one side to pet it.

Meanwhile, her father began to pace. He wasn't a tall man, but with his broad shoulders and regal posture, he made an imposing impression on all but his daughter, who knew how to set her own boundaries. "I still can't understand why you've decided to go ahead with your plans to marry Tony," Laurence said in a troubled tone of voice. "I thought the wedding was off. Why is it on again? I'd rather see you run off with one of the gorillas at Lincoln Park Zoo."

"The wedding was never off," she answered as she twisted the large, pear-shaped diamond on her left hand to straighten it. "I just postponed making the plans, that's all. Now I've started working on them again and figuring out a wedding date."

He stopped pacing and looked down at her. "But I thought you seemed to come to your senses after Jay Saunders died, and now—" He stiffened his back. "That reminds me, I've got to find you a new lawyer. Jay never had the chance to finish hammering out your prenuptial agreement."

Crystal's throat tightened and she bowed her head as she went back to stroking her cat. "Don't talk about Jay, Dad. Not tonight. I want to try to have fun for a change. I've been so upset since he disappeared. That was why I just couldn't concentrate on the details of planning a big wedding, knowing poor Jay was...was bleeding to death somewhere, or lying at the bottom of Lake Michigan, or the Chicago River, or whatever happened to him." She looked up. "How come they still haven't found any trace of him?"

Laurence's gray eyes grew downcast, too. "I don't know. I called the police the other day to ask if there were any new developments. Detective Fogarty said they're still pursuing their investigation and mentioned something about a phone call and a new lead. But as far as I know, Jay's open Jaguar with his blood on the driver's seat is still all the evidence they have. They're going on the theory that he may have been murdered and his body disposed of."

Crystal swallowed hard, trying to overcome the lump in her throat. She wanted to tell her father something but found it difficult. "I haven't felt like saying this before, but—" she paused to wet her lips "—I've always had the feeling that his death was my fault, somehow."

Her father's expression grew concerned and he sat down in the chair opposite her, studying her at eye level now. "Your fault?"

They'd often talked about Jay's mysterious phone call to her the night before he disappeared. He'd wanted her to come to his office that very evening, but she couldn't because she had a date with Tony. She had even mentioned to Tony that night that Jay had called and sounded unusually edgy. The next morning when she went to Jay's office, his secretary was worried because he hadn't come in. Later they heard on the radio that his blood-smeared car had been found abandoned in the underground parking level of his condo building.

Crystal lifted her bared shoulders in a helpless gesture, making the puffs of spun gold at her upper arms rise up and down. "Well...Jay sounded so urgent when he called me. Like he had something really important to tell me. And he wouldn't discuss it over the phone. I just assumed it had to do with the prenuptial agreement, but maybe it was something else, some information someone didn't want him to tell, so they killed him. He was such a quiet, sort of frail, scholarly fellow, he probably got in over his head in some dangerous situation and needed help. Maybe that's why he was calling on me. Maybe if I had gone to see him that night instead of keeping my date with Tony, maybe things would have turned out differently." She sighed distractedly. "I have this nagging feeling that...that he may have died because of m-me."

Laurence shook his head. "Jay would never have told you anything that would put *you* in danger. In part, I agree with your theory. I've always suspected, and so do the police, that he may have been killed because he'd learned something he shouldn't have regarding some nasty case he was working on. He was a brilliant attorney, and people whisper that he worked on some classified projects during those few years he spent in Washington. So the murderer might even have been someone out of his past who had a vendetta. But in any case, he would never have told you about that. It's just coincidence, Crystal, that he was killed the morning after phoning you."

Crystal knew that everything her father said made perfect sense. Still, the feeling gnawed at her that Jay's untimely end somehow had something to do with her. She remembered how his voice, usually carefully modulated and studiously devoid of emotion, had sounded anxious and concerned during that last phone call. He'd seemed to be completely focused on her for some reason. Then the next morning he was gone, either knifed or bludgeoned, for no bullet was ever found, and his body was apparently spirited away.

Her father rose from his seat and patted her shoulder. "Don't blame yourself. I wish to God we hadn't lost Jay, too, especially under such circumstances. I respected and trusted him. That's why I chose him to be your attorney. I'd even hoped that..."

Crystal looked up. "What?"

"Jay was from a good family and still single. He was a few years older than you, a perfect age. He was unusually intelligent with a marvelous career ahead of him, and he had a sense of responsibility."

"You mean, you hoped I'd forget Tony and fall for Jay instead?" She smiled with sad amusement and toyed with a taffeta ruffle on her dress. She knew her father would love to choose her husband for her. "I still remember Jay when we were kids at school. He was always carrying or reading a book. He was skinny—the other boys bullied him on the playground."

"He'd changed a lot since then."

She shrugged. "Oh, I don't know. He was such an egghead, he got through college and law school years ahead of his classmates. He *was* sweet, though. And caring. Like when he left Washington and moved back to Chicago because his father had died and his mother needed him. At the funeral, I remember him quietly grieving. He was a gentle soul. I always liked him, trusted him. But he just wasn't my type."

She leaned back on the couch then, remembering the last time she saw him. They were at his office. His curly brown head was bowed over the legal paperwork on his desk as he sat by the hour explaining every single detail about her prenuptial agreement. He was so conscientious about everything, she found him rather touching. At the same time, she was bored to tears by all the legal complexities, especially when she had a dress fitting and then a meeting to get to for the charity-ball committee she'd agreed to chair. She sincerely appreciated his care and concern, but—

"Yes, well, I wish you'd rethink what your 'type' is!" Laurence said, breaking her rumination.

"Attraction is something you *feel*," she told him, "not think about."

"Life isn't a fairy tale like *Beauty and the Beast*," he said as if she didn't know. "If you're an heiress planning to marry a muscle-bound thug with no family or connections he'll admit to, you'd *better* do some thinking and put aside feelings for a moment. Otherwise, if it turns out that Tony's a gold digger, as I suspect, you may come to regret a decision based on nothing more than physical attraction.''

Crystal gave him a look of impatience. She might have told him she also found Tony charming, attentive and intelligent in a street-smart way that fascinated her. But her father was in no mood to listen.

He reached toward her and changed his tone to one of reason and appeal. 'If only you'd show some common sense when it comes to your romantic life. I was afraid you'd marry that playboy Frenchman—'

''He was rich,'' she pointed out, feeling impish now as she smothered a smile.

''*Was* rich is the truth! He was flat broke when he started wooing you. Then it was that washed-up tennis player—''

''He had a roomful of trophies—''

''And now Tony,'' her father said. ''Just because he's got muscles and likes to show off the hair on his chest—''

''Oh,'' she teased, ''you don't like him because he refuses to wear a three-piece suit.''

''*None* of your men has worn three-piece suits!''

''Of course not. I look for imaginative men who don't bother with useless proprieties and customs.''

''Not someone boring and predictable, like me?''

Crystal smiled up at him with affection. ''You're my father. You're supposed to be predictable.''

''My only child, and this is the respect I get—''

The doorbell rang.

"That's Tony," she said quickly, rising to go to the door.

Laurence followed behind her. "You're going to change that dress before leaving, aren't you?"

"Nope!"

"Don't you have any modesty anymore? Any sense of respectability? Pride?"

"Sure," she told him as she walked across the white wool carpet to the long, marble-tiled hallway that led to the door. "I work out every day at my health club." Indeed, it was *her* health club, for her father had bought it for her to manage when she'd graduated college and couldn't settle on a career. He'd hoped the new responsibility would settle *her.* "People say I have the fittest body in Chicago. Why shouldn't I be proud of how I look and want to show off? It's good for business."

"But what about modesty? Your mother had such a refined sense of decorum. She wouldn't have spoiled you and let you have your way as I have," he said, talking half to himself now as he followed a step behind Crystal. "She would have known how to handle you when you were going through your rambunctious teens. She would have made you understand the proper way a young woman from a prominent family like ours should comport herself."

Crystal paused to take her father's arm as they continued toward the door. She thought of her mother, who had died of cancer eleven years ago.

Crystal had been born when both of her parents were in their forties. Her mother always called her daughter her "little miracle." After her death, Crystal had decided early on to experience all she could of life, because she'd become so aware of how unjustly and unexpectedly a life could end. In recent years, she'd begun to devote a great deal of time to her favorite charity, a cancer-research foundation.

"I miss Mom, too," she told her father in a heartfelt voice. "But I'm not like her. I don't believe in being modest. Where does it get you? I want to *live*. Be daring! I want adventure. I want an exciting man and an exciting life. I know you'd like me to be interested in the 'right' sort of man—someone you approve of from our circle of well-heeled friends. But all those budding doctors, lawyers and entrepreneurs from the families we know are focused on climbing up their success ladders. Like Jay, they're all very responsible and capable, but..."

"They bore you, I know," Laurence said with a sigh.

"Well, I can't help it, Dad. I want a man who captures and holds my attention. A three-piece suit and a briefcase do nothing to arouse my libido."

"There are more important things than an aroused libido!" Laurence told her in a hushed voice, as if there were someone in the empty house who might overhear.

"Not when you're a fit, healthy, single woman of twenty-five, there isn't!"

"All right, all right," Laurence muttered. "All people seem to think about is sex nowadays! It's in the movies, TV, newspaper headlines—everywhere. Well...maybe I've forgotten what it was like to be your age," he conceded. "But given all the untraditional relationships people accept nowadays, do you have to *marry* Tony? Can't you just have your fling with him, if you must? My God, it must be like sleeping with Tarzan, the Ape Man! But I suppose that's just what you want."

The fact was, Crystal was having private, niggling second thoughts about marrying Tony, but she didn't want to admit that to her father, knowing he'd pounce on her doubts and try to quadruple them. Whatever decision she made, she wanted it to be her own. And another fact was that she hadn't yet slept with Tony, perhaps because of her doubts. But that wasn't any of her father's business, so she didn't take the trouble to set him straight.

The bell rang again just as they reached the front door of their spacious home. As Crystal took hold of the doorknob, her father stepped away.

"Aren't you going to say hello to Tony?" she whispered.

"I'll see him later at the ball. I can wait until then for the 'pleasure' of greeting him," Laurence said with asperity. He kissed her on the cheek, then turned to walk back down the hall.

When he was out of sight, Crystal opened the door. A familiar pair of brown-black eyes greeted her.

"Wow!" Tony said, eyeing her dress with obvious approval. "You're more dazzling than Times Square on New Year's Eve."

"Same to you," she replied, smiling as she gazed over his costume. He wore tall, glistening black boots over black pants, a rich, gold velvet jacket in an old-world military cut with a very high collar, a red satin sash, and epaulets at his broad shoulders. And no shirt. His vast chest stood exposed, revealing his marvelously developed pectoral muscles and thick black hair that made a V toward his belt buckle. His black mane of hair, left long at the nape and cut to graduated lengths swept back from his face, his usual style, lent a wild aspect to the manliness of his costume. In short, he looked as if he'd jumped off the cover of a romance novel.

He lifted the mask he held in his hand to his face; it showed huge, angry eyes, a hairy face and bloodied animal teeth. The mask looked so realistic over his overwhelmingly virile body, it gave her a start, even frightened her a bit. She didn't know why it should. It was only a plastic mask, and she'd seen his chest many times when he worked out at her gym.

"Just carry the mask, so people get the idea," she suggested. "I don't think you need to wear it, except maybe when we arrive and make our grand entrance.''

"Good," he said. "It's hot wearing it anyway. Where's your mask?"

She turned to a nearby table in the hallway. Picking up her mask, which was made of gold satin, stiff gold lace and sequins, she held it by the satin-wrapped stick attached to one corner and lifted it to her face. It was purely ornamental and covered only her eyes.

"Terrific!" he said. "Are we a great-looking pair, or what?"

"We'll be noticed, that's for sure," she said with wry amusement. "I'll call and have the limo brought around."

In a few minutes they were sitting in the back of her father's long black limousine, which he'd graciously let her use so they could arrive in style at the ball, held at a large historic hotel located on the north edge of the Loop.

Tony made a perfunctory attempt to kiss her, but she held up a hand to stop him, saying she'd just put on lipstick and didn't want to arrive looking mussed. He took her rebuff with apparent equanimity. They'd been engaged for nearly two months, and already, in some ways, they almost behaved as if they were married. This disappointed her, though she knew it was probably her own fault.

She'd met him about four months ago, when he suddenly showed up at her Michigan Avenue health club and bought a membership without even taking a tour of the place. He knew a great deal about body-building, and they began their friendship comparing notes about techniques and new schools of thought regarding the proper way to train. At first, she'd found it difficult to carry on a normal conversation with him because, frankly, she was so distracted by his magnificent body. She liked the flash of his black-brown eyes and the sensuality of his swarthy skin tone. But his streetwise quickness and cleverness also impressed her. He seemed familiar with an exciting world she'd never been a part of, having been confined to the sheltered life her father had provided her as she grew up. Tony was the most dynamic man she'd ever met. There even seemed to be a hint of danger about him, which made her breath catch in her throat and her heart beat faster.

She quickly offered him a job as a trainer, and he took her up on it, saying he'd been intending to quit the job he'd had to look for something he liked better. Though she asked out of curiosity, he somehow never had explained just what and where his old job had been.

He asked her to dinner soon after he started working at her club, and that began a whirlwind courtship. The first time he kissed her and held her in his strong arms, crushing the breath out of her, her knees literally went weak. Though he suggested they make love, she'd decided to postpone becoming intimate with him, fearing she'd fallen for him too hard and too fast to keep her head. Sleeping with him, she knew, would only compound her confusion—or at least, that's what she told herself at the time.

He took her gentle refusal well, as if prepared to bide his time and wait for her. However, after knowing each other only two months, he surprised her one day over lunch at her club by proposing marriage. He even presented her with a stunning, two-karat, pear-shaped diamond that took her breath away. The size of the stone astonished her, since she hadn't had the impression that Tony came from a wealthy family or that he'd gained any fortune through his own labors. Whenever she asked about his family, he vaguely said that they were in New York and he no longer had much contact with them. As far as his work experience, all she'd learned was that he'd worked as a trainer for several athletes, mostly boxers.

His vagueness about his past didn't bother her too much at the time. In her mind, he fit the image of the "strong, silent type," who said little about himself, perhaps out of modesty. She took his ring with a sense of excitement about her future. She felt that finally she'd found a man who charged her senses, and she wanted him permanently in her life.

She also knew her father would be appalled, and that aspect thoroughly amused her. Rushing home that evening, she showed her father the ring. He'd already met Tony and, though he hadn't said much, she knew he disapproved. When he saw the ring, he went pale with anger. Seeing him so upset unsettled her, for she hadn't expected such an extreme reaction. But she was his only child, sole heiress to the family fortune who had already inherited her mother's family estate, and she'd never brought home an engagement ring before. She should have anticipated his reaction. He'd always kept a tight rein on her choices and her life, and he couldn't seem to get used to the fact that she was now old enough to have the right to make decisions on her own.

The first thing her father did was hire a private detective to investigate Tony's background, which her father decided must be unsavory. This did not surprise Crystal, for he'd had the Frenchman she'd dated for a year investigated, too, fearing she would marry him. The tennis player, also. Her father had made her read the reports the detective wrote. Perhaps learning about both men's shallow affairs, questionable business dealings, and their penchant for losing money, did make Crystal lose interest in one and later in the other. In any case, she'd broken off her relationships with her earlier suitors.

But the detective came up with very little about Tony's background. He came from a family of mixed Mediterranean heritage, the detective said, and they ran a restaurant in the Bronx. Tony had attended a local college, though he'd never graduated. And he had trained some boxers in New York after being one himself for a few years.

"See?" she'd said to her father after reading the detective's brief report. "Nothing terribly sinister here."

"Maybe the detective was bribed," her father had said suspiciously.

Crystal had only rolled her eyes and laughed. Meanwhile her father had insisted she have a prenuptial agreement drawn up and suggested Jay Saunders for her attorney. She'd met with Jay four or five times—and then Jay had met with foul play.

As she sat in silence thinking of Jay again, Tony took her hand, placed it on his knee and covered it with his own. "Why so quiet?"

"Oh," she replied with a sigh, "I was just talking to my father about Jay. They still haven't discovered what happened to him."

Tony shrugged with stiff indifference. "If he's dead, no use worrying about his remains. No difference to him anymore."

"No," she agreed, though she was irritated at the unfeeling way Tony talked about Jay's probable death. Several weeks ago, when Jay had disappeared and she was too upset to think about wedding plans, Tony had been very understanding. But his patience had soon disappeared. He'd even asked her the other day when she was going to "get over" Jay Saunders' death. "He was just another conniving lawyer," Tony had mumbled unpleasantly. But she knew Tony had always been annoyed, perhaps insulted, that her father had insisted on a prenuptial agreement.

"Thought any more about us eloping?" he asked, rubbing the back of her hand with the palm of his.

"No. I told you, I started planning the wedding again. I'm thinking maybe May or June."

"It's a lot easier to elope," he said. It was an argument he'd used often lately. "Saves your dad's money. It's simple. And—" he squeezed her hand "—we wouldn't have to wait, you know?"

Tony had been unusually understanding, she'd thought, when she told him she wanted to wait until they were married to sleep together. She'd explained that she thought it would be more romantic to wait till the wedding night. Soon, however, he began suggesting they elope, and though she kept resisting the idea, he wouldn't give it up.

Crystal hated even the thought of eloping with Tony, though she couldn't explain why, even to herself. She found it more comfortable to dabble and dawdle over the wedding plans, waiting for her instincts to tell her what to do, and not think about specific reasons. She made all her important decisions by gut feeling and impulse. Trying to think things through in a step-by-step manner, listing reasons pro and con, as her father would do, only tended to throw her mind in circles, making the decision that much more difficult. She put more trust in her instincts than anything else.

"I don't want to elope, Tony," she stated firmly.

"But why?" He quizzed her using the enthusiastic, savvy tone she used to admire but which she was beginning to find oppressive. "Why waste time with all this wedding rigmarole? We don't need that. All we need is to fly to Vegas, get married, and then we're on our way. I've got plans for our health club. I think we can franchise it. We can't move on that until we're legally married."

Our health club? she thought to herself. "Tony, let's not argue about this tonight."

"I'm not arguing. I'm just saying—"

"Let's not discuss it, then. We're going to a wonderful ball in our beautiful costumes. Let's just have fun together, like . . . like when we first met."

"Sure." Suddenly, his tone was clipped and edged with an ugly quality she didn't like at all.

She was growing tired of Tony's persistence about marrying her quickly. Sometimes he behaved as if all his plans were down the drain if she didn't. It made her wonder if her father was right, that maybe he was after her money and social position. She'd been assuring Tony that she was going ahead with the wedding plans she'd briefly put aside, just to keep him at bay. But, to be honest, Crystal wasn't sure if or when she would ever walk up the aisle with him. She felt differently about it nearly every day. She wasn't even sure anymore she really loved Tony. Electric sparks still flared between the two of them, like tonight when she'd seen him looking so virile at her door. But now, riding in the limo with him, those sparks were already fizzling. Still, no other man had ever captured her attention the way Tony did.

A quarter of an hour later they arrived at the hotel, walked up the elaborate staircase and entered the magnificent Grand Ballroom. Huge tables laden with ice sculptures and hors d'oeuvres were set up in the corners of the large room, with its high, recessed, gold-leafed ceiling and its sparkling chandeliers. An orchestra played at one end of the room, and an area in front of the musicians had been set apart for dancing. The roomful of partying people in colorful, imaginative costumes took Crystal's mind off her doubts about Tony and made her ready to enjoy the festivities she'd helped plan.

A short while later, Crystal was speaking to a group of friends. Tony had left to wait in the long line at the bar on the edge of the ballroom. She'd asked him to get them drinks. Against the sound of the orchestra playing a popular old rock tune and the general noisy chatter of the hundreds of guests, Crystal was nearly shouting to be heard by an old college girlfriend dressed as Snow White.

All at once, she became aware of a strange quietness encircling her. Everyone around her, including her friend, had become curiously silent and distracted. A vague sense of suspense in the atmosphere gave her an eerie feeling. She turned and looked about her to find out what was causing the odd silence in their corner of the ballroom.

And then she saw him.

CHAPTER TWO

Tall, wearing a black cape and a white mask, he was staring at Crystal, arm dramatically outstretched, pointing a long, gloved finger at her and singling her out with his piercing eyes. They were a translucent green, almost luminescent, intense with uncensored possessiveness. Whoever he was, he had the most compelling eyes she'd ever seen.

After she turned to face him, he slowly lowered his arm to his side. With his gaze alone, he pinned her to the spot on which she was standing, about six feet away from where he stood, and held her captive. She froze in sublime shock, as if some spotlight had suddenly been turned on her alone, separating her from the crowd of people around her. Tantalized with an odd mixture of fear and breathless expectation, she waited for him to reveal what he wanted from her.

He remained in the same dynamic posture—proud chest and squared shoulders, his long cape draping magnificently about him, his sharp eyes unblinking—and gave no hint as to what his purpose was. What was this all about? Crystal wondered. He must be staring at her in particular for some reason. As seconds ticked by, the nearby crowd began to gather in a circle about her and him, watching and waiting to see what would happen.

Crystal was barely aware of them as her mind flew. Did she know this man? He didn't look like anyone she knew, at least not with the mask that covered so much of his face. If she'd ever met anyone with eyes like his, she would have remembered. Who was he, anyway?

And then it occurred to her, as she grew aware that the people observing them were whispering and chuckling as if watching a show, that perhaps he was one of the half-dozen actors who had been hired by her charity committee to participate in the masked ball. The idea had come from another of the committee members, who had offered to arrange for the actors after the committee approved the motion. Perhaps this fellow had been assigned to dress as the romantic Phantom of the Opera and to go around and make a show of flirting with women. It was meant to be for fun, a part of the carnival atmosphere created for this Halloween extravaganza. The other hired actors were also here, no doubt, in other costumes, purposely interacting with the guests, and she just hadn't been here long enough to notice them.

Crystal felt relieved now that she had it figured out. But, God, he was good at this flirting business! He made her feel as if she were the only woman in the entire ballroom. Knowing she was part of an act now, she smiled at him, at his white mask and firm mouth and those eyes that wouldn't quit.

He responded by smiling back, his even row of teeth as white as his mask. It was a jaunty grin, as if he was sure of himself and pleased. He raised his gloved hand to one shoulder and lifted the top of the cape he wore. Taking hold of the cape with both hands as he slipped it off, he widened his stance and swirled the cape around his head. The people about them gasped and ooohed. Then he maneuvered the cape so that it swept toward her, flared out and settled gracefully at her feet, like a broad, black satin pathway between him and her.

Crystal grinned as the crowd applauded. She had to admire his showmanship! When everyone had quieted again, waiting to see what came next, the masked man held out his white-gloved hand to her, beckoning her.

"Walk across my cape and enter a new world," he told her in a low, smooth voice.

What choice did she have, with everyone watching? Besides, Crystal had never been one to shy away from any spotlight of attention. To add drama to the moment, and to coyly mock him, she lifted her own mask to her face, holding it by its wandlike stick. Extending her other hand toward him, she stepped forward onto the black cape. When she'd crossed far enough, he took hold of her hand and stepped backward, leading her across the rest of the cape until she stood on the ballroom's parquet floor again.

He gazed down at her, still holding her hand at shoulder level.

"What now?" she asked with amusement, enjoying the charade.

"Dance with me." His grandiose tone was more a command than an invitation.

His manner left her breathless. She took the mask from her face so she could place her hand on his shoulder in the traditional dance position, her mask and wand dangling from her fingers and trailing down the back of his black cutaway coat. Again, the crowd applauded. As she began to dance with him to the slow, romantic show tune the orchestra was now playing, the people began to break up into their small conversational groups again, as if the brief show was over.

Crystal wondered what came next. She supposed he would dance with her a bit to be polite and then move on to some other unsuspecting lady and go through his routine again.

As she danced in his arms, she studied the molded contours of his leather mask and the slanted holes that accented his eyes in such an unsettling way. At the same time, she questioned whether a hired actor really ought to hold a female guest as closely as he was holding her. His hand at her back kept her pressed against him, stomach to stomach, crushing her taffeta skirts.

All at once, she realized he was gazing at her grandly displayed cleavage with eyes that all but smoldered. He almost made her wish she'd followed her father's order to change into something more modest. Still, the fire in his gaze made her heart skip a beat and her head swim, and she rather liked that.

At the same time, his brazen behavior made her indignant, too. There were many wealthy, influential women attending this ball. He really ought to be more careful how he behaved. Who did he think he was?

"Are you an actor?" she finally asked in a slightly haughty tone when she thought he'd studied her physical attributes enough.

His eyes flicked up to meet hers. "An actor?" He laughed, as if genuinely amused. "No. Maybe I should be."

She felt a chill, realizing she'd been all wrong in her assumptions. "Th-then who are you?" she asked, stiffening her back as she tried to put a respectable gap between them.

He loosened his hold slightly, allowing her to separate from him a bit as they continued to dance. "I'm the Phantom in your life," he told her.

She looked askance, not pleased that he was continuing to toy with her. "What's your name?" she asked, trying to keep her patience.

"Eric."

Crystal had to laugh and give him credit for persistence in whatever game he was playing. "Sure it is," she told him, knowing the Phantom of the Opera's name was Eric in the classic book written by Gaston Leroux. "But what's *your* name, the name on your birth certificate?"

"Eric," he repeated. "My parents named me Eric."

She drew her eyebrows together, wondering whether to believe him. Meanwhile she was beginning to think his voice sounded vaguely familiar, as if she might have met him before. He seemed young, judging by the smooth, taut skin over his angular chin line, and she guessed he might be in her general age group. "Do I know you?" she asked.

"You might."

"Where? From school? Or," she said, thinking again, "do you go to my health club?"

"I was at your health club once."

"Only *once?*"

"You were wearing a workout outfit almost as revealing as this dress. I couldn't take it. Had to leave without even saying hello to you."

She laughed. "Why?"

"Didn't want to pounce on you in front of all those people on the cycles and treadmills."

Whoever he was, she was beginning to like his sense of humor. "You aren't so self-conscious now," she pointed out.

"Wearing a mask is a very freeing experience."

She smiled at his wry explanation. But she still couldn't figure out why his voice sounded familiar, if he hadn't spoken to her when he saw her at the health club. "Have I met you before, somewhere else?"

"You may have, Cryssywiss."

Cryssywiss. This was a name children at her private school had called her when she was in fourth or fifth grade. So this Phantom must be an old acquaintance. But he could be any one of forty or fifty young men who might know her since childhood.

"You're certainly being secretive!" she said.

"I have many secrets."

"Can you at least tell me why you singled *me* out to dance, with so much flair and fanfare?" she asked.

The half smile on his face faded. "To save you."

She blinked at the reply, having expected another provocative compliment. "Save me from what?" she asked, playing along.

"Marrying the wrong man."

She gave a throaty laugh at that. "Whom *should* I marry?"

He smiled with ingenuous assurance. "Me, the Phantom in your life."

"Really! Why?"

He stopped dancing and stared at her a long moment, the energy flooding into his eyes again, making her heart jump. "Come with me, and I'll show you," he told her, his voice sensual and softly commanding.

"Come where?"

"Out of the ballroom, down the hall," he said.

The heady game was too intriguing to stop now. "All right," she agreed, thinking he planned to take her out into the corridor to speak more privately, or even perhaps to try to make a pass at her. Either way, she felt more than equipped to handle the situation. If she could keep a tough-looking man like Tony at bay, she could certainly handle a man who hid behind a mask.

Tony, she thought. She'd forgotten him! Looking around, she saw him in the distance among the crowd, coming toward them with two drinks in his hands. "My fiancé will wonder—"

"Never mind *him*," Eric said in a stern tone. He quickly bent to pick up the cape at his feet. In one stroke, he swung it round his shoulders, wearing it again as he had when she first saw him. Swiftly he slipped an arm around her shoulders, bringing one side of the cape with him, enveloping her in the black material. Her mask was knocked from her hand. He began walking at a fast pace out of the ballroom, making her move along with him. The sensation of the heavy satin flowing around her like a cocoon, enveloping her with him, sent a frisson down her spine. On TV, she'd once seen footage of a bat capturing a mouse as its prey, wrapping its large black wings about the poor creature, hiding it within its folds as the bat dealt it a death bite. The image flickered through her mind as he rushed her away, and for a moment she felt like that mouse.

But then she remembered she was in a hotel full of hundreds of people and in no danger. She also reminded herself that she'd learned karate, and if this Phantom got out of hand, she'd give him his comeuppance before he knew what hit him!

She'd give Tony some explanation later. She knew he had probably seen her being carried off, so to speak. Having never given her fiancé cause to be jealous before, she wondered how he'd react. Well, she'd deal with that after she'd finished her tantalizing little game of hide-and-seek with Eric, or whoever he was. She couldn't recall knowing any boy in grade school by that name.

Eric pushed her along out of the ballroom and into the foyer, down the elaborate staircase, where she nearly tripped on her long gown, and through the lobby. He opened an obscure door, and soon they were walking swiftly down a narrow hallway. She began to grow uneasy that they had left the main part of the hotel. He moved so quickly, his long legs taking such long strides, that she had trouble keeping up in her tight gown and high heels. The stays in her dress began to pinch as she breathed deeply from exertion. "Where are we going? Why are we in such a rush?" she asked, gasping a bit.

He glanced down at her, his eyes quick now and appraising. "Sorry," he said, as he turned to look behind them. They were in yet another back hallway now—she didn't know where, they'd moved so fast—that was completely empty. When he saw no one was behind them, he seemed to relax just slightly. But he began moving again, his arm still close around her, urging her along. They turned a corner, and ahead she saw an elevator. She guessed it must be a freight elevator, since its doors were not polished and gilded as the ones in the hotel lobby were. The door was conveniently open, as if waiting for them.

She stopped in front of it. "I don't want to go any farther."

He ignored her protest and rushed her into the elevator, then ripped a thick piece of duct tape she hadn't noticed off the edge of the sliding doorframe, tape that had held the door open. He ripped a similar piece off the other side. Pressing the Close button, he waited until the doors slid together before loosening his hold on her.

By now, Crystal was alarmed. He certainly was taking this game, or whatever it was, to an extreme. Clearly he'd planned this all along, she was realizing, since the elevator doors had been taped to keep it ready for his use. "Eric, what's this all about? Where are we going?"

"I told you if you walked across my cape, I'd take you to a new world," he said in a whispery voice that gave her goose bumps.

"A...new *world?*" she repeated, not having taken his words seriously before.

"Indeed," he stated. "A quiet world, away from distractions and distortions, where a person can recognize truths and discover what he or she truly longs for. A world of revelation, where one can appreciate what had gone unnoticed in the world above."

"Wh-where?"

"Just another elevator ride away."

Her mouth was beginning to feel like cotton as the elevator kept going farther and farther down. Looking up at the floor indicator, she noticed they'd gone past the hotel's parking levels to a basement level. The elevator creaked past this to the last indicator, labeled the second basement. Here the doors slid open to a poorly lit, dreary room with a concrete floor and walls not painted for decades. Old tables and chairs, perhaps once used in the dining room, were stacked, along with cleaning equipment and a large wreath of artificial red, white and blue flowers with a banner that read, July 4, 1962.

Eric took her by the hand to lead her out of the elevator, but she resisted, jerking her hand out of his grasp. "I don't want to go any farther!" she told him. "I'm going back up." Quickly she pressed the Up button. Just as quickly, he grabbed her by the waist and pulled her out of the elevator as the doors began to close. They slid shut on a fold of her gown, and he bent to yank the material free. As he stood up again, she saw his mouth grimace, as if from pain.

"This way," he ordered, taking her firmly by the hand.

"But I told you, I don't want to!" she said as he pulled her along, limping slightly now as he walked.

"Just one more elevator," he repeated.

"How can there *be* one more elevator?" she argued, thinking he must be crazy. "We've gone as far down as we can!"

But as she finished the sentence, she found herself standing in front of an ancient-looking elevator. Again, it was open, only this time she saw no duct tape. Gloved hands on her shoulders, he pushed her in ahead of him with a gentle but unyielding force. Keeping one arm around her, as if afraid she might run out—which, indeed, she wanted to do—he slid an iron bar to one side to close the rusting old door. Once the door closed, they were thrown into darkness, for the old elevator had no light.

"Eric!" she screamed, grabbing hold of his coat.

Instantly there was a small light and she could see again, though not very well. She let go of him and saw he had a flashlight about the size of a ballpoint pen. He held it at waist level, pointed upward, and the light from below cast his face, especially his mask, in a ghostly glow with otherworld shadows. She looked away, breathing hard from fright. The elevator began moving downward then. The feeling of going even deeper beneath the hotel in this rickety, ancient elevator added claustrophobia to her sense of panic.

"I don't like this!" she told him, her voice deeply agitated. "You have no right to take me somewhere I don't want to go!"

"But you agreed to come with me," he reminded her in a reasonable tone. "Try to be calm, and trust me. You're in no danger."

"Trust you!" she exclaimed. "I don't even know who you are!"

"I'm an old friend, Cryssy. You've known me all your life. Is there anyone you can think of from your past who would harm you?"

She shrugged off the question, unable to think about the past when her present was growing increasingly scary. "My father is a very influential man," she warned him. "If anything happens to me, he'll seek you out to the ends of the earth if he has to."

The corners of Eric's mouth turned upward in a maddening little grin beneath his mask, which took on sharp edges and appeared to glow in the light of his flashlight. But his voice remained smooth and reassuring. "Your father is a good friend of mine. We've talked often."

She looked at him with disbelief. "About what?"

"About you, mostly."

"Me!" she said, her mind racing as the elevator stopped. "Is this some scheme of his to get me away from Tony?" she asked. If her father was willing to hire a detective, might he go to the extent of having her kidnapped? But why now? She hadn't even set her wedding date yet.

"Your father knows nothing about this." Eric slid the door open to absolute blackness. He pointed his penlight downward. Just outside the doorway, a large, long, metal flashlight lay waiting on the ground. He bent to pick it up, turned on its strong light and slipped the penlight into his vest pocket. His mouth pinched in pain as he stood up again.

Crystal braced herself, waiting for her chance. There was no way this man was going to take her any farther! When he reached to take hold of her hand, she grabbed hold of him, ready to bring him down with a karate move.

But instantly, she found herself hitting the floor. Next, she was flat on her back and Eric was on top of her, his knees straddling her thighs, pinning her hands over her head with his free hand. She took in a shaky breath and began to grow more frightened than she'd ever been in her life. Apparently Eric knew karate, too. At least, he'd known exactly how to prevent her attack.

He shone the big flashlight in her face, making her shut her eyes and turn away from the bright light. She tried to get her wrists free from his tight grip, but couldn't.

"Don't try that again," he told her, his voice tinged with impatience, maybe anger. "I don't want to hurt you. But I'll do what I have to, to keep you here with me.''

''Wh-why?'' Her voice came out a whisper, she was so frightened.

''So you'll be safe, believe it or not.'' He shifted the light so that it didn't shine in her eyes so much.

She squirmed, still trying to get free of his tight grasp, and then she realized why he'd shifted the flashlight. The circle of light had lowered to take in her breasts, too. Because he kept her arms pinned above her head, her breasts were almost coming free of her low neckline. Immediately she stopped squirming. But she was breathing so hard, it still made her plump mounds of soft flesh rise and fall in a provocative way she could do nothing about.

''You leer at me that way and talk about keeping me safe!'' she shouted, deciding she must keep a tough appearance however mean or threatening he became. She wouldn't give in. She'd die before she let him rape her.

''I was only... admiring you. You decided to wear that dress. You have to expect that a man will look at what you obviously chose to show off. As for your safety, I have some news for you. Your life was in danger up above. Your fiancé is a potential murderer.''

''You're crazy!'' she shot back, wondering how she could say such a thing. He *must* be mad to kidnap her this way, treat her so brutally, and then claim her *fiancé* was dangerous.

"I know you must think I'm crazed," he said in a voice whose very calmness seemed threatening now. "But I'm not. A little daft from wearing this mask, maybe, but not crazy."

Daft, but not crazy? she thought. Maybe that almost made sense. People who were insane always thought they were perfectly lucid. That was part of their insanity! How had she let this happen to herself? Here she was, down in the clammy depths of some hellhole, the prisoner of a sex-obsessed lunatic! She had to keep her wits about her, she thought as her heart pounded so fast, she feared it might stop. And then a coldness washed over her, numbing her body while all her senses grew more alert. Fright had made her slip into a new mode, a preserve-her-life-or-die-trying state of mind. For now, she'd appear to cooperate with him—until she found a chance and a way to escape.

"Don't think you can get away," he told her, still holding the flashlight near her. He seemed to be studying her face, as if reading her expression. She had no idea what his expression was, for his mask always looked the same, stark and without emotion, except for the odd light glinting in his eyes.

She shook her head, as if agreeing with him that she couldn't escape.

"Good," he said. "I'm going to let you up now. I want you to follow me quietly into the tunnels, without trying to get away. There are fifty miles of tunnels under the city. You'd easily get lost if you escaped, and I might not be able to find you. There are places down here even I haven't had time to explore yet."

She nodded her head, indicating she understood.

He smiled down at her and his voice grew sweet, as if he were speaking to a child. "Too afraid of me to even talk to me now?"

His tone and manner confused her. She nodded again, not sure what was the safest way to respond to such a question. He might be insane, but he was also discerning and intelligent—the worst combination of traits she could think of. She tried to wet her lips, but her tongue had gone dry. Then she tried to smile back at him.

"Ah, humoring me," he said, as if amused in a sad sort of way. "Well, I suppose I would, too, if I were in your position right now." He let go of her wrists and pushed himself out of his straddling position, so that he was kneeling on one knee, while the other leg, the one that seemed to be troubling him, was bent. She noticed him massage his thigh as he told her, "There, you're free. Shall I help you up?"

"I think I can manage," she said.

They both rose to their feet, though he faltered a moment as he put weight on his sore leg. But he kept a close eye on her, as if wary that she might try to outmaneuver him again. Or perhaps he was watching her adjust the bodice of her dress back into place. Probably both, she thought with anger, fear and humiliation.

When she was finished tugging up her dress, he reached for her hand. He was still wearing his white gloves, and his hand had a warm, cotton feel to it as he enclosed her cold, clammy hand in it. Shining the strong flashlight ahead of him, he drew her out of the elevator and into the darkness.

There were two narrow, parallel tracks rising from the concrete floor of the tunnel, and to avoid tripping on them she had to follow behind him, holding on to his hand. There was nothing else she could do, except try to keep a mental record of the turns they made, so that she could find her way back to the elevator they'd come off of, if she ever had an opportunity to escape. But whenever she glanced behind her, there was only blackness to see, and she soon lost track of the many turns he'd taken. Her situation seemed more and more hopeless the farther he took them into the underground, pitch-black maze. She wanted to scream. She wanted to faint. She wanted to be hysterical. But she kept it all inside, still trying to be strong.

After following him, her hand in his glove, in meek silence for fifteen or twenty minutes, she finally could no longer hold her emotions in. ''Where are you taking me?'' She begged him to answer, pulling on his hand. Her voice echoed through the tunnels like a child's.

He stopped and turned the light on her. "I'm taking you where no one will find us," he said, his voice now a deep echo, too. "Where you'll be safe."

She shook her head and began to weep, tears spilling down her face. "No one will ever find me down here," she gasped in a small, sobbing voice. "My father will never know what happened to me."

"Shh," Eric soothed. He let go of her hand and slipped his arm around her waist, drawing her against him. As she sobbed into the smooth cloth of his coat, she felt his arm go round her, the cold metal of the flashlight he held resting against her bare back.

"Wh-why are you d-doing this to me?" she asked, her shoulders shaking from her sobs.

"To protect you," he said with patience and a reassuring voice.

"How can you be p-protecting me by taking me to this awful place?" she cried, looking up at him. The light, coming from the flashlight behind her back, cast only a dim, diffused glow on his face. All she could see was the white, impersonal mask. "I don't need protection from anything. I had a nice life."

"But not a nice future, unfortunately," he told her, his voice straightforward and grim. "Tony was after your money. His plans for the future didn't include you, once you were married and he had access to the fortune you inherited from your mother. You might have found yourself dead at a very young age."

She sniffed and blinked wetness from her eyes. "How do you know anything about Tony?"

"I told you, I know many secrets. I'll tell you more later. You're with *me* now, and you're safe. Please try to believe that." He looked down at her in the semidarkness, his eyes peering through the holes in his mask, picking up the dim light and glistening slightly. Suddenly he bent toward her, and she felt his mouth press her forehead. She gripped the edge of his coat in her hand, an unconscious reaction to the realization that he was kissing her. And in such a chaste, tender way.

When he drew away, she looked up at him, still clinging to his coat. "Who *are* you?"

"I've told you my name." His low voice softly resonated down the tunnel. "That's all you need to know. Now, dry your eyes. We have only a little farther to go."

"We're actually going somewhere?"

"We have a destination, yes. You'll feel right at home, I promise."

She still knew he must be crazy, but this living nightmare was so awful, she wanted to believe him. And then he startled her again by taking his arm from around her waist and lifting his gloved hand to her face. He blotted her tears with his cotton-covered fingertips, bringing the flashlight around, pointing it at the low, domed ceiling to see her face better. The light reflected on his shiny-slick hair, which looked black in this light. He said she knew him, but she couldn't really remember anyone, especially from grade school, who had smooth black hair and green eyes. As he gently touched her face here and there with his fingertips, she longed to take off his mask and see his face.

"There," he said, when he'd finished. "Now, follow me." He took hold of her hand again, and they went back to their former method of making their way through the tunnels.

About five minutes later and another turn to the left, the light from his flashlight diffused farther than it had been as the tunnel seemed to widen. In the shadowy area to one side, she thought she could see bricks instead of concrete. The tracks seemed to be more complicated here, and they had to be careful where they stepped. He stopped and shone the light above, to an antique-looking square sign on the brick wall.

"Look up there," he directed. "What does it say?"

"Winthrop's Department Store," she read. She turned to Eric, still holding his hand. "Are we really at my family's store? The one on State Street?"

"The original store and still the one most enjoyable to shop in, in my opinion," he said, as if he was a regular customer.

"But what is this place? What are the tracks for? Where does the door in the brick wall lead to?" She eyed the door speculatively.

"This was the old railroad siding, built after the turn of the century, where merchandise and coal were brought to the store. Ashes and refuse were carted out. There was a whole little railroad system going down here at that time, serving many buildings in the Loop. Like the hotel we just came from. The door—which, by the way, is locked—leads to the subbasement of the store."

Her hopes of escaping via the door plummeted. She chattered to cover her dismay. "I remember when the subbasement flooded. We lost all the merchandise stored down there, hundreds of thousands of dollars' worth. So these are the tunnels that flooded...."

"Don't worry. If water should begin seeping in again, which is unlikely, we can quickly escape by going through the door and up the steps. I know how to get the door open."

"But what about the security system? Doesn't it extend down this far?"

"It does, but I know how to take care of that, too."

She studied him with widening eyes. "Are you a security man? Do you work for my father? For Winthrop's?"

He smiled. "A good guess. But not quite accurate. Well, we've arrived," he said as he flicked the flashlight in another direction and turned on a lamp. It was sitting on a small table. Suddenly the whole area was illuminated. "There. This has been my home for many long, lonely weeks. I'm glad to have you here, to have someone to talk to. This is your home, too, for a while."

"Home?" she repeated and looked around. She saw a small, upholstered easy chair to the right of the lamp. Across the tracks, on the wall, the bright square reflection of a mirror caught her eye. Pivoting a bit to the left, she continued her circular tour. On the floor there was a box of newspapers. Next to it she saw a large ice chest of thick, molded plastic. In back of it was a tall rack with some clothes hanging from it—shirts, jeans, a man's suit. A patch of light blue came into her peripheral vision, and she turned farther to the left to see what it was.

She froze when she saw the bed.

CHAPTER THREE

Eric touched her elbow. "Are you hungry? Thirsty? Can I offer you some wine? Or...maybe you'd like to lie down for a while."

"No!" she quickly replied to his suggestions. "I'm not hungry or...tired."

He lowered his gaze for a moment, his pale eyelids making his mask look solid white. "I didn't mean... I was just trying to make you comfortable, so you'll feel at home here."

She studied him, trying to look behind his impassive mask and courteous demeanor. He certainly made an unusual kidnapper, luring her from the ball with his sensual dramatics, throwing her forcefully to the floor when she tried to get away, comforting her like her father might when she cried, and now...behaving like a self-conscious man on a first date.

She wished she'd had some training in psychology, so she might have some clue as to how to figure him out. He must have delusions of power and heroics if he actually thought he was rescuing her from danger, from her fiancé. Tony had never frightened her the way this man did. Though, he didn't seem frightening just now....

"How long will you...will we be here?" she asked, careful not to say the wrong thing and change his current docile mood.

"As long as it takes."

"What takes?"

"For you to see me as the man I really am."

God, what kind of sense was this supposed to make? she wondered. "I can't see who you really are until you take off that mask."

He shook his head. "If I do that, then you surely *won't* see me. You never have. You've known me, off and on, throughout your life, but you've always thought of me as just another nice, dull guy. I want you to rediscover me, in a gradual way, here where there are no distractions, no Tonys to draw away your attention."

"I can see that you're not dull," she told him, humoring him with an optimistic tone. "You've proven that already."

"Good." A glint reappeared in his eyes. He swept the cape off his shoulders and threw it onto the small, upholstered chair. In his white tie and tails, he looked slim and graceful, even elegant. He began pulling off his gloves, finger by finger. When he'd removed them, he tossed them onto his cape.

"If you've been living down here, where did you get your costume?" she asked.

"Your father's store." He shook his head a bit and added in an earnest tone, "I'm not in the habit of stealing, mind you. I have a personal reputation to uphold. But these are special circumstances and I'm sure your father won't mind, once I explain. In fact, I know he'll be grateful to me for saving you."

Here we go again, she thought.

He gestured toward her with his hands. "But I'm forgetting my manners. Sit down. Let's have some wine together."

"I . . . I'm not thirsty."

"It's good wine," he assured her, walking toward the ice chest with a limp. "It's a French chardonnay, a good year. There's some cheese and bread, too, and some grapes. I got them upstairs," he said, pointing upward toward the Winthrop's sign. "It's all fresh. I removed them from the Gourmet Gifts department tonight, just after the store closed at six. I took some ice to keep it cold."

"Oh," she said, standing where she was, not knowing what to say. The last thing she felt like doing was eating. But she was afraid of refusing his hospitality.

As he walked back toward her, carrying a bottle and a plastic shopping bag with the Winthrop's logo on it, he urged, "Please, sit down. Be comfortable."

Oh, sure, she thought. She looked around again. There were only two places to sit: the bed and the chair. The chair was covered with his cape and gloves.

She was afraid to move them or sit on them, not knowing what reaction she might cause. Who knew how attached a lunatic Phantom might be to his cape? So, with great foreboding, she sat on the edge of the twin-size bed. The mattress beneath the sheets felt firm and new. She suspected his furniture had come from Winthrop's too.

He set the objects on the table, pushing the small, battery-run lamp with its plastic shade to the edge to make more room. Then he moved the cape so that it draped over the back of the chair and onto the floor. He set the gloves on top and sat down on the chair himself.

Next he took the bottle and dexterously pulled the cork out of it with a two-pronged wine opener. She wished he'd used a corkscrew—it might have provided her with a potential weapon. But perhaps he'd thought of that, and that's why he chose to steal a more benign instrument.

After taking two sparkling wineglasses out of the bag, he set them upright and poured white wine into them without losing a drop to the tabletop. Then he set the bottle on the concrete floor, under the table, perhaps so it wouldn't get knocked over. She noticed that he seemed to be a careful person in everything he did. The trait, even the sensitive way he moved his large hands as he worked, seemed vaguely familiar to her, but she could not think of whom she knew who had his deft mannerisms.

When he pushed the bottle farther under the table, she saw some thick, tall white candles stored underneath. There was also a wooden crutch lying on its side against the table legs that she hadn't noticed before. She debated whether to ask about the crutch, wondering if he was sensitive about his infirmity. Perhaps if she pretended concern, he might not mind, might even answer some questions and unknowingly provide her with information that could help her escape this surreal horror.

He handed her a glass of wine, and she took it with a forced smile. She even thanked him. He reached out with his glass to clink hers.

"To a new beginning," he toasted.

She looked at the clear wine in her shimmering glass but did not drink. "Do you have a sore leg?" she asked, inflecting sympathy in her tone. "I noticed you limp just a bit, and then I saw the crutch." She gestured downward.

Eric studied her through the contours of his mask, his cat green eyes clear and still. He said nothing. Didn't even move. Her heart rate increased as she worried whether her question had offended him. His eyes, unblinking, focused intensely on her face. As in the ballroom earlier, she found she could not look away. Her palms grew clammy again and her nerves began to tighten even more than they already were. Why was he taking so long to respond?

Suddenly he blinked.

Crystal jumped. Seeing his eyelids come down like eerie, black-fringed shades totally unnerved her. A few drops of her full glass of wine spilled onto her dress.

His eyes took note of this and he pulled a handkerchief from his inside jacket pocket. "You're still scared to death, aren't you?" he said, handing her the handkerchief.

"No, I'm not," she lied, blotting her dress.

He grinned. "I always did admire your finesse. Drink some of that wine. It will help calm you."

I don't want to be calm! she thought, keeping her eyes lowered so he couldn't read what was in them. He was so discerning, she was afraid to look at him now.

"As for that crutch," he continued, "that's the whole reason I'm living down here. There's a long story connected with it, and I was considering where to begin and how much to say. But the gist of it is, I came down here to hide."

Was he deformed, like the fictional Phantom? she wondered, her rapid imagination working. Did he have twisted legs? Did the mask hide a monstrous face, too terrible for anyone to see? The thought rattled her, and it took all her willpower to sit quietly where she was and not run away.

She began breathing hard, and her dress stays constricted her rib cage. Her confined breasts rose and fell with each harrowed breath. When she dared to look at him again, she saw where his covetous eyes were focused, and the knowledge of his lust sent terror through her.

His eyes flicked up to meet hers. The light of desire in their translucent depths quickened, as if with opportunity. He set his wineglass on the table. All at once he rose from his chair and sat beside her, on the folds of her wide skirt, making it impossible for her to get away. He placed his hand lightly on her bare shoulder, above her puffed sleeve. It was all she could do not to flinch. With his other hand, he urged her hand holding the wineglass upward, toward her mouth.

She took only the smallest sip.

"Drink some more wine, Crystal. Don't look so terrified. Everything's all right. Everything's under control."

"Are *you?*" she asked, the wine stinging her tense throat. Her situation couldn't get much more dangerous. She had to fight back. "What do you plan to do with me?" she demanded.

"Take care of you," he said in a soothing, almost amorous tone.

"If you try to rape me, I'll scratch your eyes out!" She lifted the wineglass in a threatening manner.

"Shh," he said, taking hold of her arm, making her lower the glass. With his other hand he stroked her shoulder. His strange, calm gentleness, the unexpected warmth of his hand as it caressed her shoulder, made goose bumps rise on her skin. "I'm not going to rape you." His tone was so reassuring, it made her want to cry again. "I would never take you by force, Crystal. That's not what I want at all. I want *you* to choose to come to *me,* if you're willing. If anything intimate should happen between us, it will be because you want it to happen."

"Then it never will!"

"Never say never," he told her with a smile.

She thought back to what he'd said earlier, when she'd asked how long he would keep her here. *As long as it takes* had been his answer. Did he intend to hold her prisoner until she agreed to have sex with him? Was that what he wanted? If she gave in, would he let her go?

The thought of giving in made her shudder. And even if she did, he might not let her go. His object, he'd said, had been to get her away from Tony. She doubted he'd let her go back to the real world and to Tony once she'd given herself to him. If Eric harbored some fanatical attraction to her, he might even murder her, so no other man would ever have her. Inside, she began to tremble with fright, but she forced herself to be still. She had to keep her cool. She had to find a means to get away. Fast.

What were his vulnerabilities? she asked herself as she felt his hand glide up her shoulder to massage the back of her neck. His own desire made him vulnerable. She could distract him by pretending to become attracted to him. Since he knew self-defense, however, she'd have to put on quite a show and distract him to such an extent that he didn't even anticipate her attack. Another vulnerability was his sore leg. In the elevator, she'd seen him clutch his left thigh, as if it pained him quite a bit.

And, of course, all men were vulnerable in one part of their anatomy. If she could distract him with her body, then hit him hard where it would hurt, she could get out of his grasp. If she were out of her dress and heels, she probably could run faster than him, too, considering the way he limped. Her plan was a dreadful risk. But what choice did she have? She had no intention of remaining his prisoner or becoming his victim.

But she had to be clever and make him believe she wanted him. She couldn't appear to go from fright to desire in two minutes. This would take a little time and some ingenuity.

Taking a breath to collect herself, she lifted the wineglass to her lips and took another very small sip. She needed to keep her head clear.

"Are you calmer now?" he asked, his hand gliding down her bare back. She almost wished he weren't as gentle as he was. It made it hard for her to think.

"Yes," she told him, deciding a good way to begin acting on her plan was by making conversation. "This whole situation is...well, new to me. No one ever swept me away from a ball before." She made a hesitant smile. "I am a little scared," she admitted, deciding it was a good idea to allow herself to look vulnerable. Earlier, when she'd broken down weeping, he'd comforted her. Letting him comfort her again was probably a good strategy. Seeing her appear weak, instead of displaying bravado, might make him drop his own defenses.

"I understand," he told her. "I can't blame you for being frightened. I wouldn't have chosen to do things this way. But circumstances gave me no other choice."

Turning to him as his large, warm hand rested again on her shoulder, she asked, "Why did you come down here to hide? What were you hiding from?"

"Someone was after me. In fact, they shot me." He touched the side of his left thigh with his hand.

"*Shot* you!" she exclaimed. Good God, was he wanted by the police? Was he already some kind of criminal, a fugitive from justice?

"I dug out the bullet and came down here, so no one could find me and try to finish the job."

"D-dug the bullet out yourself?" she said, truly astonished. "That must have been very painful."

"It was. I nearly passed out. Fortunately, I had some leftover antibiotics, or I might have died of infection. I bandaged myself, wiped up the blood, grabbed the medicine and came down here to recover in safety."

"Are you all right now?" she asked, finding she was genuinely curious, amazed a man could have done all this alone.

"I've had recurring fevers, from infection I believe, but not often anymore. There's a drugstore in the old Pittsfield Building. When I run low on antibiotics, I get some more. And my leg is healing. It's getting much stronger."

"Who shot you?"

He hesitated, touching her dangling curls of hair. "I'll tell you that later. Right now, I'd just like us to... get to know each other, in a way we didn't before."

A chill ran through her, knowing she had to play along. "All right. How do you mean?"

He studied her face and shook his head. "You're *still* scared. I wish you weren't so frightened of me. I'm probably the last guy you would have thought of as dangerous if you saw me at a party or met me on the street. I'm no different now, just because I have a mask on."

"You know self-defense," she pointed out.

He paused. "Yes. I learned many things when... Well, that part of my life will have to remain secret, even from you. But that's over. I gave it up. All I want now is a normal life... with a beautiful woman I've always admired at my side."

She smiled and looked down, as if made shy from his flattery. It unsettled her a bit to realize she actually did feel... well, discombobulated, if not shy. She even felt her fright fading a bit, and she wondered if that was wise. She needed to keep up her guard. But his low, sincere, reassuring voice, echoing through the underground chamber, seemed to envelop her, sensually caressing her ears from the surrounding shadows. She felt vulnerable, and though that was how she wanted to appear to him now, it wasn't the way she wanted to feel inside. What was the matter with her?

He turned all at once to glance at the candles under the table. "I know. Let's sit by candlelight. It's so much softer and soothing than this harsh light from the lamp." He got up and began taking candles from beneath the table to put them on top. "I fall asleep by candlelight every night, to save the lamp's battery. It's remarkably peaceful," he said, taking away the bag of food and setting it on the chair. He turned to her. "Hungry yet?"

"No," she replied. "Thank you."

"Whenever you are, just say so." He picked up a book of matches from the table and lit the three candles he'd set out. When all three were lit, he turned out the lamp. The cavern they inhabited was suddenly thrown into a new atmosphere of dimmer but more romantic light, which flickered and cast soft shadows. The tunnel seemed even more silent. Everything took on a golden glow. The material of her dress resonated with the light and shimmered. The glass of wine in her hand looked delicate and magical with refracted light from the candle glow. Even Eric's white mask took on a more mellow hue, she noticed as she studied his profile, with its crisp, sculptured outline of a high-bridged nose and sloping forehead. When he turned to look at her, his mask appeared alive now and had acquired a timeless character that seemed the very image of secret, serene wisdom.

"There," he said. "Isn't that better?"

"It's lovely," she agreed, her sense of wonder showing in her voice. To find herself surrounded by a mystical, warm glow when she was in such danger threw her off her guard. Ethereal beauty surrounding the threat of violence was a paradox she didn't know how to cope with.

He picked up the large flashlight, the one he'd used earlier, from the floor where he'd put it when he'd brought out the food. He set it upright next to the bed, as if out of habit, perhaps something he did every night before falling asleep so he could find it in a hurry in darkness. Straightening up, he brushed past her wide skirts as he stepped to sit next to her again, slightly closer than before.

"You haven't finished your wine," he noted.

"N-no."

"Go on," he said, his long forefinger at the bottom of her glass, pushing it to her lips.

She didn't want to drink it and cloud her mind, but she was either too afraid or too disoriented by the new atmosphere to find a way to object. After she'd swallowed two long sips, he allowed her to lower the glass. His hand came near her breasts as it followed her glass downward. His fingers paused, hesitating as if unable to resist, at the upper edge of her bodice while she lowered her glass of wine to her lap. He touched the stiff material that held her breasts so tightly, making them plump with innocent allure in round, soft mounds. She thought she felt his fingers trembling slightly. Or maybe it was she who was trembling. She realized that this might lead to a chance to escape, that she must let him touch her, make him distracted by her feminine curves.

"You're so beautiful," he whispered. "Many times I've longed to touch you."

"Have you?" she asked, managing a smile.

"Many times I've dreamed of you. The dreams that came from my fevers were so real, it was almost as if... as if you had caused the fever to come upon me. And only you could take it away."

His fingertips glided upward an inch and moved with exquisite gentleness over her skin, pausing with unnerving sensitivity in the valley between her breasts. She couldn't help it, she took in a shaky breath, trying to keep her nerves steady. But she had to play along with this. "Take your fever away? How?" she asked with coy innocence.

He withdrew his hand and studied her face closely, as if he suspected she was baiting him. "We'd better not speak of that," he said.

She looked down at her wineglass, disappointed that she had failed to encourage him to continue his seductive fondling. "It's just that one usually gets rid of a fever with cold compresses and aspirin," she tried to explain, covering herself.

"Is that how you get rid of Tony's fever?" he asked, his tone changing.

The question threw her. "He's...never had a fever, that I know of," she improvised.

"Not for you?"

"Well..."

"Or have you nursed him so much, he has no need to go into heat anymore?" Now there was a streak of scathing sarcasm in his voice. "How many times a week—or a day—do you minister to his needs? He's such a he-man, he must need a lot of attention."

"You hate him, don't you?" she said, looking at him with new eyes. "You're jealous. It's some vendetta. You want to get me away from him, to get back at him."

"Not because he sleeps with you, because—"

"He doesn't." If he was going to do her bodily harm to get back at Tony, it might help her case if he knew the truth.

His eyes widened to the full circumference of the holes in his mask. "But—you're engaged." He lifted her left hand, indicating her ring.

"I know, but we never... I never let him..."

He took her chin sternly between his thumb and forefinger, making her face him, nose to masked nose. "Don't lie to me," he said, taking on a threatening tone. "I won't tolerate a lie, telling me what you know I'd like to hear, to humor me."

"I'm not lying. I never went to bed with him."

"Why not? Is there something wrong with his sex drive?"

"No. Well, I don't know." She fumbled for an answer. "He asked me to, but I just...it didn't feel right. I didn't want to. I told him it would be more romantic to wait."

"Why marry him, if the idea of sleeping with him doesn't feel right?"

His personal questions annoyed her. "He's an exciting man. We have a lot in common. He takes an interest in my health club, knows a lot about bodybuilding. I just wanted to wait until the time was right."

"But he was eager for you to elope."

"How do you know that?" she asked, astonished. Not even her father knew that Tony was pressuring her to elope.

"You told me."

This was incredible. "I never told anyone that."

"You have a bad memory, don't you? Or maybe your conversations with me were all so unmemorable, you forgot them afterward."

Crystal shook her head in confusion.

"Do you remember every word that Tony says to you?" he asked.

"I don't know," she answered, lifting her shoulders.

"God, don't do that," he said, eyeing her cleavage again. "I can't imagine how he kept his hands off you. But maybe it was because he was only after your money."

Crystal was beginning to wonder if what Eric said was true. He seemed to have so much information. "Was he? How do you know?"

"I found out." Eric's jaw clenched, as if wanting to say more but stopping himself. "Do you know what I think?"

"What?"

"I think you chose a man like Tony because you wanted to rebel against your father, against the life he expects you to lead. You were attracted to Tony in particular because you like men who are virile and athletic, with animal magnetism, who have muscular bodies and the word *stud* stamped on their foreheads," he said, almost spitting sarcasm.

Then he shifted his position, leaning more toward her, and his tone softened. "You never caught on to the fact that a man like me can offer you so much more. A lasting relationship is more than genetic biology and hormones, an alpha female attracted to an alpha male. A lasting relationship takes true love from the depths of one's soul. It has to do more with the harmony of the spheres than X and Y chromosomes.

This is the kind of love I can offer you. If you'd let me.''

Crystal swallowed, having no response. He'd left her speechless. He was so intelligent, civilized and romantic, he didn't seem at all like the type of man who would take a woman prisoner. Yet here he was, powerful and moody, threatening in his white mask and black suit, looming over her. She was sitting here on his bed, afraid to try to escape, and...and now...this was truly scary...a part of her didn't really want to escape anymore. She wanted to sit and listen some more, and watch him quietly lust after her in such a poignant way that he made her feel more desirable than any other man ever had.

His voice grew soft and mesmerizing now, echoing around her like silk. "I care for you a great deal. I'm living like a fugitive for you, because of you." He lifted his hand to her chin and slowly ran his fingertips along her jaw, then quarter inch by quarter inch down her throat. The sensation of his touch on her sensitized skin made her shiver in a sublime way, made her quiver with repressed excitement. "I want your time and your full attention, here, where there is nothing else for us to do, no one to capture your interest away from me. This is a situation I never enjoyed in our life aboveground. Here I can make my desires—and yours—clear to you."

He slid his fingers, which had been caressing her throat, around the back of her neck, beneath her hair.

Leaning even closer, he pulled her head toward his, until his mouth found hers. His lips were warm, firm and insistent. An involuntary little sound of fear came from her throat at the vibrating passion she felt from him. His other hand went round her back and pulled her closer, making her chest arch forward while her head went back under the force of his kiss. She lifted her hands to his shoulders to try to resist, but it was useless against his masculine strength.

And then she reminded herself that she shouldn't resist. She should respond, get him so worked up with desire that he lost track of what was happening, so she could get away.

When his mouth left hers to move down her throat, she gasped for breath. Again, it was an involuntary reaction—he'd pressed her so hard, he'd kept her from breathing. But her quick intake of air made her breasts rise, and this, again, drew his attention. His mouth moved from kissing her throat downward to hover over her pulsing cleavage. His hand at the back of her neck moved over her shoulder, his fingers trailing over her collarbone, then to the top of one plump, jutting breast. He fondled her skin, tested its softness, then moved his hand down over the edge of the dress to cup her breast. Bending his head, his lips fixed hotly on her skin.

Crystal's heart began to pound. This felt too good. She wasn't supposed to get aroused herself. Not really. She'd only intended to look aroused. Maybe she was playing her part too well, getting into her role too... *Oh, my God,* she thought as he lightly bit her flesh. She closed her eyes at the erotic sensation. Her heart was beating so fast, and he'd pushed her back into such an extreme arch, that she couldn't catch her breath.

"Eric," she protested, pushing on his shoulder. "Please. I can't... breathe."

He straightened and pulled her upright with his hand at her back. She felt a bit dizzy and looked at him with dazed eyes.

"You're so beautiful," he whispered with reverence, his fingertips touching one breast, "and I've wanted just to touch you for so long. Did I hurt you?"

"No, I—I just couldn't breathe. This dress is very tight."

"I've noticed. Little show-off," he said in a teasing tone. "You like to make men pant after you, don't you?"

Did she? "I like to look good, that's all."

"You look exquisite," he said, running his fingers along the top edge of her dress, feeling the contours of her flesh again. He'd lost all hesitancy about touching her now. It was as if he felt he had the right. "I'm beginning to understand. You like to dress sexy, feel sexy, because you aren't getting any, that's why. And you like to drive men mad. You enjoy the attention. It gives you a feeling of power, doesn't it?"

"I—"

"You always drove *me* mad," he went on, "but I don't think you ever noticed. Or cared. You're so sexy, you take it for granted. You're so desirable, you know you can take men for granted. You even got engaged to a man you apparently could either take or leave, if you could so easily put off making love with him. But I've made a vow to myself that you'll never take *me* for granted again."

"A vow? To m-make love with me?"

He stared at her, his luminescent eyes burning with ever-kindling fire. "I didn't say that. But if you're willing—"

"I—I'm not sure," she said, thinking about her tone, wanting to sound hesitant and a little helpless.

His eyes grew round beneath the almond-shaped slits. The light radiating from them softened. She never knew a man's eyes alone could look so tender. "What would make you sure?" he asked in an ardent, sweetly patient tone.

She breathed in and out while thinking fast, her body still desperate for oxygen to support her galloping heart. Her deep inhale made her breasts move beneath his fingers and she became aware again of his touch. Instinctively she took hold of his large hand, pressing it into her cleavage to give him a silent, tantalizing answer. But she grew transfixed as she felt its masculine heat warm her breasts and seep through her to her pumping heart.

"I can feel your heart," he whispered with a little smile. There was a sense of awe in his tone. "You're excited by our kisses, too."

She nodded, feeling incautiously dazed again. This wouldn't do. She had to keep her head!

But he swept her up against him, into his arms, for another long, exhaustive kiss. His lips and tongue were so thorough, she briefly lost track of what was happening, aware only of sensation and of being overwhelmed. When he finally withdrew his mouth from hers to kiss the side of her throat, she opened her eyes wide and inhaled deeply to get hold of herself. But then his hot mouth was at her breasts again, kissing and nibbling, and she felt that spiraling, dizzy sensation return. She gave a little cry and felt herself going limp in his embrace.

He stopped, lifting his head to look up at her face. "Are you all right? I've never made a woman faint before! Here," he said, finding the zipper at the back of her dress and pulling down the tab. Immediately her dress loosened and she could breathe again. As she clung to him, reviving with deep breaths, she felt the dress fall away a bit from her body. Just as she grew conscious of this, he pushed the puffed sleeves down her arms and off her hands. "No," she said, but her voice was hardly a whisper as cool air met her bared breasts and midriff.

"My God, you're lovely," he told her, his voice sheer sensuality. With reverence, he brought his hand up to softly caress one breast, testing her pink nipple with his thumb. She closed her eyes at the sweet gentleness of the sensation, almost comforting, easing her fright and encouraging her dazed state to turn to one of pleasure. He brought his other hand up to caress her other breast in a similar manner, until her nipples contracted and turned to pert nubs against his palms. She closed her eyes and felt tears start behind her lids. Considering all the men she'd dated, some of whom she'd allowed to caress her, none had ever made her feel like this. She hadn't realized... didn't know... a man's touch could be so reassuring and sweet. How could she feel so comfortable now with a man whose identity she didn't know? She shouldn't feel safe with a man who had kidnapped her, who seemed to threaten her very life. She opened her eyes, looked at his white mask, tried to come to her senses about where she was and what could happen to her.

But when he saw her open her eyes, he smiled and leaned in to kiss her again. This time he pressed her down onto the pillow and settled his body half over hers. She felt the weight of him on her chest, the smooth satin of his coat lapels brushing against her nipples. As he kissed her mouth, he pushed her dress downward past her waist. He broke the kiss, rose up on his elbows and looked down at her, his eyes devouring her.

Feeling naked beneath him and totally vulnerable to a man she didn't know, she impulsively lifted her hands to his mask to pull it up and off his face. He reared back, out of her reach, and grabbed one wrist, then the other, in one of his hands.

"No, Crystal. Not yet."

"I want to know who you are—"

"Not *yet.*" He pushed her hands downward, to rest one on top of the other between her breasts. "I will be the one to decide when you will learn my identity. We're doing very nicely together just as we are. No use complicating our pleasure in one another with unnecessary details. We're deeply attracted. We have something rare and magical happening here between us. Let's play out this fantasy. See where it leads us. Then we'll talk."

He gazed down over her body, then at her dress, whose top was crumpled around her hips. "This is in the way," he said, moving to tug at the dress. "You don't need it anymore." He got up, pulled the dress down her legs and tossed it onto the chair.

She lay startled, mind racing again, dressed now only in her sheer gold panty hose and panties. Her shoes had slipped off when he pulled off the dress. It was just as well he'd removed her tight, long gown, she told herself, trying to keep calm. She could move much faster without it. She didn't need the high heels, either. But when he reached for the waistband of her panty hose, she writhed away, to avoid his hands.

"Don't be afraid," he told her. "You want to see where our passion leads, too, don't you?"

Earlier she had silently led him to believe she did, and there was no point in going back on her plan now. Escape, she reminded herself. Her escape was the most important thing. Let him touch her and fondle her. Let him get engrossed in her body again. All the better to catch him off guard. Only... she got so confused herself....

He pulled off the panty hose and discarded them to one side, apparently too hasty with desire now to be neat. When he reached for her panties, she stopped his hands. "Please," she said, using a supplicating tone. "Not yet. I'm ... shy."

He smiled and reached out to touch her cheek in an affectionate way. "The woman who wears such sexy outfits is really modest underneath?" He chuckled as he straightened and took off his cutaway jacket, tossing it haphazardly on the chair over her dress. "I might have guessed. You never were a hussy," he said, removing his white bow tie, which he also tossed away. As he loosened his shirt collar he added, "You were just spoiled and used to getting attention—ever since you were a child. You fascinated me, even then."

He looked over her form, lying meekly on his bed, almost naked. The rawness in his gaze unnerved her, but she pretended to be at peace.

"You're still spoiled," he said, coming toward her, one knee on the bed, gliding his frame over hers, making the bed shake. "And I plan to give you plenty of attention." He settled his body over hers, his legs tangling with hers, his chest heavy on her breasts and rib cage. Crystal braced herself, telling herself she did not like the manly weight of his body on hers, did not like the feel of his thigh between hers. As he began kissing her in another heated, lingering match of passion between them, he showing all his desire and she trying to keep hers tethered, she felt something else. His erection, beneath his zippered pants, nudged her inner thigh, hard and insistent. As his kiss dazed her senses again, her mind went wild with ideas and images. How would that length of hardness feel inside her? How would he make love? Would he take his time? Would he be gentle and passionate, or would he turn savage? What would he say? How would he fondle her? Could he make her go mad with ecstasy? Could he fulfill her, satiate the deep desire she'd kept to herself all these years? Was *he* the man she'd always secretly hoped for and never truly found?

Why did she want to know? the reasoning part of her mind questioned. He was holding her prisoner. He was dangerous! She shouldn't be *wanting* to give her body to a man whose very purpose was to molest her or worse. He'd made her crazy. She had to get away from him.

But how? He wasn't lying in a position that would enable her to knee him in the groin. She'd have to get him to move somehow.

Then he slid a bit to one side of her, his masked face lingering over her breasts as he fondled them with one hand. His right leg remained between hers. But he drew his left, injured, thigh upward, crossing her thigh, as he made himself comfortable lying half over her, half on his right arm.

The flashlight, she told herself. The heavy flashlight was standing on end beside the bed. She could easily reach down with her hand and grasp it, she was sure. If he was distracted enough, he wouldn't notice....

"I adore you," he whispered, leaning down to kiss her chin. "Only you. All my life." He kissed her lips softly. "I always thought I'd outgrow it. When I was a teenager, I thought it was leftover puppy love. When I was at college and away from you, I thought my longing for you must be a teenage crush I couldn't get over. But the longing never went away. Every time I came back to town and saw you somewhere, at a party, or on someone's yacht, the feeling came back again, strong as ever. When I learned you were marrying Tony, I went into a tailspin. Until I realized how dangerous he was for you. Then I knew what I had to do. You realize now that he's not the right man for you, however attractive you once found him, don't you? Now—now that you see how you can respond to me? As if...as if we were meant to be lovers?" He smiled.

Crystal's mind was in such a confusion of fright, desire and astonishment at his heartfelt declaration of passion that tears invaded her eyes. She'd waited all her life for a man to tell her things like this; why did the one who said them have to be a masked, maniacal Phantom?

The shadowy recesses of the tunnel and the steady flames of the candles on the table beside her seemed to float and softly spin as she felt his ardent mouth on her lips, her cheek, her chin. He kissed her throat while stroking her breast with his warm, big hand, teasing her nipple until she winced in pleasurable pain. She didn't want this to stop. She wanted to travel this path to passion he'd set her on, experience the destination of bliss he offered.

When he brought his seeking mouth to her breast, she unconsciously brought her hand up to the back of his head and squirmed beneath him with undeniable excitement.

"Oh, Crystal," he murmured, the need in his tone resonant in the cavern as his heated whisper echoed in the silence. "I knew you'd want me, too."

His feverish mouth fixed hotly on her nipple. A helpless cry of unbearable arousal escaped her throat. She couldn't stand this anymore. He began to suckle her breast, drawing in hard on her nipple, sending zooming sensations through her limbs, to the secret recesses between her thighs. She began to breathe raggedly. What should she do? She was about to lose control, and she had to make a decision. This was all part of her *plan*, she reminded herself. She'd gotten him successfully distracted now. He was lost in her body, intent on only one thing. The problem was, she now wanted what he wanted. Should she follow her raging desire? Or should she use what might be her one opportunity to escape?

She knew what her answer ought to be. Oh, God, why did she want to *stay* and be his prisoner? She indeed must have caught his madness. The only sane thing was to escape, to get back to the real world, away from darkness, candlelight and this masked, seductive Phantom who'd woven some kind of sensual spell over her. She *must* do the sane thing and save herself.

While he continued to fondle and suckle her breast with adoration, she dropped her hand to one side of the bed and picked up the metal flashlight. It felt heavier than she'd imagined it would be. But that suited her purpose. Stroking the back of his hair to make sure his head stayed down, she lifted the flashlight. Gripping it tightly, she took aim at his left thigh, trying to remember the place he'd pointed to when he'd talked about his bullet wound. Trembling, trying to block the sweet sensations his lips drew from her sensitive nipple, she gritted her teeth and swung, hitting him squarely and very hard on his thigh.

He stiffened, cried out, and rose up on one elbow, grabbing his thigh with his hand. She took the opportunity to move out from under him, then hit him again on his shoulder at the base of his neck.

"Ohh," he cried as he slumped forward in pain. She knew she ought to hit him on the head and knock him out, but somehow she just couldn't. And she didn't need to, she told herself. His leg would hurt so much, he'd never catch up with her.

She got off the bed, leaving him in a heap, writhing in pain. Remembering the door to Winthrop's, she turned on the flashlight and ran up to it. He'd told her it was locked. But maybe he was just bluffing.

She tried the old, rusting door handle and could not budge it. Never mind, she told herself. She'd find her way back to the hotel and the elevator they'd come down on. Most important was to get out of his sight, away from him as fast as she could, so he'd never catch up to her.

Seeing his long cape draped on the chair, she grabbed it to cover herself. As she ran past the bed to go down the tunnel by which they'd come, she saw that he was trying to get up. He glared at her as she swiftly went by.

"You vixen!" he cried out, looking after her as she ran out of his sight down the tunnel. "You led me on. You tricked me. *Damn you!*" His voice, echoing after her as she ran, sounded like a harsh sob now. There was silence for a second or two. Crystal kept running, flashlight pointed ahead. And then she heard, "Come back! I love you—"

CHAPTER FOUR

Eric clenched his teeth, feeling agony as he slowly pushed himself to a sitting position, careful of his searing, throbbing thigh. The muscles at the base of his neck, numbed by her blow, were beginning to register pain, too. His mask felt claustrophobic, and he tore it off and threw it to the floor in anger. A lot of good it had done him! he thought, his heart tearing in two. He bent his head and buried his face in his hands, elbows on his knees.

"Crystal, Crystal—why?" he asked in a broken voice, as if she could hear, as if she gave a damn about his feelings.

He knew very well the answer to his question, he thought, angry with his own stupidity. Why should she love him just because he was saving her from a man who meant her harm? She probably still didn't believe her fiancé was a nasty piece of work. And she just wasn't attracted to her "Phantom," mask or no mask. He might as well accept it.

But did she have to make him think she was enjoying his kisses? That was the worst of it, to have truly believed she was actually, finally, responding to him, and then to have her turn on him so suddenly, to feel her injuring blows and watch her run away. Pretending to enjoy his lovemaking had only been her ploy to escape him—why hadn't he anticipated that? He ought to have known better. But he'd wanted so much to believe Crystal wanted him, could love him, that he'd let his guard down. He'd trusted her. What a fool he'd been!

He drew in a long, anguished breath and rubbed his thigh. Well, why *should* she trust a man in a mask who said he was trying to rescue her? Even though it was true, it sounded farfetched. And the way he'd brought her forcefully into these tunnels—why should she believe it was for her own safety? If he had been her, would he have believed it? He ought to have given Crystal more credit for questioning people's motives.

On the other hand, she'd chosen a man like Tony to be her husband. She hadn't managed to see his ulterior motives, the lethal danger lying beneath his swarthy good looks. If she could fall for a dime-store hunk, why not for an elegant masked man? Wasn't one cartoon character as good as another?

He forced a grim laugh at the sad, comic irony of his misguided method to attain the woman he loved. But laughing only made his shoulder hurt. As he massaged it, he told himself it was time to give up. To hell with wishing and waiting for Crystal to be his bride. He'd never win her. If he couldn't do it with a mask, candlelight and wine, how would he ever succeed?

Give it up! Get over her! he told himself with angry impatience. He'd put in enough time and energy in his life planning and hoping for her. After getting his university degree, he'd worked for a few years with a top-secret special force in the military, because he wanted an all-consuming challenge. After highly specialized training, he'd performed a number of secret missions, slipping in and out of foreign countries and high-security buildings for the government. During this time, he'd worked to hone himself into the sort of man he wanted to be—brave, strong and self-reliant. Now he was such a man, and Crystal still took no notice! Damn her beautiful, blind eyes.

There were lots of women who could appreciate what he had to offer, Eric reminded himself. If Crystal couldn't love him, he'd let someone in his life who would. At this moment, he could list several women whom he sensed were interested in him, and knew of two who had even asked mutual friends to arrange dinner parties in order to meet him. In the past, he inevitably would wind up putting such women aside after a few dates, always preferring to hope and wait for the one woman he wanted: Crystal. It was high time he gave up on the impossible and reassessed his priorities.

But, though Eric had to admit his failure to win Crystal's heart, it was still his duty to keep her safe, the other aspect of his mission tonight. To do that, he realized, he'd better be a lot tougher with her from now on, especially with his renewed injury slowing him down. And he'd better not let his Achilles' heel, his deep desire for her, get the better of him again. From now on, he'd have to keep her too damned afraid of him to even think of seducing him in order to attempt another escape. As long as she feared him, he could keep her safe until he was sure he could return her to her father without risk.

He turned to look down the tunnel where she'd run, his neck stiff and hurting as he did so. He hoped she hadn't gotten too far away. She'd get lost, he was quite sure, in this underground labyrinth. With fifty miles of tunnels, he only hoped he could track her down. He needed to get up and get going—

His eyes came across the mask lying at his feet, and he reached to pick it up. With an exhale of fatigue, he put it back on his face, stretching the elastic over his head. He might as well stay a Phantom in her mind when he found her again. It would be too humiliating for him now to reveal who he really was.

Had he recovered enough to try to stand up? he wondered with trepidation. What if he couldn't walk yet? He might not find her in time. His leg still throbbed, but perhaps the worst of the pain was over. Placing a hand on the bed, he tried to stand up. Wincing with agony, he fell back again.

He remembered the crutch and slid sideways on the bed to reach for it. Bringing the padded top of it under his armpit and putting pressure on his good leg, he managed, falteringly, to rise up on his feet.

Slowly, getting used to the pain and finding the best way to use his muscles, he made his way to the box of newspapers. To one side of the papers lay an extra flashlight, similar to the one Crystal had taken. He bent to pick it up, painfully, then hobbled over to his discarded swallowtail jacket. In an inside pocket he found the extra batteries he'd placed there earlier. It was a precaution he always took when moving through the tunnels. He put the batteries in his pants pocket, deciding it was easier to move in the shirtsleeves and vest he still wore. He threw the jacket back onto the chair.

He set off then, moving as fast as he could, which wasn't very fast, in the direction she'd run. "Crystal," he called out, his voice coming back at him from all directions. "Stop where you are! You'll get lost—"

Crystal hesitated when she heard the distant echo of Eric's voice. Stop? No way! She increased her pace, thinking that, though his voice seemed more distant, he sounded stronger than he had the last time he'd shouted to her—when he'd cried out that he loved her with such pain in his voice. Who was he? she wondered again, that he would love her so much? Who could he be?

No time to think of that now. She had to find the hotel they'd come from and escape up the elevator. The long cape was proving to be a hindrance, however. She'd tried to drape it around her, but it was too long, and she tripped on it more than once. She tried bundling it up and carrying it, but it proved cumbersome with the flashlight she was also carrying. Deciding speed was more important than modesty right now, she tossed it aside. Maybe she'd be able to find some old piece of cloth to put around her in the storage areas of the subbasement. Then she'd find a phone and call the police.

She'd tried to re-create the turns they'd made but didn't remember exactly how many times they'd turned. And there were so many choices. She'd passed through a number of intersections, some of them with tunnels going off in more than four directions. Here and there her flashlight would pick up street names that long ago had been hand-painted on the concrete walls. She'd passed State and Madison about ten minutes ago, though she wasn't sure she'd taken the tunnel in the right direction from there to bring her to the hotel. State and Madison was considered the center of Chicago; the city's street numbering began at that intersection. It had been so frustrating to know that if only she could go straight up through the earth to the surface, she would have known exactly where she was. The Carson, Pirie, Scott & Company department store, a competitor to Winthrop's to this day, was located at that corner. She had even found and tried the entrance to its subbasement but couldn't get in.

Now she must be several blocks away from that point but hadn't seen a street marking since. Perhaps some of them had disintegrated or gotten washed away in the flood. A few of the tunnels had almost been blocked off by abandoned wooden freight cars, apparently the ones that had been in use in the early part of the century.

Crystal was beginning to get tired from moving so fast. She'd stopped running once she felt relatively safe from Eric's grasp but had kept up a steady pace searching for her way out. It was frightening to be all alone in these shadowy, silent tunnels, her only possible companion a madman who claimed to love her. Besides that, her flashlight beam seemed to be growing weaker. She couldn't see quite as far down the tunnel as she could before and the light seemed darker, more yellow. God, what would she do if her batteries failed? She had to find the hotel—

"Crystal! Where are you?"

A chill went through her. Eric's voice sounded distant but significantly closer than it had before. He was coming after her! Now she wished she had knocked him unconscious. Stupid! Why had she felt sorry for him? Now he'd apparently recovered quickly enough to go searching for her.

She began to run again, coming to another intersection. As she raised her flashlight to look for street signs, it went very dim. She shook it, and it brightened again. As she ran on, not seeing any sign to indicate where she was, the light began to fade once more. She tried tightening the top of it, but this had no effect. Growing panicky, she slapped it against her palm. The light went out.

Suddenly she was standing in blackness so dark, she couldn't even tell which way was up. She almost lost her balance. "No!" she shrieked, feeling the flashlight to find the top of it. She loosened and tightened it, but the light would not go on. Putting out her hand, she tried to find the wall. Her hand came up against it, and when she stepped forward, she found herself walking into the wall, hitting her forehead on concrete as it domed upward to form the ceiling. This threw her off balance again as she stepped backward. Her foot encountered the raised rail of the track and she tripped. The flashlight slipped out of her grasp. Cold concrete slammed against the side of her body, stunning her. Her ribs and shoulder hurt, and she realized she'd fallen. Reaching out, she searched blindly but couldn't find her flashlight, unable to see anything, even her hand. As she rose to her hands and knees, she knew she was absolutely helpless now. She would die here in pitch darkness of thirst and starvation.

Crystal began to sob, frightened to the core. There was only one hope—that Eric would find her. The man she'd run from in fear was now the only one who could save her.

"Crystal?" Eric's voice echoed down the tunnel out of the distance.

"I'm here!" she called out, still sobbing.

"Where?"

"I don't know," she said between heaving breaths. "My light went out."

"Damn you! I knew you'd get lost!"

His harsh words made her cry even harder.

"Stop crying and keep talking!" his voice echoed. "I have only your voice to go by."

"I'm here. I passed State and Madison a while ago."

"In which direction?"

"I don't know!"

"Not very smart, were you?" His chiding voice seemed to sound a bit closer.

"I was just trying to get away from you!" she cried, needing to justify herself and answer his derision. "You kidnapped me. You had me pinned down on your bed! Why shouldn't I run?"

There was no reply. Only silence broken by a distant, shuffling sound.

"Eric?"

Silence.

"Eric!"

"What?"

"Y-you wanted me to keep talking."

"Then keep talking. I don't have to answer every complaint."

She realized it wouldn't do her any good to make him angrier than he already was. Swallowing what was left of her pride, she said, "I'm sorry."

"Sorry? For what?"

"For... for complaining."

"Really? Are you saying now you enjoyed your visit with me?"

"I... in some ways," she improvised.

"What ways?"

"I liked the... the candlelight. And the wine."

"What about me? Did you like me?" he asked in a baiting voice.

"S-sure—"

"Liar."

"It's hard to like someone wearing a mask, Eric."

"Why did you pretend to, then?" he countered in a snide tone. "Those heated kisses. Those whimpers of arousal. You're a wonderful actress."

Crystal bit her lip, hating the need to justify herself in order to be rescued. Even if he found her, she'd be back in the same situation with him. Only now he sounded dreadfully angry. He'd probably try to get back at her, perhaps force her, even beat her. Maybe she'd be better off if he didn't find her. She could just die here alone in the darkness and avoid his revenge.

After a few moments of silence, he yelled, "Crystal?"

She hesitated in agonizing fear, not knowing what to do, what was better, to die alone or be tortured, maybe even murdered.

"Crystal!"

Now she was too afraid to answer. His voice was getting so close.

"Crystal, don't play games!"

No, no more games, she thought as an icy, invisible veil of terror overtook her nearly naked body. Death couldn't come too soon, she decided.

All at once a beam of light streamed down the tunnel. She looked up in its direction from her cowering position on the floor. The beam grew stronger, fixing her in its path, like a floodlight on a criminal. Soon she could see a vague shape moving behind the enlarging light, a white-and-black figure that hobbled as it moved. She heard the steady beat of a stick against concrete, and then caught a glimpse of his crutch.

When he was only a few feet away, he stood looming over her as he leaned on the crutch and shone the light directly into her face. She turned her head, instinctively covering her naked breasts by crossing her arms over her chest. Tears of humiliation and fear streamed from her face.

"You're a sorry sight," he whispered. "Never thought I'd see you so cowed." His voice grew intimate and angry. "But still sexy as can be. All soft and naked and helpless." He shifted the flashlight to the hand that worked his crutch, and with his free hand began unbuttoning his shirt.

Crystal looked up in alarm. Was he going to force her here? She began to get up to run again.

"Stay there!" he ordered in a voice so imperative and authoritative, it made her freeze.

"Please, don't!" she begged, on her knees in front of him. "I...I'll cooperate, if you promise not to hurt me."

He looked at her as he pulled the white shirt out of his pants waistband. "Cooperate?" he asked with sardonic interest. "What does that mean, exactly?"

She'd once read that it was better to cooperate with an attacker and stay alive than fight him and be murdered. She didn't know if it was sound advice, but at this point she had no idea what to do and was ready to try anything. "If...if you still want me..."

"What? You won't hammer me with a flashlight again?" His eyes flicked to one side. "Which reminds me, hand that up to me." He pointed toward her spent flashlight, lying between them.

To do this she had to take one protective arm away from her chest to pick up the flashlight. She covered her breasts as best she could with her other arm and handed the flashlight up to him, shaking with the fear that he might use it on her as she'd used it on him. "Don't—"

He took it and shoved it into his waistband, beneath his unbuttoned vest and shirt. "Stop pressing your arms into your breasts that way. It only...makes you look sexier. Wait." He leaned his crutch against the wall and began taking off his vest and shirt. The beam of light from his flashlight flicked up and side-ways from his movements, but there was enough light to see his broad, smooth chest and muscular shoul-ders. The masculine formidability of him as he loomed over her kneeling form made her tremble. Despite what he'd said, she instinctively drew her arms closer to her chest.

"Please, Eric..." she whispered in terror.

She was answered by his white shirt thrown against her torso. "Put that on and keep yourself covered. And don't waste your breath asking for mercy. I don't want you anymore."

Stung by the material flung against her skin and feeling confused, she grabbed hold of the shirt and quickly slipped it on. The sleeves were far too long and the shoulders much too broad. As she lapped the sides of the dress shirt's pleated front over her chest, she could feel his body warmth still clinging to the cloth against her breasts. The sensation reminded her of his earlier caresses. She looked up at him with large eyes as he slipped his vest back on, leaving it open over his bare chest. He reached for his crutch, still resting against the sloping wall.

"Don't look at me like that. Get up!" he said, sounding like a drill sergeant.

She did as he ordered, reaching to the floor to push herself up. As she let go of the shirt, it fell open. She grabbed hold of the sides and pulled them together to cover herself again.

"Button that."

With shaking fingers, she followed his instructions, angry at being ordered around so much. She had the luxury and security to be angry, now that he'd claimed no further interest in her. Or was there some perverted corner of her mind that had begun to feel injured at his sudden rejection of her, when earlier he'd wanted her so? She must put that thought out of her head! What, did she *want* him to take her by force?

Certainly not.

But... to hear his voice speak gently to her again, to feel his sensual caresses... to be swept away by his passion...

Crystal, you must be crazy, she told herself. She ought to be glad to hear him say he didn't want her.

He pointed with his crutch, holding the flashlight with his other hand. "Walk on the other side of the track, beside me, where I can see you."

She saw that with his crutch to deal with, and the flashlight, he couldn't pull her along behind him as he had when he'd first led her into the tunnels. And there was only room for one on either side of the narrow track. But as she crossed the track to walk parallel with him, she felt the distance between them. The few feet of space ought to have made her feel more at ease. But somehow she would have preferred holding his hand. This made no sense, she knew. Why should she want to feel him comforting and protecting her, as he had when he'd led her down here? This was a man who had kidnapped her! If it weren't for him, she wouldn't even be in this situation.

Her perverse thought pattern must be due to the fact that she was dependent on him now for her survival. She'd heard of a syndrome kidnap victims experienced after being held hostage for a while, where they found themselves in sympathy with the one holding them prisoner. Eric was both her dangerous captor and her only hope of survival. That must be the reason why she had found herself so vulnerable to his sensual seduction; so much so, that now that he'd grown harsh with her, she missed his tender ways. She supposed it was reasonable to prefer to be pampered and petted by your captor than shut out in the cold by him.

They'd been walking for some time now in silence, Eric with his eyes straight ahead, only glancing at her occasionally to see that she made the turns he took and was still following him. All she heard was the shuffle of his hobbling gait and the regular sharp sound of his crutch against the concrete.

"How's your leg?" she ventured to ask.

He turned bitter eyes on her. "Your pretense of caring is touching."

"You can't blame a prisoner for attempting to get away," she said, trying to reason with him. "I could have hit you on the head and knocked you unconscious, maybe even killed you."

"Thank you for your restraint."

"I'm serious! I considered knocking you out. But I didn't because . . . well, you seemed to have tried to be kind to me, even though you did kidnap me. I found I didn't really want to hurt you."

"How sweet," he mocked. "If you had knocked me out, you wouldn't have survived yourself! If you had any common sense—but, of course, you don't—you'd have known enough to take extra batteries."

"It was a new situation for me," she countered, using sarcasm of her own. "I'm not used to trying to escape a masked man who's got me pinned down on his bed, about to— I didn't stop to think about where you might keep extra batteries!"

"Let's not talk about what happened on the bed."

"All right." But somehow, she did want to talk about it. They walked half a block in silence and then she said, "Why did you say you loved me?"

"When did I . . . ?" And then he left off, as if remembering.

"You shouted it after me when I ran off," she said, reminding him anyway.

"Must have been due to the agony you put me in with your flashlight. Momentary delirium from extreme physical pain, that's all."

"Did I hurt you that much?" she asked in a softer tone.

"Yes."

She bowed her head and walked a few steps in silence. Then she looked at him and said, "I'm sorry, Eric."

He kept his eyes straight ahead, limping along on his crutch, taking in a breath as if debating what response to give her. Finally, he spoke in a cold manner. "You're not forgiven. And you're not to speak to me anymore unless spoken to. You're my prisoner, and you'll behave as such until I free you."

"You do really plan to free me?" she asked with surprise.

"Haven't I told you that all along?" he retorted.

"Yes, but—"

"You didn't believe me. Well, that's your problem. I'm just following my duty to rescue you."

"Why?"

"Out of..." He exhaled. "Because of my friendship with your father. I knew how miserable he would be if you married Tony, if any harm came to you because of your prospective husband."

"What do you know about Tony?" she persisted.

He considered a long time before he answered. "Tony is the man who shot me. He tried to murder me."

She hesitated in her steps. "He did? Why?"

"Your father had asked me to look into his background. He'd gotten a report from a detective that he felt was, let's say, incomplete. I suspect Tony found out and bribed the detective to give him a clean report. With my background in surveillance, I managed to find out quite a bit about him, none of it good. Tony's got mob connections in New York. He's done time for theft. By the way, I suspect your engagement ring was stolen."

Crystal looked in horror at her ring.

"He likes to live the good life," Eric continued, "and there have been other women he's taken for a ride. He needed to get out of New York because things got too hot for him there. When he came to Chicago, he discovered you at your health club—the perfect heiress to suit his aspirations. And you, naturally, fell right into his arms. When your father insisted on a prenuptial agreement, he didn't like that at all. That's when he began to insist on eloping, isn't it?"

"Yes," she admitted.

"And when he found out that I was on his case— one of his 'family' members in New York tipped him off, I think—he knew I'd already learned too much and that I'd warn you that he was only after your money. He was looking into life insurance, by the way, which said to me that he might have had a plan to murder you once you were married. That way he'd get insurance *and* the fortune your mother left you. He'd be sitting pretty. Knowing how impulsive you can be,

I was afraid at any moment he'd talk you into eloping, to avoid the prenuptial agreement. So once I had
the information I needed on him, I acted with great
haste. I didn't check adequately to make sure my
tracks were covered. He caught me off guard, shot me
and left me for dead.''

Crystal listened to all this, horrified and mystified
as she walked along beside him, barefoot. She wondered who he was that he had a background in surveillance. And somehow he knew that she was
impulsive and that Tony wanted her to elope. When
Eric mentioned the prenuptial agreement, she thought
of Jay. ''Do you know what happened to Jay Saunders, the lawyer my father hired to do the prenuptial
contract? He disappeared and no one ever found him.
Do you think . . . could Tony have murdered him?''

Eric didn't answer for a long moment. ''That's quite
possible.''

''Unless . . .'' She looked at Eric, so tall and manly
in the darkness, despite the crutch. Jay wasn't so tall
and was of a slighter build, as best she could remember. And his hair was lighter in color and curly, the
type that would fall in short, springy locks over his
forehead. She had no idea what color Jay's eyes were.
And his voice . . . ? All she remembered was that it was
conscientiously businesslike, so lacking in emotion
that it was almost a monotone. Eric's voice was altered by the echo effect in these tunnels, so it was hard
to compare. She remembered she'd thought it sounded

vaguely familiar in the ballroom. Still, she couldn't imagine Jay sounding as sensual and passionate as she knew Eric could. Besides, Eric had said that his first name really was Eric—that is, if she could believe him. And she found she was beginning to.

"No, you couldn't be Jay," she muttered, disappointed. For a moment, she thought she might have solved the mystery of who Eric was.

Eric kept walking and said nothing.

She had many more questions. "But why—"

"Didn't I tell you not to speak unless spoken to?" He interrupted her with stinging impatience.

"Yes," she replied, feeling chastised. Why was he so angry again? He'd been tolerant enough to answer her questions about Tony, and now—

"Then do as I say! I'm tired of talking."

She gave him a spiteful look but kept her silence until they returned to Winthrop's.

The three candles still glowed softly on the table by the bed. The light blue bedsheets looked rumpled. The atmosphere lay as silent and shadowy as before. Everything was just the same as when she'd run away. Only, she now wore his long shirt, which extended to her thighs, and Eric was the one partially clothed. Their state of dress was somewhat reversed from before, and she liked that. She felt more comfortable, less embarrassed, more in control. And...she liked looking at him, with his unbuttoned vest leaving his upper body half-uncovered. He had no chest hair, and not an ounce of excess flesh. His ribs showed slightly and his midsection formed a marvelous washboard hardness. His chest, shoulder and arm muscles also looked lean and superbly developed. She wanted to ask him where he worked out but remembered with annoyance that she was forbidden to speak.

He tossed her spent flashlight onto the newspaper pile in the box and walked to the bed. Using his crutch to assist him, he lowered himself to a sitting position on the edge of the bed, grimacing with pain.

She stood a few feet away, watching, and decided she must say something. "Can I get you anything? Do you have a painkiller you can take?"

"You're going to be my nurse now?" he snapped.

"Just wanted to help."

"There are some bottles of water in the ice chest. I'd like one. Get yourself one, too. And eat something."

"All right," she said, going for the water. She came back and handed him a plastic liter bottle, keeping one for herself. Picking up the bag of food he'd set aside earlier, she brought out green grapes, Brie cheese and French rolls. There was a plastic knife to spread the cheese. She divided the grapes into smaller bunches and then broke a roll in half. After spreading one half with cheese, she held it out to him.

He'd been drinking the water from the bottle and looked at her as he twisted the cap back on. "I didn't say I wanted bread."

"You should eat, too."

"I'm not hungry," he told her in a testy voice.

"Eric, do you have some aspirin to take for the pain?"

His eyes flicked to a drawer in the small table, which she hadn't paid attention to before. Without waiting for instructions, risking his wrath, she opened it. Inside were two bottles of prescription drugs with no label to tell who they were prescribed for. The medications he'd stolen, she guessed.

"Is one of these a painkiller?" she asked.

"Yes, but I'm not going to take it," he replied, as if making up his mind at that moment.

"Why not?"

"It makes me tired."

"Well, so what? Oh," she said, realizing, "you're afraid I'll run away again if you fall asleep."

"You're getting quicker on the uptake minute by minute!"

"I won't run away," she told him.

"Really?" he said with sarcastic amusement.

"Really. I won't run. Being alone in the dark like I was is the most frightening thing I've ever experienced. I know now I'll never get out of here without you to show me how, or to unlock this door to Winthrop's," she confessed, indicating the door in the brick wall behind them. "So I'd be foolish to run away again. You can trust me to stay here now."

"Can I?" he baited. "The way you trust me?"

She bowed her head a moment. "It's hard to trust someone wearing a mask who refuses to tell me who he is. But...I'm beginning to believe what you've told me—about Tony and all. You seem to know so much. And you have taken care of me, even if you are nasty about it sometimes."

"Nasty?" he said with arch drama.

"The way you've been ordering me around. Even right now you're still in a foul mood."

"Ah, so my hostage is complaining about her conditions."

"Yes!"

"Sorry it's not the Ritz, with personal maid service. This was the best I could do."

"It's not that. It's just...if you could be kind again, the way you were at first..."

"Before you faked ecstasy and thrashed me with a flashlight?"

"I didn't fake—"

"No, you're right, you didn't take your playacting quite that far. A little writhing, a few soft moans and gasps just to keep me going, but you did them *very* well. The blows with the flashlight, however, were quite real."

"I'm sorry! But if you'd told me more then about why you brought me down here, I might have trusted you more—the way I'm starting to now, since you've explained some things."

He bent his head, elbows on his knees, and set the bottle of water on the floor. "All right," he muttered. "You have a point. I was just afraid if I told you everything, you'd have all the pieces of the puzzle you'd need to figure out who I was. And I wanted to keep that secret, so...so we could have a chance to get to know each other in a different way than we had before." He chuckled with grim self-mockery. "It didn't occur to me that once I told you things that would be obvious clues to my identity, you *still* wouldn't figure it out!"

"Why don't you just tell me and get it over with?" she pleaded in frustration.

"At this point, it would be too embarrassing for both of us," he replied in a dismal tone. "I prefer to remain anonymous for now." He glanced at his watch. "It's 2:00 a.m. You'll learn who I am before this new day is over."

"Is that a promise?"

He held up his hand, palm facing her. "Promise."

"And when will we...leave here?"

"I want to give the police a few more hours, then I'll call them to find out if everything's been taken care of and Tony is safely locked up."

"You're working with the police?" she asked in astonishment.

"Yes," he said, sounding tired. "You think I would appear to kidnap someone without getting the cooperation of the local authorities first?"

She sighed sharply. "Eric, how am I supposed to know what you might or might not do? I don't know who you are, so how could I guess something like that?"

"Put on your thinking cap!"

"Are you a police officer?" she asked.

Eric brought the heels of his hands to his forehead, pressing them against his mask. He leaned to one side and fell back onto the pillow. "No, no, no!" He brought his hands down and looked up at her. "Would you do me a favor and stop guessing? It's damned humiliating to me that you can't figure it out!"

"Not telling me is humiliating to me!" she retorted.

She watched him try to bring his legs up onto the bed. He moved with obvious pain. Stepping to the bed, she bent to help him lift his sore leg onto the sheets.

"Ouch. God!" he exclaimed.

Tears stung her eyes, knowing she had caused his misery. She leaned over him. "Please take the painkiller," she told him, reaching to touch his chest. She drew back her hand with alarm, "You have a fever!"

"The infection's probably coming back," he said, his voice thick with fatigue. "Give me two of the tablets in the green-capped bottle, will you?"

"Sure," she answered, getting the bottle from the drawer. Reading the name of the drug on the con-

tainer, she recognized it as an often-prescribed anti-
biotic. She poured out two pills, picked up the bottle
of water, then handed them to him. He sat up uncomfortably to swallow them. "What about the painkiller? Take it, Eric. If you fall asleep and rest, it
would do you good."

He stared at her, his green eyes stern.

"I'll stay here with you," she promised. "Where
would I go? Back into the tunnels to get lost again?
I'm not that dumb."

"I was beginning to wonder."

She pressed her lips together, accepting his insult
without retort. "Please take the painkiller. I don't like
to see you suffer this way, because of me."

"It's nothing new," he muttered.

"What do you mean?" she asked.

"Give me a tablet from the other bottle," he instructed, ignoring her question.

She got the bottle and gave him a pill. As she
watched him swallow it, she wished he'd answered her.
Did he love her, as he'd called out when she ran away?
If so, she wondered why and how he'd fallen in love
with her. When? For how long? And why had he never
told her? But then, there had been a number of men
over the years since high school who had told her
they'd loved her. Maybe Eric had been one of them.
But if he had been, she didn't think she would have
forgotten. It would have stood out in her mind like
neon.

Relieved that he'd taken the painkiller, she put the bottle back in the drawer. "Will you eat something?" she asked.

"Give me the bread and cheese you made up," he acquiesced.

She smiled and quickly took it off the table where she'd left it to hand it to him. Making up her own half roll spread with cheese, she took it and her bottle of water and sat beside him on the bed. He rested his weight on one elbow and ate with the other hand. She handed him his water when he'd finished. After he'd drunk some, he set it on the floor and lay back on the bed.

"You really look tired," she told him with concern.

"How can you tell with my mask?"

"By the way you move. The fatigue in your voice. You will get better, won't you?"

"I've recovered from worse than this. Done eating?"

"Yes," she said, setting down her water.

"Lie down with me," he said.

"Wh-what?"

"Don't worry. I'm too tired to molest you, assuming I wanted to. And I've told you, I don't."

She didn't know how she would deal with being physically close to him again. The image of him looming over her, caressing her, flashed in her mind. She didn't care if he was ill with a fever. The very thought of lying on the bed again with him, next to his body, unsettled her. "I'd rather not."

He grabbed hold of her arms firmly. "Lie down with me," he ordered softly, pulling her toward him.

"But—"

"Don't argue! You're still my prisoner. And fever or no fever, I'm still a hell of a lot stronger than you." He pulled her down until she was on top of him. "If I fall asleep, I want to be sure you'll stay here."

"But I told you—"

"Call me crazy, but after beating me with a flashlight while you pretended to make love, I find I can't quite trust you yet. The memory—and the pain—are still too fresh. I want you here, next to me. If you make the slightest move, I'll know it. The drug makes me drowsy, but it's a light sleep." His tone grew harsh as he raised a threatening forefinger an inch from her face. "You so much as blink an eye, I'll wake up. And you'll have hell to pay."

She almost wanted to cry. Things were going better between them, she'd thought. Why did he have to turn mean again? Why did he want to make her feel scared once more, just when they'd begun to relax with one another? Maybe his fever made him moody and ill-tempered.

Crystal obeyed him and did not try to writhe out of his insistent embrace. She squirmed over him until she felt reasonably comfortable stretched out beside him, half lying facedown on his chest, her head resting at his shoulder, her hand on his vest. He clasped both his arms around her snugly. The sensation of being held by him, against his bared chest, made her breaths come faster, though she tried to hide it. She might have begun to like the situation, if he weren't acting as her prison guard.

"You ought to get some sleep yourself," he advised her, voice empty now of emotion.

"Sure, now that you've made me feel so comfortable!" she retorted.

"Didn't I tell you not to speak to me?"

"Fine with me!"

She felt a tenseness in his fevered body, but after several minutes of silence between them, he seemed to relax. Soon she heard the regular breathing and felt the gentle rise and fall of his chest that indicated sleep. She relaxed then herself. Exhausted, she soon drifted off.

The sound of her name, spoken feverishly, awoke her. Startled, Crystal lifted her head from Eric's chest. His eyes were closed and he appeared to be asleep, though he seemed quite restless. His breathing was uneven and she could tell he was dreaming, for his eyes seemed to be moving back and forth beneath his eyelids. He held her closely against him with one arm, and she noted that his body temperature still felt too warm. She remembered him speaking of his fever dreams. Glancing at the candles, she saw that they had burned down enough to indicate that a few hours had passed.

All at once, his arm about her shoulders tightened, and his hand curled around her upper arm possessively. "Crystal," he murmured hotly in his sleep. His other hand, lying on his stomach, moved toward her and his warm fingers came up against the side of her breast.

His seeking fingers tantalized her, made her remember his caresses earlier in the evening. She moved slightly, shifting her body so that her breast lifted from his chest. Her heart rate began to pick up at the very thought of his hand fondling her. She debated, wondering if she should give in to her own temptation. This was wild, this was being more boldly sexual than she'd ever been in her life. And she didn't even know who he was. She began to tremble. God help her, but she wanted this. She'd waited all her life to be touched the way Eric had touched her. She wanted to feel his touch again.

Taking hold of his hand, she gently guided it to cover her breast, glancing up at his face to see if she'd awakened him. She hadn't. If he was dreaming, calling her name, he'd think he was dreaming this, too, she told herself.

It seemed to work. He took tender hold of her breast and caressed her through the white cloth while his breathing grew more labored and his head shifted to one side. His other arm around her back began moving up and down in long strokes over the shirt covering her body.

Crystal closed her eyes for a moment, savoring the heated manipulations of his long fingers. Carefully she slipped her hand beneath his as it fondled her breast, and she began unbuttoning the shirt. When she'd finished, she slowly pulled the open edge of it to one side, gradually uncovering her breast beneath his seeking hand. As his hot fingers met her bared skin, she closed her eyes again, feeling a pleasure so sweet, she could have wept. When his thumb found her nipple, she gasped at the acute sensation coursing through her nervous system, making her feel alive with sensual electricity.

Suddenly, his hand stopped. His head lifted from the pillow. She looked up and found him staring at her, clearly wide-awake now. His green eyes looked stunned, perhaps angry. When he realized what he was doing, he pulled his hand away, as if he'd been touching fire.

"Did I unbutton this?" he demanded, sounding bewildered and irritated.

"No," she whispered, barely able to breathe. She knew he'd want answers for her action. Her heart throbbed. What would she tell him?

"No? Then—"

"I unbuttoned it." There, she'd admitted her desire. She held her breath.

His eyes darkened with suspicion. "Why?"

"You were asleep," she said. "You started to touch me. You called my name. I wanted to…accommodate you."

He sat up more, resting on one elbow, looking down at her. His action made her slide off of him a bit, but she stayed as close as possible and bravely drew up on one elbow to face him. The shirt slipped open farther, revealing the inner curve of her other breast.

He took the edge of the shirt and pulled it over her bared chest with an angry jerk of his hand. "Accommodate me?" he repeated with sarcasm. "Why? So you can clunk me over the head this time and knock me out completely?"

"You were sound asleep. If I'd wanted to do that, I could have, without unbuttoning this shirt."

"Then why did you uncover yourself? I told you, I don't want you anymore."

"But you called out my name in your sleep. You reached for me. You held me close."

"I was dreaming."

"About me," Crystal said with bold assurance.

"I don't remember."

"Yes, you do. You woke up from your fever and found this time that your dream was real."

His eyes grew more fierce. "You still haven't answered my question. Even if I was dreaming, why did you go along with it? Why are you suddenly going into your seductress act again? What little plan have you got now?"

Crystal swallowed and bowed her head. "It's not an act. And I don't have a plan."

"Then why did you have me touch you?"

She looked up, hesitant about what she should say. She was still working things out in her own mind. How much should she reveal of her secret feelings, when she didn't even know who this often frightening, angry man was?

"I wanted you to..." she paused, short of breath "...to caress me," she whispered with a passion springing from the depths of her soul, "the way you did before I ran away. I wasn't acting when I responded to you then. I *wasn't* acting. No one has ever made me feel the way you did."

He stared at her with unblinking severity. "Then why did you hit me and run?"

"It was the most difficult decision for me, Eric," she told him with all her sincerity. "You made me desire you. I *wanted* so much to—" She wet her lips, too shy suddenly to say the words. "But I had to remind myself that you'd kidnapped me. You hadn't explained very much yet about why, about Tony. I didn't know what to believe. I thought you were a madman. A seductive madman. I had to tell myself not to give in to the desires you'd aroused, that it was more important to try to escape. I was very frightened of you, and I felt I had to run for my life." She chewed her lip a moment, then added, "I'm still afraid of you. Your moods change so quickly. I know I'm risking your anger." She reached out with trembling fingers and touched his chest. "But I want you. I began to realize how much after you said you didn't want me."

Eric's eyes had become a steady, wary glow peering through his mask. "Why do you want me? Explain what it is you're attracted to. The mask? The mystery and excitement of it all?"

She lifted her shoulder, unconsciously making her closed shirt come apart a bit. "I don't know," she replied, trying to answer him honestly. "Maybe. I'm not very experienced with men. I've only... you know, given myself... once."

Eric's eyes narrowed to slits. "Once? You're twenty-five, aren't you?"

"Yes."

"And the provocative way you dress! You're a tease. I thought—"

"I know. Everybody probably thinks that. Even my father. I don't want people to guess how... how unsophisticated I am when it comes to sex, especially now in my mid-twenties. So I dress to look like I'm more experienced and relaxed about it all than I am. And I think you were right when you said that... that I want to look sexy, to feel sexy, to be *fulfilled* that way—b-because I'm not."

She sighed, feeling as if she was unburdening herself of a secret she'd carried for years. "The men I meet, that I'm attracted to initially—well, things never seem to pan out the way I hope. In college, I fell for the football team's quarterback. Like a schoolgirl, I thought he was handsome and heroic. I was so ecstatic when he asked me out. We got along great. I thought I was in love. I wanted him to be the first... and he was. I looked forward to my first time, to finally experiencing what everyone was talking about. I'd dreamed of it and fantasized what it would be like for years. And when I finally went through with it..." Tears glazed her eyes. "It was so disappointing. He was finished in about two minutes. Then he rolled over and went to sleep. The next day he told the whole team what a great time I'd given him. I broke up with him immediately, only to have his teammates start hitting on me one by one. It was awful! And I'd thought he was so wonderful."

Eric shook his head, the muscles in his jaw clenching.

She continued despite the harshness about his mouth, somehow wanting him to understand. He'd been sympathetic and comforted her when he'd first brought her into the tunnels. She wanted him to be that way again. "I was deeply hurt and disillusioned," she told him. "I've been afraid to take another chance with a man—even the one I was planning to marry."

Eric's voice was disparaging. "With the men you choose, I'm not surprised."

"What's wrong with the men I pick, then?" she asked.

"They're smug hunks who only think about themselves. They see you in your provocative little outfits, know whose daughter you are, and they target you as a prime catch. They don't care about *you*. You seem to pick men who only want to use you. Find a man who *loves* you—loves you for yourself, and not because you have money, connections and a gorgeous body."

"You seem to like my body," she pointed out.

"But I liked *you* long before you had that body," he argued. "Now that you do, I . . . well, I'm only human."

"So you're saying you do want me now?" she asked, smiling a bit at having caught him. "A little while ago, you were still claiming you didn't."

His eyes glowed with consternation, making Crystal feel light as air. "I'm not admitting anything," he told her.

"Why not?"

"I still don't trust you." He fingered the cuff of the shirt that covered her small knuckles. "Who knows what you've got up your sleeve. I don't need any more injuries. Physical or otherwise."

Crystal's shoulders sank a bit. "Have I hurt you in the past? Did I say no when you asked for a date or something?"

"You never hurt me intentionally. But you always rejected me in small ways. When I'd ask you to dance, for example, you'd sweetly dither and then introduce me to one of your girlfriends.''

That was Crystal's usual way of handling boys, and later men, she wasn't interested in, so this information gave her no further clue as to who he was. ''Did you ever ask me out to dinner?''

''Yes.''

''And?''

''You said you were busy.''

''Oh.'' She bowed her head, wondering how she could have been so foolish. ''How long ago was that?''

''Years.''

''Not very persistent, were you?'' she chided, growing braver by the moment.

''I decided to bide my time, hoping you'd grow up and wake up—that one day you'd look around and discover me. I was a fool.''

''I've discovered you now,'' she said.

''Yes, but look what it took!'' he spat out bitterly.

''Well, I'm here. You're here. We're together.'' She willed herself not to be shy or scared and fingered the button on his loose vest. ''Why don't we do something about it?''

He stared at her, eyes so bright they could cut steel. ''You really want to?''

Her heart pounded. ''Yes.''

''Are you taking the Pill?''

The question threw her. "No. But you didn't worry about that when you almost made love to me before."

"I was carried away by the moment and wasn't thinking. I even trusted you! I'm trying to keep my head now. Why would you risk getting pregnant?"

"You're suspicious," she said, growing downcast. "You still think I'm trying to trick you."

He nodded his head. "Why are you so anxious, that you're suddenly willing to take risks? Think about it— you avoided sleeping with your fiancé, but you're willing to throw caution to the wind to make love with a man in a mask?"

Her heart sank, realizing he didn't believe her. "Because I think you *would* 'make love' with me. The way you touched me . . . the way you spoke, the words you said to me. No man ever treated me the way you have. You've given me a taste of what I'd only dreamed of. I put Tony off because down deep I had the feeling I'd be disappointed. I didn't want to face that fact, so I avoided the truth and toyed with wedding plans anyway. I've gone for years wanting so much, more than I thought any man could give me. I didn't know someone like you existed. I suppose I *was* looking for the wrong thing." She touched his mask, wishing she knew who the right man was. "I want this experience with you, Eric. Whatever happens after we're back in the real world, I want to have had this experience. I think...I know...you can give me what I've longed for. Please..."

She leaned up to kiss him, and he kissed her back, hesitantly at first, but then his mouth grew fervent. He broke away suddenly and gripped her arm.

"I'm serious about what I said. You might get pregnant." He drew his face closer and whispered ardently. "I'd love to father a child with you."

The words shocked her. "I...I think it's a safe time of the month for me."

He nodded slightly. "If not, don't worry. I want to marry you anyway."

Was he mad, as she'd earlier thought? Or was it his fever that made him say these extreme things? Or did he say them out of love?

His hands slid under her shirt, pushing it aside to caress her. Her doubts about his sanity got lost in the mesmerizing pleasure of his touch. He pulled her against him, her breasts compressing against his hard chest. They kissed and writhed together in sudden, heightened need. She felt wanton, more free than she'd ever felt in her life. When his mouth released hers, she took in a deep breath in a long, sensual gasp and whispered, "Eric, oh, Eric."

The heel of his hand lifted her breast as his mouth slid hotly from her lips, down her throat, over the soft mound of flesh to her nipple. A poignant cry of need escaped her as his heated lips fastened onto the pink, aroused little nub. He sucked hard, driving her mad. Flames shot through her limbs, arousing her secret place hidden beneath her panties. She wanted him to touch her there, too, and her hips and thighs squirmed with desire.

As if reading her, he let go of her breast and slid his hand down her abdomen and stomach, then under her panties. She cried out when he touched her sensitive tissues, slick with moistness from her arousal. Her cry echoed all around her as she sank down against his shoulder in tortuous ecstasy, catching a glimpse of his mask and the candles, which seemed to softly spin in circles against the silent blackness.

His fingers penetrated her as he covered her mouth with his again. His other arm moved completely around her back, so that his fingers just reached her nipple to tease it. Crystal thought she would die of the sheer, maddening pleasure he gave her. Still she wanted more. As she kissed him and withstood his hot caresses within and without, she reached down to his pants waistband and then below. Through the cloth, her stretching fingers felt the engorged length of him, which both frightened and fascinated her.

"Eric?" she breathed.

He responded by letting go to unfasten his pants. His voice was ragged as he said, "My leg is still too sore. You'll have to be on top."

Her eyes widened with a feeling of inexperience and inadequacy. "I don't know how...."

He kissed her mouth, tenderly this time. "I forgot, you're practically a virgin. Take off your panties," he told her. She did as he asked, not even thinking to be shy now. She tossed the panties to one side. Meanwhile he'd loosened and pushed his own garments out of the way. "Face away from me," he whispered.

"What?" she asked with surprise.

"It's all right." Hands on her soft buttocks, he guided her over him, helped her draw him into her aching feminine recess. When she felt him slide inside, she closed her eyes, first at the thick, huge feel of him within her tight body and then at the more profound sensation of having an emptiness within her filled. She'd never felt so whole before.

"Lie back," he said, pulling her down with him, her back against his chest, as he fell backward onto the pillow. He cradled her in his arms as she lay her head beside his, the side of her forehead touching his mask.

She realized how much she wanted to know who he was, this man she was making love with, who had professed with such emotion that he wanted to father her child. Reaching up, she took hold of the edge of his mask. But he quickly grasped her hand, preventing her.

"No, Crystal," he said with an ache in his voice. "Let this be a dream. Let us have this moment. There'll be time enough for reality later."

She touched his chin as he let go of her hand. "All right, Eric. Then be my dream lover."

His arms, cradling her, tightened their hold as he moved his pelvis upward, farther into her. She closed her eyes at the transcending sensation his strong, hard member aroused. As if that weren't enough, he slid one hand down to caress her pleasure point between her thighs, making her writhe over him in sublime delirium. "Ohhh," she breathed. "Oh, Eric..."

His other hand settled on her breasts, for it was large enough to reach both at once. He lightly rubbed the palm of his hand over her nipples, while his other hand coaxed new sensations from her heated body and his masculine hardness continued to move more and more urgently within her. Crystal felt dizzy with erotic pleasure.

"Sweet woman," he whispered through his ragged breaths. "I've longed for you, Crystal. You're everything I've ever wanted." He continued to gently torture her until both were writhing with spiraling, undeniable urgency. All at once, he pressed her breast possessively and moved with long, startling thrusts inside her, which made her cry out with fear mixed with overwhelming need. She felt an intense pressure rising in the lower part of her stomach, and it gripped her attention entirely. Something monumental was about to happen, and it made her want to run again. And yet she was paralyzed with the need to see this through, even if she died of the experience.

"Eric," she cried with a scared little sob, and she took hold of his hand at her breast. "Please..."

"Don't be afraid," he whispered. She felt his hot breath scorch her ear and heard his words echo all around her. "Don't be afraid."

She opened her eyes wide, unsure, frightened at what was happening to her body, which seemed to be about to go out of control.

And then he said, "I love you, Crystal."

The words whispered into her ear, then echoed into the atmosphere. She smiled, wanted to cry but couldn't because she was so riveted to the sensations emanating from below her navel, to the feel of his urgent thrusts inside her. She began to breathe in high little gasps.

And then all at once she reached some new plateau, a brief moment of transcending peace where the world seemed to stop and only the candles glowed in serenity. With a last, hard thrust, he pushed her beyond that brink, and suddenly she felt as if she were plummeting. She closed her eyes tightly. Her body exploded with sensation, and she was swept into paroxysms of pleasure so intense, she cried out in a joyous fright, as if she were on a roller coaster, only a thousand times more profound. He held her closely as his own body convulsed, and she felt him pulsing inside her as he called out her name.

Breathing fast, she felt the waves of sensation coursing through her begin to subside. A cool feeling, a slight, buzzing dewiness came into her head. She opened her eyes to the shadowy darkness about her and saw points of light, like stars.

They, too, gradually faded, and she lay back against him, spent, exhausted and more abundantly happy than she'd ever been in her life.

When his own breathing had calmed, she heard Eric ask, "Are you all right?"

"Oh, yes," she told him, stroking his hand on her breasts. "More than all right! Now I know what I'd been waiting for." She turned and drew her head away slightly, so she could look at him. "You've brought me into that new world you promised when I stepped across your cape. And you've spoiled me. I'll never be satisfied with anyone but you."

She saw the sheen of tears filling his eyes. "God, I wish that to be true. Remember you said that, once we're up above in the unforgiving sunlight instead of this soft candleglow. Whatever happens, remember it was I who awakened you...with a kiss." He stretched his neck to gently kiss her on the mouth. She reached up to touch his mask, to caress it with her hand as she kissed him, tears beginning to stream down her cheeks.

"Don't forget me," she said with tender earnestness, "when we're up above. There must be other women who want you. Don't forget you said you love *me.*"

He smiled and gently dug his fingers into her thick, curled hair, which she knew must be quite mussed by now. "I've never been able to forget that I love you," he told her. "How could I now? I want to go on making love with you. I want you to be mine."

"I love you," she told him, still stroking his mask. "I'll be yours. But—" she hesitated at lifting the mask "—who are you?" she begged. "Whom do I love?"

He lifted his hand to his mask, as if considering taking it off. His lids shifted downward, veiling his eyes as he seemed to weigh his options. She touched his hand, stretched to kiss his chin. He looked at her briefly with wide, sad eyes. Finally his gaze settled on some point in midair only he could see. "No, not yet. When you find out, you...you'll probably be shocked to realize who you let make love to you, shocked to know it was I who gave you such pleasure. You'll be embarrassed, no doubt. And you'll have a lot of thinking to do. I don't want to go through that with you right now, to watch your expression of joy turn to confusion and...and disappointment."

"I wouldn't react that way, Eric."

He made a little smile. "Maybe not. But I don't have the emotional resilience right now to test it out. You'll learn who I am soon enough, Crystal. Until then, let's just keep our fantasy a little while longer."

"Eric," she told him, running her fingers over his lips. "You still don't trust me. My love won't change."

He kissed her fingertips. "Reality destroyed the love of more renowned hearts than ours. Romeo lost Juliet. Heathcliff never regained Catherine. In Leroux's book, the Phantom never won Christine." His tone grew ironic. "She went off with her handsome hunk, Raoul."

"But those are just stories, Eric."

"And this," he said, pointing to his mask, "is just a costume."

CHAPTER FIVE

Eric glanced at Crystal, standing next to him, as he spoke to police on the phone. He almost lost track of his conversation. Her dreamy brown eyes shone as she looked up at him, as if she'd found the end of a rainbow. Her lustrous auburn curls were disheveled and her eye makeup had smeared. She looked absolutely beautiful, all sensually mussed, bare legged, still wearing his white dress shirt, though she'd buttoned it again. He'd thrown on an extra shirt before bringing her up here, but Crystal hadn't wanted to discard the white shirt to put on her ball gown again.

They were in Winthrop's subbasement, at a telephone in a small, makeshift office between storage rooms. It was 6:00 a.m. Sunday, and the store wouldn't open for a few hours yet.

Eric hung up the phone. "Detective Fogarty said they arrested Tony a few minutes after we left the charity ball. He's safely behind bars."

"What did they charge him with?" she asked. "Attempted murder?"

"Yes."

"How did they know?"

"I'd secretly phoned them from here, after hours, then met with Detective Fogarty in an empty underground parking structure I designated. This was at 1:00 a.m. a few nights ago. I'd read in the society column that you were scouting out places to hold your wedding reception, so I knew you were going ahead with your plans to marry Tony. I'd finally recovered enough to do something about rescuing you. I was still afraid he'd talk you into eloping. That was my only fear, that you'd run off and marry him before I had a chance to intervene. The paper had a write-up about the Halloween ball, which I knew you would attend, since you told me you worked on the charity committee that sponsored it. I suggested my plan to Detective Fogarty and the police agreed to cooperate."

Crystal's eyes widened. "I mentioned the ball to you?"

"More than once. You always had an appointment with your dressmaker or a committee meeting to hurry off to."

She looked at him blankly. God, it was deflating to him that she couldn't guess who he was. He supposed that her former image of him precluded even the notion that he might be the masked man who had rescued her, with whom she'd just experienced such heights of passion.

She seemed annoyed with herself for not being able to figure out the puzzle. "What about the police?" she asked. "They didn't wonder who you were? Why would they agree to your plan?"

"I wasn't wearing this mask and I gave Fogarty my complete identification. He checked my background, got verification about my past experience. After that, he was happy to follow my lead. Oh, yes, I'd also given him the bullet I took out of my leg. That was a tangible piece of evidence, besides my eyewitness account of Tony's attempt to murder me. Detective Fogarty just now told me that they searched Tony's apartment after they arrested him. They found a gun, and it matched the bullet I gave them. So they have ample evidence to convict him."

She opened her mouth to ask another question, but he stopped her with a kiss. "Shh! No time now for lengthy explanations. The police are on their way. They told your father everything after Tony was arrested. Fogarty was going to call him now, to let him know we're resurfacing. But I think you should phone your dad yourself, so he hears your voice and knows you're okay."

Crystal nodded and phoned her father. Eric smiled as he listened to her side of the conversation, watched tears come into her eyes as she reassured him. He held his breath, however, waiting for the possible moment when her father might reveal his identity. But apparently, it didn't happen. Crystal hung up and wiped away her tears.

"He was so happy," she told him, smiling. "He was very grateful to you."

"What did he say?"

"He said, 'I'd never have guessed that young man could still be your salvation, but he was!' What did he mean?" Her expression grew startled. Eric's heart almost stopped. "I should have asked him!" she exclaimed, in a huff with herself. "He knows who you are, doesn't he?"

"I assume the police told him."

"Oh!" she fumed and reached for the phone again.

"Hey," Eric said, taking it out of her hand. "People will be here any moment. We've got to find you some decent clothes. You can grill your father with questions later."

"All right," she conceded, disappointed. "Dad said he was coming here for me in the limo. I'll ask him then." She glanced up sharply. "Unless you want to make a grand, last-minute revelation."

Eric found, despite all his recent heroics, that he was quickly losing his nerve. She'd disappointed him too many times over the years. He still couldn't trust her to look beneath his romantic, mysterious mask and love him anyway. If he took off the mask, he couldn't bear to see the admiration in her eyes turn to dumbfounded shock. Let her find out on her own. Give her time to adjust, to get used to the idea. Then maybe…

He swallowed. "No," he told her, using a harsh tone again to keep her, and his own emotions, under control. "No time." He took her firmly by the hand and led her down a hall to a stairwell. "We've got to do some shopping." He glanced at her as they climbed the steps. "You know how you look? Like you've spent the whole night making love. You won't want your father to see you so... deliciously mussed." He tried to say the words with sarcasm.

He must have failed, for she slid her arms around him and leaned against him as they walked onto the main floor of Winthrop's, full of elegantly displayed merchandise, but empty of people. "I don't care how I look. I don't want to see anyone. I just want to be with you." She looked up with needy, sweetly sensual eyes. "When will we make love again?" she whispered.

Eric felt his pulse begin to race. No time for that, either, he told himself with regret. But to know that she wanted him again made him higher than a kite. He wondered if she'd still feel the same way once she found out who he was. The brief, heady sensation of flying left him.

"I don't know, Crystal," he stated in a terse manner.

"Don't say you don't know," she begged, sadness entering her eyes.

This was more than he could deal with at the moment. He had to keep emotion aside right now and deal with particulars. The police, her father and probably reporters would be here any time now. He brought her to a women's clothing section. "Here," he ordered, "find yourself something to put on." He pointed to a nearby rack. "There are some dresses."

Crystal reluctantly fingered some of the dresses on the rack, her heart obviously not in a shopping mood. Looking more and more rebellious, she glanced around, as if searching. All at once she moved down a few racks to a selection of women's dress pants. She grabbed a black pair, checked the size, took them off the hanger and bent to put them on. When she'd pulled them up, she stuffed the long ends of the white shirt inside them.

Eric watched, bewildered. With irritation, he said, "Don't you want to find a fresh shirt—blouse—to go with the pants?"

She looked up at him, defiance in her eyes. "No! I want to wear your shirt. You gave it to me, and you made love to me while I wore it. I won't take it off."

Tears suddenly filled her eyes, her face crumpled, and she walked up to cry on his shoulder, as she had once before. "Why are you angry with me again? Now that we've made love? Everything's going to change, isn't it?" She looked up with pleading eyes. "You'll stay with me, won't you?"

His heart melted. "I'll always be near, if you want me," he assured her as he held her close.

"I do, Eric," she said, reaching up to touch his mask, poignance in her eyes. "Believe in me."

With reluctance born of doubt, he hesitated, then kissed her, softly reeling at the warm passion in her lips. Sliding his hand over the side of her shirt, he found her breast and caressed its soft, feminine warmth. She made a whimper and pressed her pelvis forward, against his rapidly swelling member. Oh, God, he thought. He wanted her. Maybe they had a few minutes yet—

But then, from a nearby glass revolving doorway, he could hear a commotion on the sidewalk outside. He lifted his head and looked around. Photographers were taking photos of them through the glass window nearby. Beyond, he could see a black limousine and behind it a police car, with another pulling up in front of the limo.

"They're here," he whispered. He kissed her once more, hard, fearing it might be for the last time. "We have to go, Cryssywiss."

"Why did you call me by that silly old name again?" she asked, pain and confusion in her eyes.

"I gave you that name when we were kids." His arm around her, he urged her toward the revolving door, which someone, probably a Winthrop's manager her father had called, was unlocking. He made her walk into one of the revolving door compartments, followed in the one behind and pushed them round to the outside world.

The air was crisp and cold and the feel of it on his shirtsleeves awoke him briskly from the remaining haze of arousal her kiss had given him. He realized they'd become the center of a small hubbub. Photographers, who either had kept watch on her house and followed the limousine, or kept tabs on police reports, snapped photos, particularly of him in his mask. Now he wished he'd taken it off. Reporters shouted questions at them and put microphones in front of them. Laurence Winthrop ran up and pulled his daughter into his arms, extending a hand to Eric.

"Thank you! I'm so glad you're alive. And that you found a way to get my little girl out of that murderer's clutches. I'm so relieved!"

Eric nodded and murmured, "You're welcome," feeling ill at ease now. His natural quietness, his reluctance to be a center of attention, came back despite the mask. When Detective Fogarty came up and asked him to ride to the station in his police car, Eric was happy to comply. But he had to say goodbye to Crystal.

She was still holding on to her father, but she turned and took his hand when he approached. "Come home with us," she said.

He shook his head and kept his emotion from showing in his voice. "The police want me to go down to the station and give a full report."

"But—"

"I have to go now," he said abruptly. The disappointment in her eyes was breaking his heart, but he had no choice and he knew it was better this way anyway. He squeezed her small hand and began to step away.

"When will I see you again?" she called after him.

"I don't know," he told her, then quickly turned to catch up to Detective Fogarty. He couldn't bear to look at her face, her pleading eyes, anymore. She might never look at him with such adoration and love again.

Crystal watched Eric get into the police car. From her position behind and to one side of the car, she could see through the side window that he was taking off his mask. But all she could see was the back of his head. As the car sped away, she had the urge to run after it, to bring Eric back. Why was he so impersonal toward her when they parted? Earlier, he'd told her he loved her. Had she said something, done something, to make his love grow cold? Why had he suddenly called her Cryssywiss, as if she were still a child?

Her father led her past the shouting reporters into the waiting limousine. As she walked beside him, her mind sped back to the past. All at once a vivid memory flashed into her consciousness from some remote part of her brain. She saw a thin boy, a few years older than she, with curly hair. He was teasing her, but she didn't mind it. He said, "Crystal's a funny name for you. You're not like a cold sphere of glass or a hard piece of quartz. You're too lively and full of energy. You're more like the fizz in a pop bottle. Cryssywiss suits you better. That's what I'm going to call you." And he did call her that all through grammar school. Her classmates picked up the name, too. It was the only nickname anyone had ever invented for her.

Tears stung Crystal's eyes as she remembered very well now who that boy was. He was known as E.J. then. He'd been named Eric after his father, and his parents called him by his initials to avoid confusion. After a while the other children just started calling him Jay for short, and that name stuck with him into adulthood. Jay Saunders. He was her Phantom. Why hadn't she pieced it all together before?

The driver closed the door of the limousine and suddenly she was safely isolated from the frenzy outside, but certainly not at peace.

"You were on the early TV and radio reports this morning," her father told her. "The morning newspapers, too. All about how a man dressed as the Phantom of the Opera whisked you away from the costume ball and you hadn't been seen since. They're already calling him the Phantom of Chicago."

"You knew who he was, didn't you, Dad?"

"Yes." He paused, smiling. "Though I'll admit, I'd hardly have recognized him with that mask and his hair slicked back. You knew, didn't you?"

"No," she said with regret. "For a moment I thought he might be Jay." She remembered how annoyed Eric had gotten after she'd ruled Jay out as a possibility. "He kept telling me his real name is Eric. I'd forgotten he'd been named after his father."

Her dad chuckled. "He seems to have had some fun fooling you while he was rescuing you."

Crystal's heart felt cold suddenly. "You think he was just playing a game with me?" That might explain why he was so vague about when he would see her again.

"I have no idea," her father said, still amused. "I knew nothing about all this until after I saw plainclothes police escort Tony out of the ballroom. They put handcuffs on him in the foyer and took him away. I'd only just arrived and didn't even know you were missing. When I questioned what was going on, the police told me the whole story. They said that Jay had been with a confidential quasi-military government team while he was in Washington. Getting himself in and out of tight places, taking risks, apparently is nothing new for him. Once the police had verified his background, they put a great deal of trust in him to get you out of harm's way so they could capture Tony. Tony is the one who shot Jay, did he tell you that?''

"Yes—at least, he told me *he'd* been shot by Tony.''

"Do you know he dug the bullet out himself? He told police that he saw Tony just as he was getting into his car that morning, but couldn't get out of range before Tony shot him. He slumped over the wheel, pretending he was dead, and made the horn sound. Tony ran off. Jay tied his handkerchief around his bleeding leg, went back up the elevator to his apartment, dug the bullet out, bandaged himself, wiped up all traces of blood at his apartment so no one would know what happened to him and went down into the tunnels. Turns out, his grandfather worked in them, years ago. That was before his father had made the family's fortune in real estate. Anyway, his grandfather once took him into the tunnels, after they were no longer in use. That must have been when Jay was still a kid.''

Crystal shook her head, still marveling at it all. "Jay,'' she whispered. She'd always thought of him as the quiet bookworm she remembered from school days. In later years, whenever she'd seen him at some social gathering, she hadn't thought he'd changed much. He'd grown more handsome, of course. The skinny gawkiness had disappeared. But in her mind, he wasn't the stunning sort of male she always had sought, and besides that he seemed too much a scholarly sort. Who would have guessed what passions and courage lay underneath? Oh, she'd been stupid!

She realized now how superficial she'd been in her approach to men. All she'd looked for was physical attraction—the way ''Eric'' had seemed at first to be mainly attracted to her feminine attributes. But he'd made her realize what depth of passion a man could feel for a woman, the deep, abiding love he had apparently felt for her for years. And best of all, he'd made her feel that wondrous emotion for the first time. She'd fallen in love with him. Thank God she'd learned better. Now she knew what she wanted.

She only hoped he still wanted her.

She laid her head on her father's shoulder, sad and troubled. ''When will I see him again, Daddy?''

''We'll have to have him over for dinner.''

She lifted her head. ''When? Tonight?''

''Well, that's short notice for our cook, but...oh, I'm sure it can be arranged.'' He smiled. ''What's your hurry? Are you more impressed with Jay now than you were?''

She nodded her head and tears filled her eyes. ''I love him, Dad. I want to be with him.''

But that night, Jay couldn't be reached. She phoned his apartment, even his office, both of which had been sealed off by police ever since his ''disappearance.'' Her father phoned Detective Fogarty at the station, asking for Jay, but the police officer said Jay had left after spending the entire morning giving them a full report. She worried whether Jay was still ill with his fever.

Later, growing desperate, Crystal phoned his mother's home. Mrs. Saunders said he'd stopped by to see her that afternoon, to assure her he was all right, but then he'd gone out. She told Crystal she'd never believed he was dead and that she was happy he'd kept Crystal out of harm's way. "He always had a soft spot for you," Mrs. Saunders said. "Maybe you didn't know."

Days passed and Crystal heard nothing from Jay and could not reach him. Meanwhile, his photo, with and without his mask, was on every front page and on the TV news. So were photos of her and of the two of them together, taken that last morning in front of Winthrop's. The Phantom of Chicago had captured the city's imagination. Details, revealed gradually by police, were eagerly reported to the public. But Jay did not appear on any show to be interviewed. Crystal had refused all interviews, too.

She wondered where he was and why he hadn't called or tried to see her. She spent her days at home, not even going to her health club for fear reporters would be there. Recent events in her life had been so dramatic, so confusing, she just couldn't deal with the media. Her fiancé had turned out to be a potential murderer. She'd been kidnapped and held prisoner by a masked man who had turned out to be Jay, who she'd thought was dead. And Jay had turned into the most exquisite lover she could imagine. She longed to be in his arms again.

Didn't he miss her, the way she missed him? Why was he ignoring her this way? Had it all been a game to him, an adventure, a fantasy to be played out? She remembered him speaking in those terms. Now that the fantasy was over, was he off looking for some new adventure—or some new woman—to pursue and conquer?

Had he become bored with being a lawyer working in an office after his undercover work for the government? Was that the reason he'd chosen to rescue her, because he needed some exciting challenge to undertake again? Of course, Tony had shot him, and he wanted his attacker apprehended. But dressing as a phantom and kidnapping her had been quite an inventive way to accomplish his goal. He'd said he'd done it because he loved her, but maybe that was all part of the fantasy, too.

Still, she didn't regret making love with him. She could live on the memory of those moments for the rest of her life.

By the end of the week, she'd gone from worry, tears, utter despair, to bitter anger at Jay's failure to contact her. She'd stopped trying to call him. And she was darned if she was going to stay here at home and look like she was waiting for him. She told her father she'd like to go up to the family's summer cottage in Wisconsin to be by herself for a while, away from lurking reporters. If Jay wanted her, she decided, he could go searching for her. If not, then she'd just as soon be alone—to get over him.

She drove up by herself on Sunday. November was the wrong time of year for Wisconsin. The trees had lost all their leaves. The air was chilly and the small lake on which their quaint stone cottage was located looked gray and dismal. After she'd arrived and unpacked her bags late in the afternoon, she built a fire in the fireplace. Intending to relax, she got out of her jeans and sweater. She slipped on the shirt Eric, or rather Jay, had taken off and given her to wear, the shirt she'd had on when he made love to her. She'd been sleeping in it every night since they'd parted and had reluctantly washed it before packing it in her suitcase. After buttoning it, she got her quilted robe out and put it on. Pulling a heavy easy chair closer to the fire, she sat down to read the latest bestseller.

But she couldn't concentrate. The fictional adventure wasn't nearly as fascinating as the one she'd lived with Jay. Where was he? she wondered again with sadness. She'd begged him not to forget her once they came back up into the real world. But it seemed he had.

Her sad ruminations were interrupted at twilight by the sound of knocking at the small cottage's front door. She got out of the chair and turned on the light in the darkening living room. The fire had gone down to glowing embers. She rushed to the door, thinking—as she constantly had been during the last week—that any ring or knock might be Jay. But when she reached the door, she hesitated. Only her father knew she was here. It was getting dark, and she was alone in the cottage. The place was quite secluded. She wondered if she should answer it.

The knock sounded again.

Crystal chewed her lower lip as her heart rate accelerated. "Who is it?" she finally asked.

"That depends on who you want it to be," a male voice said. "You have two choices."

She smiled with joyous disbelief and immediately opened the door. Before her stood a tall man in a wool tweed jacket, an open-collared shirt and dark pants. His brown hair was curly—above his white mask. His green eyes studied hers, wary, as if bracing himself.

"Jay!" she exclaimed, ignoring his grim demeanor, laughing and crying all at once. After pulling him in and shutting the door, she grabbed him by the upper arms and shook him. "Where have you been? I thought you forgot me!" she sputtered at him.

He seemed a trifle disoriented by her reaction. "I've been ... well, staying away on purpose. I wanted you to have time to think, for our life to get back to normal. As normal as it can be with all the reporters. I've been lying low to avoid them, too.''

"Where were you? I called everywhere."

"So I heard. I have an aunt who lives in Evaston. I stayed with her for the week and didn't tell anyone except my mother, and I swore her to secrecy."

"How did you know I was here?"

"I finally called your home this morning. A week had gone by, the length of time I promised myself I'd stay away from you. Your father answered and told me where you'd gone. I left right away and then got lost trying to find this place."

"Promised yourself to stay away a week! I was right about you. You *are* insane. Keeping us apart a whole week, when we could have been together. And why do you still have that mask on?"

He bowed his head a moment. "I thought about it a long while." He looked up, eyes translucent and serious. "I decided it might be best if we make the transition together."

"Transition?"

"From being Crystal Winthrop, heiress in danger, and Eric, the Phantom of the Opera, to just Crystal and Jay, who've known each other since grade school."

She nodded. "All right." Without hesitation, taking him by surprise, she reached up with both hands and grasped the side edges of his mask. He stiffened for an instant, as if fighting the instinct to stop her. But he did not interfere, and she gently slid the mask upward and off his face.

Crystal smiled up at him, happy and content to see Jay's familiar, angular face, his high forehead, dark eyebrows and narrow nose. She reached up with one hand to lightly touch his brow, his high cheekbone. Now she couldn't figure out why she'd never noticed what handsome, quietly arresting features he had. Why had she never noticed his luminous green eyes? Perhaps because most of the time she'd seen him recently was in his office, when he'd had his head bowed as he studied her prenuptial agreement. Before then, she'd never taken the time to notice him. She ran her fingertips through the short brown locks that fell over his forehead, liking it so much better in its natural state than straight and slicked back.

"Jay," she said on a sigh. She rose up on her toes to kiss him. He still seemed taller than she'd remembered Jay as being but realized that she'd usually seen him at his office when she was wearing high heels. When her lips met his, he curled his large hands about her waist and drew her against him.

As his mouth moved with eager insistence over hers, she felt the flame that had been languishing inside her burst forth into frenzied fire. She threw her arms around his neck and pressed her body to his. He responded in kind, pushing away the lapel of her quilted robe to find and caress her breast. The feel of his hand fondling her softness through the shirt made her melt with heating desire.

"Jay, make love with me," she whispered. She drew away, tossed the mask in her hand onto the couch and began taking off her robe. "I've thought of nothing else this whole week. I want to make love with you!"

When she'd let the robe drop to the floor at her feet, he took hold of her shoulders and studied her intently, as he'd done so often in the tunnel. "Wait," he said.

"Why?" she asked, disappointed, her body aching for him.

"There's something I've wanted to ask you for years."

"What?"

"Will you marry me? And by *me,* I mean Jay, not Eric."

She grinned and slid her arms around his neck. "Of course I'll marry you, Jay! In fact, let's elope!"

He seemed slightly alarmed. "Crystal—"

"Why not? I don't want to plan a big wedding. I've had enough of that."

He smiled and shook his head. "But, Crystal, you've only just discovered that you can be attracted to me. I've felt that way about you for a long time, but maybe you should take some time to think about this. I asked you to marry me because I wanted you to know how I felt and what my intentions were. But *you* ought to be sure before we go ahead with it.''

"I'm sure."

"But, sweetheart, we've only had one long night together.''

"That night was a lifetime. You think after making love with you that I could settle for anyone else? I told you, you've spoiled me.''

"Maybe we ought to be engaged for a while, so you can take some time to think before we actually take vows that aren't meant to be broken.''

"I'd rather go back to being your prisoner,'' she said.

He paused, his brows drawing together. "Why?"

"Because then there was no way I could escape you. I want to belong to you,'' she told him with heartfelt passion. "I want to be your prisoner forever.''

He shook his head. "I want a *wife,* not a prisoner.''

"Okay, I'll settle for that. I'll settle for it *now.*''

Jay inhaled and let the breath out in a long, beleaguered sigh. "You always did tie me in knots. Talking with you has always been a new experience in logic for me.''

"This is love, not logic!" She began to unbutton her shirt, a tried-and-true method to drive all traces of logic from his intellectualized brain.

"You're still wearing that?"

"I've practically lived in it. It was all I had of you."

When she pulled the unbuttoned shirt apart, his eyes shone with painfully impatient need. "Crystal—" He gathered her roughly in his arms, kissing her with such force, the air was pushed from her lungs. She clung to him as he kissed her thoroughly, feeling limp with desire and lack of oxygen. When he left her mouth to kiss her throat, bending over her, she felt a wondrous, dizzy helplessness. She experienced a feeling of falling and then her back met the soft cushions of the couch. He stopped to throw off his jacket, then settled his body over hers, his hot mouth coming down on her breast. She whimpered with pleasure, then sighed wantonly as his lips fixed on her nipple.

"Ohhh, Jaaay..." she moaned, burying her fingers in his hair.

Lost in ardent pleasure, she squirmed and arched her back as his hand found its way downward to stroke her intimately. Moments later, when he entered her, she closed her eyes in ecstasy, tears streaming down her cheeks at the joy of loving him again.

As she shifted her hips to accommodate him, she was barely aware of nudging some object in her way.

She heard it lightly fall to the floor and then got lost again in the heated throes of their passion.

The mask lay forgotten, tilted as its top corner leaned crookedly against the side of the couch, its almond-shaped eyes hollow now. But the mask's silent, fixed expression appeared curiously wise and content.

* * * * *

LORI HERTER

Chicago is my hometown. I grew up in the suburbs, graduated from the University of Illinois, Chicago campus, and worked in the Loop. Chicagoans learn to take snow-blitzed winters and summer tornado warnings in stride, developing a down-to-earth perspective on life. Paradoxically, I'm a born dreamer and live in Southern California now, yet I'll never lose my Chicagoan's underlying grip on reality.

However, when I saw Andrew Lloyd Webber's version of *The Phantom of the Opera* in Los Angeles, starring Michael Crawford, I admit my grip got shaky. My heart palpitated. I had to remind myself it was only a show. When it ended, I yearned to see it all over again. Why? I wanted to reexperience the Phantom's powerful emotion, his desperate love, his frightening, mesmerizing sensuality. The Phantom made me discover things about myself I never knew.

When Silhouette invited me to write for the Shadows anthology, I felt honored. I knew just what I wanted to do: Create my own Phantom. I wanted to tell this dark fantasy in a contemporary setting I knew, to make it seem . . . well, real. The city's underground labyrinth provided the perfect lair for my Phantom. There in the darkness, he would nurture his desire for his chosen woman and scheme to make her discover things she never knew.

I wrote this story in a fever. I'm over it now. Sort of.

Oh, let's get real. Both Chicago and the Phantom will be a part of me forever.

Lori Herter

And then there were three...

Three authors-- who brought you a taste of romance and danger, who kept you spellbound in the *Shadows Short Story Collection*--are back and better than ever...with more surprises and adventure! You won't want to miss...

ONE OF THE GOOD GUYS—Carla Cassidy
Silhouette Intimate Moments, coming in November 1993
P.I. Tony Pandolinni was hired to get the dirt on Libby Weatherby. Instead, he became her protector—only to realize that his heart was on the line.

THE WILLOW FILE—Lori Herter
Silhouette Shadows, coming in March 1994
A spurned lover's ghost haunts the halls of an old hotel. And when a lonely woman falls prey to the ghost's darkest desires, only a mysterious stranger with his own demons can challenge the past....

SIMPLE GIFTS—Kathleen Korbel
Silhouette Intimate Moments, coming in summer 1994
You met Jake Kendall in *Jake's Way* (IM #413)—now read about his sister, Lee, as she faces love and danger in the very masculine form of police captain Rock O'Connor—an American Hero you'll never forget!

Look for these three exciting stories, all coming your way...

Only from

ᐁ *Silhouette*

SILHOUETTE® Shadows™

NEW! FOR NOVEMBER

IT ALL BEGINS AT NIGHT....

The dark holds many secrets, and answers aren't easily found. In fact, in some cases the truth can be deadly. But Silhouette Shadows women aren't easily frightened....

Brave new authors Cheryl Emerson and Allie Harrison are about to see how scared *you* can get. These talented authors will entice you, bemuse you and thrill you!

#19 TREACHEROUS BEAUTIES by Cheryl Emerson
Widowed Anna Levee was out to discover who had mysteriously murdered her brother. Trouble was, the best suspect was slowly stealing Anna's heart. What if Jason Forrester decided he wanted her life, as well?

#20 DREAM A DEADLY DREAM by Allie Harrison
Kate McCoy assured herself it was just a dream. The erotic fantasies she remembered were strictly her imagination. But when Jake Casperson knocked on her door, Kate discovered her nighttime visions were about to become reality....

Pick up your copy of our newest Silhouette Shadows books at your favorite retail outlet...and prepare to shiver!

SSHNEW

**Fifty red-blooded, white-hot, true-blue hunks
from every State in the Union!**

Look for MEN MADE IN AMERICA! Written by some
of our most poplar authors, these stories feature fifty of
the strongest, sexiest men, each from a different state in
the union!

Two titles available every other month at your favorite
retail outlet.

In November, look for:

STRAIGHT FROM THE HEART by Barbara Delinsky
(Connecticut)
AUTHOR'S CHOICE by Elizabeth August (Delaware)

In January, look for:

DREAM COME TRUE by Ann Major (Florida)
WAY OF THE WILLOW by Linda Shaw (Georgia)

You won't be able to resist MEN MADE IN AMERICA!

Relive the romance...
Harlequin and Silhouette
are proud to present

by Request™

A program of collections of three complete novels by the most-requested authors with the most-requested themes. Be sure to look for one volume each month with three complete novels by top-name authors.

In September: **BAD BOYS**

Dixie Browning
Ann Major
Ginna Gray

No heart is safe when these hot-blooded hunks are in town!

In October: **DREAMSCAPE**

Jayne Ann Krentz
Anne Stuart
Bobby Hutchinson

Something's happening! But is it love or magic?

In December: **SOLUTION: MARRIAGE**

Debbie Macomber
Annette Broadrick
Heather Graham Pozzessere

Marriages in name only have a way of leading to love....

Available at your favorite retail outlet.

HARLEQUIN®   ˅ Silhouette

What a year for romance!

Silhouette has five fabulous romance collections coming your way in 1993. Written by popular Silhouette authors, each story is a sensuous tale of love and life—as only Silhouette can give you!

Three bachelors are footloose and fancy-free... until now.
(March)

Heartwarming stories that celebrate the joy of motherhood.
(May)

Put some sizzle into your summer reading with three of Silhouette's hottest authors.
(June)

Take a walk on the dark side of love—with tales just perfect for those misty autumn nights.
(October)

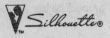

Share in the joy of yuletide romance with four award-winning Silhouette authors.
(November)

A romance for all seasons—it's always time for romance with Silhouette!

Silhouette®

If you've been looking for something a little bit different and a little bit spooky, let Silhouette Books take you on a journey to the dark side of love with

▼ SILHOUETTE® *Shadows* ™

Every month, Silhouette brings you two romantic, spine-tingling Shadows novels, written by some of your favorite authors, such as Heather Graham Pozzessere, Anne Stuart, Helen R. Myers and Rachel Lee—to name just a few.

In October, look for:

THE HAUNTING OF BRIER ROSE
by Patricia Simpson
TWILIGHT PHANTASIES
by Maggie Shayne

In November, look for:

TREACHEROUS BEAUTIES
by Cheryl Emerson
DREAM A DEADLY DREAM
by Allie Harrison

In December, look for:

BRIDGE ACROSS FOREVER
by Regan Forest
THE SECRETS OF SEBASTIAN BEAUMONT
by Carrie Peterson

Come into the world of Shadows and prepare to tremble with fear—and passion....

If you're looking for more titles by

CARLA CASSIDY,

don't miss these heartwarming stories by one of Silhouette's most popular authors:

Silhouette Desire®

#05784	A FLEETING MOMENT	$2.89 ☐

Silhouette Romance™

#08884	FIRE AND SPICE	$2.69 ☐
#08905	HOMESPUN HEARTS	$2.69 ☐
#08924	GOLDEN GIRL	$2.69 ☐
#08942	SOMETHING NEW	$2.75 ☐
#08958	PIXIE DUST	$2.75 ☐

Silhouette Shadows™

#27004	SWAMP SECRETS	$3.50 ☐
#27011	HEART OF THE BEAST	$3.50 ☐

TOTAL AMOUNT	$
POSTAGE & HANDLING	$
($1.00 for one book, 50¢ for each additional)	
APPLICABLE TAXES*	$ _____
TOTAL PAYABLE	$ _____

(check or money order—please do not send cash)

To order, complete this form and send it, along with a check or money order for the total above, payable to Silhouette Books, to: *In the U.S.:* 3010 Walden Avenue, P.O. Box 9077, Buffalo, NY 14269-9077; *In Canada:* P.O. Box 636, Fort Erie, Ontario, L2A 5X3.

Name: _____

Address: _____ City: _____

State/Prov.: _____ Zip/Postal Code: _____

*New York residents remit applicable sales taxes.
Canadian residents remit applicable GST and provincial taxes.

CCBACK2

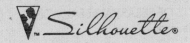